A HUSBAND FOR ESYLLT

WELSH REBELS

VIRGINIE MARCONATO

OLIVERHEBERBOOKS

A Husband for Esyllt Copyright 2024 © Virginie Marconato

Cover art by Dar Albert at Wicked Smart Designs

Published by Oliver-Heber Books

0 9 8 7 6 5 4 3 2 1

Prologue

"Thank you. You can leave us."

At Esyllt's command, the two guards bowed and left the room. Once the sound of their footsteps had been swallowed by the spiral staircase, she looked at the man they had deposited on the chair she had readied in preparation for him. Following her instructions, they had not only covered his eyes and bound his wrists but they had also tied him to the back of the chair.

A smile curved her lips.

He was not going anywhere, at least not until she'd had what she wanted from him.

Taking advantage of the fact that he couldn't see her, she looked her fill. Far from ranting and writhing in protest, Lord Sheridan's squire was sitting stock still and his breathing was even and calm, much calmer than her own. It unnerved her. If he didn't feel in a position of inferiority, then she wasn't quite sure how she would gain the upper hand. Intimidation had never been her weapon of choice, and she wasn't sure how to wield it in front of such a man. That he was a seasoned warrior was obvious from his physique, and that he was used to dealing with women intent on seducing him was all too clear. The way he had ogled her during the banquet had been indecent.

That was the only word she could think of to describe it. Indecent. And it had made her body burst into flames.

Esyllt swallowed hard. Had she not been too presumptuous? Perhaps. She had neither the strength to fight a warrior nor the skill to handle a seducer. In truth, she even lacked the will to go through with this mad plan of hers.

Still, he was here now, so she had better not waste the opportunity, because there would not be another.

Silently, she edged closer. After one last glance at his perfect chest molded in a tight tunic, she set about untying the cloth from his eyes. The gesture was disturbingly intimate, something she had not anticipated. Perhaps she should have asked one of the guards to do that for her because, sitting as he was, the squire's mouth was level with her breasts. Though she reminded herself that he was not here for her pleasure, she could not help but shiver at the thought of him placing his lips on her.

Damnation, she should have approached him from behind to untie the knot, it would have been a lot less intimate. From such close quarters, he could probably smell the floral water she liked to dabble between her breasts and if he moved but an inch forward, he would touch her.

When the cloth finally fell to the floor, she took a step backward to look at him.

The man lifted his eyes to hers. Oh, those eyes! She had no choice but to call them green, but they looked almost transparent, and his dark coloring only made them more piercing. Black stubble covered his jaw, and his short hair was disheveled, testimony to the fact that he had been dragged to her bedchamber straight from bed. His mouth was set in a hard, disapproving line. Oh, that mouth! The sensual curve of his lips made her blood run ten times faster in her veins.

"Would you care to explain what is happening, my lady?" he said when it became obvious she was too fascinated to speak.

A shiver traveled down Esyllt's spine. The gruff voice made it clear he was beside himself with fury, even if he appeared calm. She had better get this over with as quickly as she could.

"Your master and I are to be married at dawn."

His arched brow indicated he was already aware of the fact and did not see what it had to do with his abduction. She carried on, making sure to look anywhere but at him. It was one thing admitting to her rash plan, quite another doing so while looking him in the eye.

"It is not my wish to be married again, much less to an Englishman, but I have not been given any choice, as you can imagine. I'm only a woman, after all. My personal preferences do not count. The whole thing has been decided without my consent by the local Welsh lords for reasons I do not agree with."

That was the least she could say.

Freshly widowed, she was to be used as a pawn in their game of domination. At first, she had been surprised to hear Gruffydd ap Hywel, one of her late husband's friends, who was fiercely opposed to the English rule, demand that she marry a man he considered an oppressor, but she had quickly seen that he merely meant to use this union as a way of ridding himself of a powerful lord. Once married and settled in a hostile land, away from allies who would never even get to hear of his disappearance, Lord Sheridan was to be disposed of. Though she didn't agree with those underhand methods, Esyllt had not been able to voice her protests. She was only a woman, as she'd said, and thus unfit to have an opinion, much less behave in accordance to it.

She looked at the man on the chair, hoping he would sympathize with her plight. His stern stare indicated that he did not, however, so she carried on.

"I cannot refuse to marry Lord Sheridan. However, if *he* were to decide that he would rather not marry me after all, then it would be quite diff—"

The man did not even let her finish. "What makes you think he would change his mind now? He's been negotiating this union for weeks, enduring endless discussions in the process, he's traveled for days in foul weather to come and claim his Welsh bride. He's hardly going to cry off now because you took his squire hostage."

Despite the uncomfortable and humiliating position she had put him in, the man spoke calmly. Esyllt could not help but admire his equanimity. Her task would have been a whole lot easier if he had been a more impressionable man. Alas, there was nothing meek about him.

"I am not taking you hostage," was all she could say.

"Am I to assume this is how guests are treated in Wales then?" A glance at the ropes binding him to the chair made his meaning clear. "A most endearing custom, to be sure."

Esyllt bit her bottom lip. His composure was unsettling. True, she posed no real threat to him but still, she had imagined a proud warrior would be furious to find himself bested by a woman. He didn't appear furious, only mocking.

The time for arguing was over. She had to get on with the second part of the plan.

"In a moment Lord Sheridan is going to walk into this room. My men have gone to get him. When he enters, he will find his bride and his squire... coupling."

The word, or rather the image it created in her mind, sent heat to her cheeks.

"Will he really?" The man's lips twisted into a smile. "You might need my cooperation for that."

She gave a movement of impatience. They were wasting precious time. "We are not going to actually do anything, of course."

"How then is he going to think that we are, in your words, 'coupling'?"

Without a word, Esyllt untied the laces of her gown and let it fall to the floor. In preparation for this moment, she had donned a garment that could be discarded without the help of a lady's maid. Underneath, she wore nothing but a very revealing shift.

The man's eyes widened in shock. Clearly, he had not expected such a bold move.

Before he could say anything or lose her nerve, she lifted her shift to come straddle his lap. He was so tall and strong that her feet didn't touch the floor, something she had not anticipated and that did little to help her hold on to a semblance of composure. Unbalanced, she gripped his shoulders to steady herself. Under her palms, she felt rock hard muscles.

Dear Lord. This was a lot more unsettling, a lot more arousing than she had expected, a most unfortunate turn of events. *She* was supposed to be in control of what would happen, not him.

"What does it look like now?" she asked, her voice huskier than she would have liked. "Lord Sheridan will think me the most shameful wanton, a wild creature governed only by lust and possibly carrying his squire's bastard child. After that, he will no doubt demand that—"

"Let me stop you right here," the man cut in. "Lord Sheridan, whatever you may think of him, is not a fool. I am tied to the chair and I am fully clothed. He will know that in these conditions, nothing could have happened between us."

Damnation, he was right. At the moment, it looked like he was here against his will, not the impression she wanted to give. She needed to make it seem as if he were not her captive but her lover. The ropes may well have to go. But if she freed him... Then she would have no way of controlling him or ensuring his cooperation.

As if he'd read her mind, he gave a side smile. "I'm risking a lot just by being here, and we both know it. It is in my interest to remain tied up, so as to avoid Lord Sheridan's wrath. But if you want him to believe we are coupling, you will have to untie me." He paused then looked at her from under his long, dark lashes, as if in consideration. When something in his eyes flashed, she understood he had taken a decision. "Of course if you were really determined—"

"I am." This was not in question.

"Well, then, I suppose we do not have to pretend. If you were willing, something *could* happen between us. For real. It could be compensation, shall we say, for the risk I'm taking."

Esyllt inhaled sharply when he bucked upward to show her just how ready he was to aid her in her plans.

"Y-you..." she stammered, in both shock and confusion. Never had she felt such an uncompromising proof of masculine desire nudging at the place between her legs. Her late husband, God rest his soul, had never achieved such iron hardness. "You are hard!"

"What did you expect?" The corner of his lips curled. "A beautiful lady is sitting astride me, her bare flesh is pressing against my most sensitive part, and by her own admission, she wants to couple with me." The green eyes seemed to catch fire, which in turn, sent molten lava down her veins.

"I never said I actually wanted to couple with you," Esyllt croaked.

"No, you didn't say it," he conceded. "But you do."

How did he know that what had only started as a pretense, as a means to an end, nothing more, had inflamed her whole body?

"Untie me, my lady. Then I could give you what you really want. For a moment in your arms, I'm ready to take any risk." His voice was so low she had to lean in to hear what he was saying. As she did so, her breasts brushed against his chest. The pleasure shooting through her at the intimate contact had her bite her lip to stifle a moan. "The whole thing would be more believable if we were in a bed, don't you think? Not many people couple on a chair in the middle of the room, you know."

Yes, perhaps it would be more believable in a bed, but would it be better? Esyllt couldn't think straight. All she knew was that she wanted to lie under this man, feel his hard heat over her, if just for a moment. She stood up on shaky legs and reached for a knife. Before she had time to wonder about the wisdom of her decision, she sliced the rope holding the squire captive.

Slowly, he brought his arms around and stretched, easing the pain in his muscles. When he stood in front of her, taller and stronger than she had imagined, Esyllt gulped. What had she done? She had freed a dangerous beast, that was what, one who would not be captured a second time.

Her heart started to beat loudly in her chest. What would he do now?

Had it all been a trick so she could free him? Would he now do as they'd agreed, or would he throw her over his shoulder, bring her to his master, and expose her plans to him? His loyalty was to Lord Sheridan, not her, and he did not need her to satisfy the desire she had so foolishly awoken. Anyone could do it. He could have her delivered to Lord Sheridan, then go in search of the first willing woman available and bed her instead. The inconvenience would be minimal, and the potential reward great.

"That's better. Your men were none too gentle with me, no doubt because I'm English. Now, where were we?" he purred. "Ah, yes, the coupling."

He swept her into his arms with breathtaking ease and placed her on the fur covers with more care than she had expected. Luck was with her, it seemed. He did not appear as if he would hand her over to his master. Perhaps he despised him and he was enjoying playing him for a fool. Perhaps he wanted her more than she had thought. Whatever the reason was, he seemed prepared to indulge her and go along with her plans.

"So you want Lord Sheridan to think you are a wanton. How far are you prepared to go?"

He knelt on the bed and started to tug at his clothes. Transfixed, Esyllt watched as he undressed, revealing his body bit by bit. The tight tunic was discarded, then the undershirt. Soon he was looming over her, bare-chested, and magnificent. The muscles on his stomach were rippling under a skin that looked smooth as silk. Esyllt could barely breathe.

Where had that man come from? Straight from her shameful fantasies, evidently. He exuded carnality, and raw masculine strength in a way no one she had ever met did.

After throwing his clothes to the floor, he came to lie over her, trapping her under his much larger body.

"You want to make it look like we are coupling, then?" he whispered in her ear.

She did. It was her only option, Esyllt told herself. She was in bed with this man to escape a marriage she did not desire, she had freed him from the ropes because she had no other choice, she was lying under him because it was the best way to make Lord Sheridan believe she was not a suitable bride and *not* because she wanted him.

A burst of heat exploded between her legs when he pressed his shaft against her mons. Though he was still wearing his braies and her own flesh was covered by her shift, she could feel how hard it was.

How was she going to stand it? Her body felt like melted wax already. If the door did not open soon, she might disgrace herself and beg this man to take her.

"You might want to open your legs for me, my lady," he drawled, looking at her from under his lashes in the same manner as before. Evidently, he was all too aware of the effect this lethal look had on women. "At the moment it doesn't look like much is happening."

Oh but it *was* happening.

"Yes." The word barely made it out. Somehow, the air had left her lungs.

He waited, holding his weight over her, until she parted her thighs. After what felt like an eternity, she did. He smiled, a devilish smile if ever she'd seen one.

"Do I have your permission to lift your shift?"

"Lift my—"

"Men and women can couple while dressed, though it is a pity in my opinion, but one thing is for sure, nothing must come between their intimate flesh. I'm sure you're aware of that, having already borne a daughter."

She nodded, allowing him to do as he wished, knowing all the while it was a mistake. There was no need to go that far. Anyone walking into the room right now would be shocked by the sight meeting their eyes. She was lying in a bed under a near-naked man, with her legs spread open. There was no room for misinterpretation.

Slowly the man ran his hand up her calf, lifting the hem of her shift as he went. Dimly, Esyllt wondered why he thought it appropriate to stroke her thus. He could just have gathered the fabric up without making it feel like a caress.

No, it wasn't *like* a caress, it *was* a caress. And her reaction to it was shocking.

A finger brushed the place between her legs and she almost swallowed her tongue when the pleasure of the touch made her buck upward.

"How much of a wanton do you want to be, my lady?" he purred. "You don't even have to pretend. I could have you right here, right now."

Esyllt's mouth fell open because suddenly he was... there, poised at her most secret entrance, ready to slip in. When had he unlaced his braies? How had she not realized what he was doing? Her body didn't care about the answers, it welcomed what her mind was struggling to comprehend. He gave the tiniest nudge, and it was all she could do not to arch her back and urge him inside.

"I..." She could not agree to such a shocking thing, could she? Pretend, that was all they were doing, that was all they needed to do. In a moment the guards would arrive with her betrothed and it would be over.

"It would be good for Lord Sheridan to hear you moan when he is brought up to your room. I could help to make it convincing... If you wanted me to, of course." He gave a low, sensual chuckle. "I only ever consider bedding willing partners, but I don't think that is an issue here, is it?"

Esyllt thought she was going to expire from the tension coursing in her body. The man ground his hips in scandalous invitation, but still he did not press inside of her. He was waiting for her to agree. Oh, Lord, where were the guards? If they did not arrive soon, she would not resist the need to wrap her legs around the squire's waist and draw him in. She would beg him to plunge inside her and yes, she would moan.

"Surely there is no need to do anything else," she managed to say, her voice little more than a croak. "Our position is already compromising enough. Lord Sheridan—"

"No one is coming," the man said in a persuasive whisper. "Let me give you what you deserve, my lady. You're so wet, I can barely control myself. Your body wants me, I'm sure you can feel it. Just say yes."

He had not stopped his teasing for a moment; her core was pulsing desperately, as if to draw the man's hardness in. Could she give in? It was clear he was leaving the decision to her, and she wanted to agree.

"My men have been sent to get Lord Sheridan, they will soon—"

"They will not find him. No one is coming," he repeated. She shifted her hips, and the movement caused him to slide inside her just a fraction. She could not help a cry of relief at the sensation.

Oh, yes, more, she wanted more of that!

Esyllt stopped resisting and allowed him to push in another inch. Closing her eyes, she let her body take over. She was poised on the edge of something devastating, and suddenly, she wished no one would come to her room, not yet, at least. The idea that they would be interrupted before she could find out just how pleasurable having him make love to her could be was too dire to contemplate.

"How do you know they won't find Lord Sheridan?" she asked, feeling him withdraw then slide back in, a little further. She bit her lip and he withdrew again, then plunged in all the way. Yes. Like that was perfect. Just one more thrust and she would...

Erupt.

That was what it felt like. Instinctively, she knew that was what was about to happen. She would erupt. And she was desperate for it.

"I know because *I* am Lord Sheridan, and I am currently not in my bed but in yours, coupling with you."

He stilled, and she froze.

For a long moment Esyllt stared at him, this man who was buried to the hilt inside her. Her mind refused to accept what she had just heard. Her body was pulsing, poised on the edge of explosion and he was telling her that he had tricked her.

"You?" she said in a deathly whisper. "*You* are Lord Sheridan?"

"Me." He ground his hips against her and it was all Esyllt could do not to scream. That movement had almost been enough to make her erupt. "I am your future husband."

All thoughts of pleasure fled her mind. "No!" she roared and bucked upward, trying to lift him off of her. Instantly, he flattened her onto her back, pinning her in place.

"Don't even think about it, or I will tie you down with the rope you kindly provided me with." He lowered his head so he could speak in her ear. "Listen to me, my lady. This marriage was decided by my king, it is not about my or your personal gratification, and it will go ahead, no matter what you say, no matter what you do, no matter how devious or debauched you are, no matter who you take to your bed beforehand or after."

"I'm not debauched," she protested. "I told you what I wanted to—"

He stopped her with another thrust that made her body arch in supplication. "You wanted to show your groom how much of a wanton you were. Well, you have. Rest assured that I will not forget how readily you surrendered to a stranger's advances, how you welcomed him inside your body."

He slid back out, then in again. Esyllt could not stop a

whimper from escaping her lips. She was so close, if he could only—

"I could put an end to your misery now," he drawled, reading her mind. "It wouldn't take much, I don't think. You are on the edge of surrender."

His next thrust was excruciatingly slow, not enough to cause the friction she needed. Then the wretched man withdrew and stood up. As he fastened his braies, his honeyed voice kept playing in Esyllt's mind.

Let me give you what you deserve.

Oh! Indeed. He'd not really wanted her; he had only exacted his revenge over her in the most humiliating way, by showing her that she could not resist him. This mad plan of hers had ended up in disaster.

She covered herself with the furs, fighting the urge to cry.

"Get some rest, my lady. You have a wedding to go to in the morning."

Chapter One

North Wales, February 1296

Earlier that day

"Lord Sheridan is here."

Esyllt straightened her spine. The dreaded moment had finally come. The man Gruffydd had selected to be her husband was about to walk into the great hall. She didn't know anything about him, save for the fact that he was English and recently widowed, like she was. It did not seem to matter to the old Welsh rebel that she was about to be shackled to a total stranger. The only thing that mattered to him was the possibility of ridding himself of a powerful lord.

The futility of the enterprise struck her anew. What was he hoping for? To keep offering her up to Englishmen he could then kill off? Even supposing the foul plan could work this time, how many more times did he intend to use the same method before suspicions were raised? And even if, by some miracle, he got away with it, he would only have disposed of three or four men at the most, hardly a significant contribution to his cause... Was she the only one to see how ridiculous this all was?

Apparently so.

From her place on the dais, she watched the door at the other end of the hall, waiting for her groom to appear. A moment later, a tall, blond man entered, and it was all she could do not to gasp. She was so opposed to this union that in the last few weeks she had convinced herself that the man was an ogre, one who could never appeal to her senses or her sensibilities, one who was as coarse as he was unwelcome, not unlike Gruffydd himself, in fact. Well, at least she could be reassured on that score. Her future husband was nothing like the gnarled old man. He was young, strong, and uncommonly handsome. More than handsome. With fine features, a muscular body and an air of masculine ease, he was... perfect.

Just when she was thinking that she had never seen a man who appealed to her more, a dark-haired man drew to his side to whisper something in his ear. His squire, she imagined. Once he had delivered his message, he looked straight at her and Esyllt received the force of his green gaze like a punch to the gut.

Arglwydd mawr!

Her future husband's beauty was instantly eclipsed. Where did these Englishmen come from? Lord Sheridan's golden looks had overwhelmed her, but his squire's dark beauty was almost too intense to bear. She lowered her eyes, like someone blinded after having stared straight into the sun.

From that point on, Esyllt lost track of everything that was being said around her. All she could do was try not to stare at the man standing behind Lord Sheridan while the Welsh lords welcomed him in.

The whole thing seemed to last forever, but at long last, the Englishman was free. He nodded one last time at Gruffydd and then walked over to the dais where she was waiting, heart pounding in her chest.

"My lady. Finally we meet." His voice was rich and pleas- ant, his manners perfect but she could barely speak, such was the tightening in her throat. Where was the squire? She forced herself not to go in search of him and answered her betrothed's greeting instead. Not doing so would be a great slight, one not so easily forgiven.

"We do."

He smiled at this far from warm opening, but she did not let it bother her because at that moment she caught sight of the handsome squire, who was taking his place at one of the benches with the rest of the English retinue.

"Shall we eat? I see you have a veritable feast prepared for us. I even recognize most of the dishes, something I had not dared hope for."

As in a dream, Esyllt accepted Lord Sheridan's hand and sat down next to him, readying herself for what she already knew would be the longest meal in her life.

What cruel twist of fate had made her see a man with the beauty of a fallen angel on the day she was meeting the husband who'd been chosen for her? It had been hard to reconcile herself with the idea of this marriage but against all odds, she had been struck by Lord Sheridan. Then, a heartbeat later, she had been forced to see that she would never be satisfied with him because she would forever be thinking of another man.

As a succession of dishes were placed in front of her, she did her best not to stare at the squire. A servant offered him some roasted goose, and she watched as he selected a leg and bit into it. For a reason she could not fathom, her insides convulsed. He deposited the half-eaten leg on his trencher, and the corner of his lips twitched. Esyllt's heart plummeted in her chest. He had seen the effect he was having on her and he was making a point of letting her know it.

She swallowed hard. This wouldn't do. The last thing she wanted was for the squire to report to Lord Sheridan, whom she imagined already wary of the Welsh, that his future wife was lusting after other men.

Or...

An idea struck her. Could this be the way out of this marriage she'd desperately been looking for? Gruffydd would not be able to blame her for not cooperating if Lord Sheridan was the one calling a halt to the proceedings.

And she had just found the perfect reason for him to do so.

Feeling much lighter than she had in weeks, she selected a piece of meat from the dish in front of her. As luck would have it, it was goose. She bit into it with relish. Cooked to perfection, flavored with rich spices and honey, it melted on the tongue.

Just like that, her appetite was back.

Connor Hunter, Lord Sheridan, watched his future wife place what little remained of her goose leg on her trencher and frowned. She had not eaten a single thing since she'd sat down and now she was smiling to herself and eating with appetite. Why? What idea had just crossed her mind? What made her green eyes sparkle so? Not that they needed anything to dazzle. They were already bright enough to ensnare any man. He should know, he who had been struck at first glance.

His future wife was one beguiling woman.

Instead of being pure perfection, which would have been rather dull, she was a study in contrasts. Her delicate face was framed by a veil as white as her skin, and her voice was soft and measured, but her full, red lips hinted at sensual delights no man could resist and her tight velvet dress hugged the body of a temptress. Connor suspected she was as fiery on the inside as she appeared demure on the outside. There was some welcome color to her cheeks, a color that added to her allure and was due, in part at least, to him and the heated gazes they had exchanged.

From the moment she'd seen him, her demeanor had changed. Before she'd spotted him next to Matthew, she'd been pale and drawn, obviously wary of the English retinue and dreading the meeting with the man she was set to marry.

Then he had appeared and she had looked entranced.

By him.

And the feeling was mutual, because the future Lady Sheridan was a rare beauty and, even more importantly, not as modest as she wanted to appear. Connor could make his peace with being married to a woman like that. He had feared being sold to another meek woman like Helen. It had not taken him long to see that was not the case.

While her attention was focused on Matthew, the man she took for her future husband, Connor was able to observe her at his leisure. It had been a stroke of genius on his brother's part to suggest the deception. It gave him the opportunity to take in everything without being seen—or bothered—by anyone. Who would pay attention to a lowly squire when his master was in attendance? No one. And they would answer his questions more honestly.

Of course the Welsh lords would be furious tomorrow when they were told that the man they had taken for an insignificant squire was none other than Lord Sheridan himself, and the one they had lavished their attention on only his low-born foster brother. But in the meantime, he would have had a chance to find out what the people at Esgyrn Castle really thought about this marriage and the fact that they were going to have to answer to an English master from now on.

Not that he couldn't guess. The Welsh despised, feared and hated the English who had taken over their land in equal measure, which was hardly to be wondered at. He suspected he would feel the same in their place.

And him, what did he think of the Welsh? He wasn't sure yet. What he had heard was not exactly encouraging. Many of his countrymen considered them little more than savages unworthy of trust or even attention, but Connor wanted to see for himself where things stood. Unlike Matthew, he was prepared to give them the benefit of the doubt. His brother would never have agreed to a match with a Welsh woman, but he was not so worried, and now less than ever because, on a personal level, his bride appealed to him.

All he had known about her before he'd come riding through the gate of Esgyrn Castle was that she was a twenty-six-year old widow with a young daughter. He had not asked any more details, and no one had thought it appropriate to describe her to him. He had assumed this was down to her being too plain to be deemed worth a description. Nothing could have been further from the truth, so much so that he was amazed no one had thought to use her striking looks in her favor. The man who had handled the marriage negotiations on the Welsh side, a Gruffydd ap Hywel, evidently viewed her as nothing more than a pawn in a political game and not a woman in her own right.

A mistake, but Connor was not so blind.

The second Lady Sheridan would be nothing like the first. Helen had been rather plain and thin. He had never admired these delicate damsels who moved as furtively as mice and ate like birds, who seemed as breakable as glass and were as easily offended as old clerics. No such problem here. His bride to be was elegant and feminine without appearing fragile in the least.

Esyllt ferch Llewelyn—Heavens, but that was a mouthful, one he might never be able to pronounce properly— was a proud she-wolf, not a timid doe. She moved with decision, she spoke with intent, and she looked at people without blushing.

Well... almost.

When she looked at *him*, she most decidedly blushed. This was a most welcome development, as it would help start their marriage on a good footing.

Her hair, he decided, must be of a most fetching color,

something between blonde and auburn. It was impossible to tell under her veil, but her eyebrows were the color of an autumn leaf. He would delight in finding out just what shade of bronze her hair was on their wedding night. At the idea of lifting her shift to see if her intimate hair matched it for fire, his body gave a jerk.

At that precise moment Esyllt looked up at him. Her lips parted as if, even after so many glances in his direction she was still surprised by how appealing she found him. This unexpected desire they felt for each other would make for satisfying nights and compensate in some way for the trying days ahead. And if they were compatible in bed, as he was starting to suspect they might be, it would only help build a satisfactory relationship outside of it.

Perhaps this would not be such a disaster.

He moved out of her line of vision for a moment, wishing to see if she searched for him when she found him gone. It wasn't long before he saw her crane her neck to see where he had disappeared to. He smiled to himself.

Yes. This marriage might not be so bad after all. He'd never thought to gain any sort of personal advantage through it. That had never been the point, but perhaps, against all odds, he would. He had chosen his first wife for practical reasons, and had not thought twice about doing the same a second time, despite a lacklustre marriage. Everyone knew that to marry for love was an unattainable dream, perhaps even unwise, as it could make you act the fool. But if his union to Esyllt could bring him more satisfaction than his union to Helen had, he was not going to complain.

He would take what he could by night, and be on his guard by day, at least until he knew whether he could trust his Welsh wife or not. Then, once he knew where matters stood between them, he might relax.

Satisfied with what he had seen so far, he slipped away toward the kitchen, intent on learning more about the workings of Esgyrn Castle before going to bed. Tomorrow it would be too late, as he would be restored to his normal role as master of the place.

And married.

Damnation, where had the squire gone? He'd been here only a moment ago, now he was nowhere to be seen. Esyllt craned her neck, in vain, before resigning herself to the fact that he had left the banquet.

Without the devilishly handsome man to distract her, she had no choice but to focus her attention back on the conversation around her. Gruffydd was acting like the man in charge, which did not surprise her, but she let him do what he pleased. She noticed that Lord Sheridan didn't contribute much to the conversation either. Or, at least, that he didn't ask the interpreter to say more than a few words at a time, because, as could have been expected, her future husband could not speak a single word of Welsh. Even a simple greeting had been beyond him.

The fact that he relied on his English interpreter to translate his words to the lords grated. Could he not have trusted her to do that? He'd brought a man from Sheridan Manor, not knowing whether the two of them would be able to converse. It was a sensible decision, one she could not fault. However, now that he'd seen she was more than proficient in his language, surely he could have dispensed with the man?

This unwillingness to see her as a woman in her own right, merely a wife he was forced to marry, didn't bode well for the future of their marriage. Attractive as he may be, her husband didn't think her worthy of interest or capable of intelligence.

"You will be married tomorrow at dawn," Gruffydd concluded, as if everyone had not already been aware of the fact.

Lord Sheridan nodded. Esyllt remained silent. What was there to say?

Besides, this marriage would never go ahead, not if she had anything to say about it, because meeting her betrothed had only strengthened her resolve to foil Gruffydd's plans. It had not taken her long to see that she and the Englishman would never get along. If he was not prepared to see her as a reliable, trust-worthy ally, then his breathtaking physique did not matter, and there was no point to this marriage. The plan that had started to hatch in her mind moments ago was slowly taking form, now that she was not distracted by the handsome squire's smoldering gaze. Long before dawn, Lord Sheridan would consider her unfit to be his wife, and with luck, before the week was over, his retinue would be gone.

She would be free.

Her first action would be to call Siân back to Castell Esgyrn. When she'd been told about the arrival of the English, she had sent her daughter away to her mother, just in case her stepfather proved a violent man who would object to his wife having a child by her late husband and treat the little girl like a burden. It was one thing being used by Gruffydd, but she refused to let her young daughter pay the price.

Her immediate fears on that score were allayed. Lord Sheridan did not seem like a child abuser or indeed a wife beater, but she preferred not to have to worry about her daughter at this time.

"I shall retire now, if I may," she said, heart thumping hard in her chest. The moment to put her daring plan to execution had come. Would she be brave enough to see it through? That was the question. "I need to look rested in the morning, my lord, if I am to please you."

"My lady. No need to fret. You already look enchanting. Any man would be honored to call you his wife."

Lord Sheridan took her hand and kissed it with exquisite gallantry. His brown eyes sparkled, daring her to protest at this treatment. Esyllt had no choice but to acknowledge the compliment. At least the man had exquisite manners and seemed determined to give the illusion that this marriage pleased him on a personal level. Was she not making a mistake? After all, if she rejected this suitor, Gruffydd would only find her another, one who was less attractive and did not even bother to pay her compliments.

No, she decided. She had to go through with her plan. The compliment was only for the benefit of the audience watching their every move. If he'd really valued her and wanted her to feel important, he would not have acted as if he didn't know she could speak his language until now. That he thought her a pretty trinket could not compensate for the slight on her abilities. She could not be married to such a man.

"I thank you, my lord. I will see you on the morrow."

On the way out of the great hall, she went to give the castle steward her instructions. As soon as the banquet was over, he and two guards were to find Lord Sheridan's squire and bring him to her room, securely bound.

Then she would take over.

Chapter Two

"Do you take this man to be your lawfully wedded husband?"

Esyllt stole a glance to the man at her side, so tall and determined, and almost laughed. Though in reality she'd been asked a question, not issued an order, she knew she did not have any choice. Unflinching green eyes met hers, confirming it. She was to say yes, without further delay. Behind Lord Sheridan, Gruffydd bared his teeth in menace, urging her on.

With the two men in league against her, she would never be allowed to get away with a refusal now.

"I do," she whispered.

The Englishman had already given his agreement, and so the deed was done. Only one thing remained to make this union indissoluble. Consummation. Her heart skipped a beat. No one knew that it had already taken place late last night, after a fashion. They were married, as surely as if they had both wanted it.

Her new husband held out his hand to her. Knowing it was futile to resist, Esyllt took it and let him walk her out of the chapel in a dream-like state. In the bailey, people were offering their congratulations, but she barely heard a word. All she could think was how different this wedding was to her first one. She had been a shy seventeen-year-old virgin then, surrounded by friends who had her happiness at heart. The people present here today were only interested in what this union meant for them.

Well, she would not be so easily cowed. To prove it to herself, if no one else, she disentangled her hand from the crook of her husband's arm. She could stand by herself, thank you very much, she didn't need the help of someone only intent on keeping her in line.

"My dear Lady Sheridan. May I offer my most heartfelt congratulations on this happy occasion?"

Esyllt found herself face to face with the blond man who had posed as her husband the previous evening. The satisfied gleam in his eye was enough to make her want to scream. How dare he provoke her thus, or behave as if he had not deceived her in the most shameless manner? He made to take her hand, but she snatched it away in anger.

"You will forgive me for not greeting you, my lord, as I do not know who you are," she said, straightening her spine.

The infuriating man exchanged a glance with her husband, as if her defiance had been fully expected and amused him.

"This is my brother, Matthew," Connor said, taking the hand she had refused the other man as he introduced him.

"Brother!" The two men looked nothing like one another. If they had, she might have realized something was amiss, at least doubted that he could be his squire. But the two men facing her were as different as night was from day. How could she have suspected foul play?

"Foster brother, actually. I will explain it all in due time."

"Yes." There would be a lot of explaining to do, she thought wryly. They did not know anything about each other, yet the man by her side was now her husband, they would have to spend the rest of their lives together.

Esyllt bristled at the thought.

Here she was, married for the second time. Just like the first time, she hadn't had any say in the decision. For all that, her first union had been more satisfactory than she had hoped, and made a mother out of her. But there could be no comparison between the two men who would have shared her life. Gwyn had been some thirty years older than her, easy-going, a father figure more than anything else, a companion, and Welsh, like her. Lord Sheridan, was a man in his prime, a fit warrior. There was nothing easy-going about him. He was the image of ruthless determination—and of course, he was English.

How was she going to survive marriage to a man like him? He was impossibly daunting, and what was even worse, impossibly alluring, which meant she could not dismiss him out of hand. If she had been less drawn to him, she might have found it easier to ignore him.

But unfortunately, she could not ignore him. It was too late for that.

Because she had not known who he was upon first acquaintance, she had not thought to guard herself against any feelings he stirred in her. It had seemed harmless to admire his perfect features and strong body when she'd thought him unimportant, so she had not tried to stop herself. As a result, she had been struck much harder than was wise. Despite all that had happened since then, it was impossible to forget her first impression of him, that of a man she admired for his beauty and self-possession.

And because she had thought his brother Matthew was the man she was to wed, she had taken an immediate, strong aversion to him instead. This was the man she was being sold to, the

Englishman who repulsed her and would soon call himself her master—or so she had thought.

But the quiet squire in the corner, watching her with piercing green eyes... She would never forget the jolt she'd felt when their eyes had met for the first time.

Esyllt had heard of people being struck by thunder and surviving the shock. It seemed to her that the instant the thorough devastation she had felt blaze through her soul when she had seen Connor was much akin to what these people described. As she'd had no reason to steel herself against any feelings she might have for him, she'd been hurtled headlong into the abyss. She had erected her defences against Lord Sheridan, an English stranger, all her strength had been focused on him, leaving her weak and vulnerable for anyone else.

Connor had crept under her skin while her attention had been engaged somewhere else and now she wasn't sure how to get him out. The decoy had worked and had damaged her soul more than either man could have predicted.

Yes, they could well be satisfied with themselves.

"Shall we go and eat?"

She could only nod.

All during the banquet she fought to keep her composure. What would happen now? Would he demand to bed her and enjoy proving to her just how much of a wanton she was? If he did, she would be unable to refuse. They were husband and wife, so she did owe him access to her bed. That was bad enough. But what was worse was the fear that, once he started touching her, her body would melt for him, regardless of what her mind was telling her.

If last night was anything to go by, she was right to be fearful.

As the sweetmeats were served, wild panic engulfed Esyllt. Everything was spiraling out of control but she could not allow her ill-advised desire for this man to wreak havoc through her. The reasons why she had opposed the match were still valid, even if Lord Sheridan had since proved to be a sinfully handsome man and fiery lover. In fact, it only made him more dangerous, because he'd also been exposed as a manipulator without scruples, ready to use the feelings he provoked inside her to gain the upper hand.

She needed some time and distance from him to regain control and a clear head. But how could she get it? She could not demand he leave Castell Esgyrn when he'd just arrived. He would refuse, if only to spite her. She could not pretend to be a wanton, and hope to disgust him that way. She had tried that, but doing so had only succeeded in giving him more ammunition against her. What other choices were there? Could she make his life hell so that he regretted his decision to marry her?

It was worth a try, and might even make her feel better.

"You think you've won, my lord," she said, leaning in toward him. "But you might think differently when you get to know me better and see what I'm capable of."

"Is that so?" His smile made it clear he was not impressed in the least. "Worry not, wife, I'm not afeared."

No, indeed why should he worry? Next to him, she was insignificant, in every sense of the word. Not only was she Welsh, but she was a woman. He could have sent her sprawling to the floor with a flick of the wrist. Standing next to him in church earlier, she'd gotten the full measure of his power. He was the most forbidding man she had ever met, and now that they were married, he effectively owned her. He could behave in any way he wanted with her. Last night she'd been unforgivably devious and wanton with him. If he wanted to make her pay for the trick she'd played on him, no one would come to her aid. Not Gruffydd, who had arranged this union for his benefit, not anyone from the English retinue, who would always be on their master's side, not a member of her family, who had not even been invited.

She could only rely on her own wits to protect herself and her daughter. This man could even now be plotting to dispose of her, just like Gruffydd was plotting to dispose of him.

An idea popped into her head. He'd said he was not afeared. But what if she gave him reason to be, make him keep his distance that way?

Her chest tightened at the prospect of wielding such a weapon. It could prove a dangerous one, but she would use it, because there was no other choice.

If she managed to instill some fear in him now, it would be her best protection in the future. He might well leave her alone. After all, last night he'd made it clear he felt nothing but contempt for her, so she had nothing to lose.

"I killed my first husband," she said, squaring her shoulders. "And I don't think you would want to be next."

For a moment the very air around them seemed to still. Then Connor's eyes narrowed.

"Did you just say you killed your first husband?"

"Yes," she forced herself to answer, addressing her silent apologies to Gwyn. Heavens, what was she reduced to, using his death thus? But what other choice did she have? "You never wondered why I was a widow at such a young age?"

Connor was not so easily impressed, as she could have guessed. "No. Six-and-twenty is not such a young age to be widowed, considering your husband was well into his fifties at the time of your wedding."

"He was forty-seven."

Esyllt bit her lip. The threat had utterly failed to rankle him. Perhaps it was for the best, for in truth she already regretted having claimed to being a murderess.

"So. You disposed of your first husband. What shall I do

with this information?" Connor asked, crossing his arms over his well-muscled chest. It was odd to have this conversation in the middle of the great hall, surrounded by dozens of people, amongst which were English people who could understand what they were saying.

"What do you mean?"

"Am I supposed to flee in fright, and go back to England? Try and repudiate you even though it could be argued that the marriage has already been consummated?" She winced at the idea. Being repudiated now would only make matters worse. "Kill you before you get the chance to kill me? Tell me. What am I supposed to do?"

Kill her? This time Esyllt recoiled in horror. Was he seriously considering the option? "No!" she rasped. "Of course I don't want you to kill me?"

"Then what?"

"I-I don't know."

"A charmingly honest answer, wife." Connor took her hand and kissed it. A few people nodded at the gallant gesture, and she realized that they would look to onlookers as happy newlyweds when they were in fact discussing the best way for her husband to get rid of her. "I could always call an investigation first, find out what really happened to your first husband," he carried on, sounding as if he were really giving the matter some consideration. Perhaps he was, or perhaps he only wanted to rankle her. She already knew he liked to unsettle her. "I don't know about here, but where I come from, murder is frowned upon."

Oh no, what had she done?

What a fool! She felt as if she had seized a sword to hit him in a fit of madness and had been disarmed in the blink of an eye, only to find the sharp blade pointing at her throat.

"Don't worry. There will be no investigation. I shall make

up my mind about you myself, Lady Sheridan. Nothing or no one will be allowed to sway me. What you did years ago matters less than what you do now."

She blinked at him. Her ridiculous claim had failed to scare him, but at least it would not be used against her—for now. The worst had been averted, but he would bide his time and observe her, waiting for the first misstep.

Had she foolishly handed him the means of her own destruction?

Slowly, she disentangled her fingers from his grasp.

"If you will excuse me, I will retire to my room now. I feel a headache coming on."

"But of course. I will join you presently."

Join her. Oh God. Did he mean... Of course, as far as everyone was concerned, the marriage was still to be consummated. Though she was not a virgin and he was not her first husband, it was still expected that they consummate their union.

When she stood up, the people around them exchanged knowing glances, chief amongst them Gruffydd, who was eager to see this match he had worked so hard for made indissoluble. Esyllt felt her cheeks go crimson and hastened away. She was a woman of six-and-twenty, not a shy maid, and married to a man she did not love, so why was she so embarrassed at the idea of what was going to happen?

Once in her room, she sent her maid Seren away as soon as she had unlaced the back of her gown. She needed to be alone with her thoughts, needed to decide what to do next.

As she let her satin gown slide to the floor, her decision was made. She would not let Connor claim his marital rights. After what he'd had the gall to do to her last night, she would not allow him access to her bed, at least not willingly. Surely if she made her feelings clear, he would not force her? He had not allowed his masculine urges to take over even when he had been hard and buried deep inside her, so she was pretty confident he felt no real desire for her.

Oh, if only the reverse were true.

The memory of what had happened sent blood to her cheeks and heat to her core. *She* had been the one overwhelmed by the moment and desperate for more, while he had managed to remain detached. This marriage was a political move for him, not a way of satisfying his lust. He probably had dozens of women available for bedsport. He didn't need her.

It wasn't long before the door opened, and for the second time that day, Lord Sheridan walked into her room.

The circumstances could not have been any different. Tonight he was not a prisoner bound with ropes, in a position of weakness. Tonight she knew who he was, and he was entitled to use her as he wished. They were now husband and wife, not two strangers lusting after each other.

Heart in her throat, she waited for him to speak.

The woman standing in the middle of the room, looking utterly ravishing in her nightgown, was married to him. Possessiveness swelled within Connor, at the same time as his cock lengthened in his hose, a most disconcerting reaction. Considering the trick Esyllt had played on him the night before, he should feel resentment and wariness in front of her. His desire for her as a woman should be dampened at the very least. But it was not. Which was perhaps not so odd. After all, the last time they had been together alone, he had been inside her. It was hard to forget that fact.

Although she had now discarded her wedding finery, she had lost none of her appeal. Her hair was falling over her shoulders in a shower of gold streaked with copper, the color just as fascinating as he had hoped. And even in her nightgown, she was all about elegance. That seemed to be part of her as much as the green of her eyes was. She was also taller than most women, even without her boots, a welcome discovery. As he towered above most men himself, he would have felt uncomfortable in front of a short wife.

He would have to keep her hidden from his king, he decided. Edward had a notorious wandering eye, and he would not let anything or anyone, much less someone as insignificant as Lord Sheridan, get in the way of his desire if he wanted to sample the Welsh lady's charms, and Connor could not see how he would not.

Esyllt was just too beautiful.

Pushing those unhelpful considerations aside, Connor closed the door behind him. The king was not here right now. There would be time enough to worry about a visit at court later.

"I imagine you have questions," he said, coming to a stop in front of her.

"Erm... Yes, I do." He could tell she had not expected him to worry about that. He was pleased to surprise her. His wife would be made to see that they did not have to be enemies all the time—least of in the bedroom. And there were legitimate questions she would be asking herself. It was only fair he answered them, if he wanted her to answer his later.

"Ask them, I will ask mine afterward."

"I hope you are not here to consummate our marriage," she said taking a step toward the window when he moved forward.

"That is not a question."

Nevertheless, it was not hard to see that it was all she had thought about ever since they had exchanged their vows in the chapel. Connor hesitated. What could he say? Without a doubt, he wanted to take her to bed, but he could tell she didn't want him to touch her. Her fists were bunched tight and there was a wild gleam in her eyes that made him uncomfortable. Was she afraid of him?

"Well, are you here to bed me?" she demanded.

"Whether I want to or not is irrelevant. As your husband, it is expected of me, and well you know it," he said dryly. He did not care for her tone, or to be made to feel like a brute for doing nothing more than what was required. Though he would not force her tonight if she was so opposed to marital relations, he was still master of the place and he had no intention of letting her forget it. "But it is obvious that you do not wish me to bed you. I believe you would strike me if I tried to touch you and that is not the way I mean to start our marriage. Brute force is not my preferred method when bedding a woman."

Had he expected her to dissolve in apologies? Perhaps. If so, he was to be disappointed. She merely straightened her spine and glared at him.

"No. Much better to resort to trickery, apparently."

Oh, so she was not afraid to remind him of his little game. Even better, since they both knew she was the one to blame for it.

"I was not the one who initiated our... coupling." He said the word with relish and saw thunder and lightning flash in her eyes. Why was he provoking her so, he wondered? Perhaps because she reacted to it so beautifully. No knight worthy of the name had ever tried to break a docile mule, there simply was no need. But a half-wild, spirited horse posed a stimulating challenge for any determined warrior. "You were the one who had me bound with ropes and brought to your room. You sat on me of your own initiative, bared your legs, and then allowed me to get you into bed. At no point did you offer any resistance. You opened your thighs willingly, you let me inside your delicious body, and you melted for me." Her color increased every time he added something to the list, as did the temperature in his own body. "But I believe I will not be so lucky tonight."

No.

The word never passed her lips but he saw it in her eyes. His manhood, made hard by the description of all they had done the previous night, twitched in protest. How would she respond to his provocation? By ignoring it, it seemed.

"Why did you ask your brother to take your place?" she asked, lifting her chin.

Ah. He should have guessed this would be her first question.

"It was his idea, not mine," he explained, helping himself to a goblet to wine. Esyllt's lips thinned but she refrained from making any comment. Good, she was learning to curb her tongue. "He is highly suspicious of the Welsh and feared some sort of attempt on my life upon my arrival. It seems he was right to be wary of the welcome I'd get, even if I'd wager he never foresaw something like what happened."

Connor allowed a smile to touch his lips. Matthew had talked of men coming to stab him in the dead of night, not of half-naked women trying to entice him into bed. If he heard what had actually happened, he would laugh in disbelief.

"Finding yourself between a beautiful woman's legs is not exactly dangerous, neither is it what I would call a predicament," his brother would tell him with a suggestive wink. "I'm sure you could handle such a situation."

Indeed he could. Or at least... He would, in normal circumstances. But last night, his enjoyment had been cut short. Never had he left a woman's bed with his shaft still hard as steel and it was not something he would recommend to anyone. He had meant to punish her but in the end he had suffered just as much from the unsatisfactory ending to the seduction.

"How dare you laugh!" Esyllt cried out when he let out a

snort at the memory of how he had been forced to palm himself before going to sleep. His release had left him hollow. "Don't laugh!"

"Do you mean that laughing is only allowed at certain moments here in Wales?" He emptied the rest of his goblet of wine in one gulp. "Well, I'll be sure to familiarize myself with your customs. Laughter is apparently considered a high offense if done at the wrong moment, whereas the attitude to murder is surprisingly lax and guests can expect to find themselves abducted in the middle of the night. Who would have thought?"

"Do you think we could have a serious conversation?" his wife asked with a tilt of the head. To Connor's surprise, he felt his lips quiver anew. Perhaps despite the lack of sensual gratification, his wedding night would not be a total waste. Esyllt's spirit seemed enough to offer some compensation for the relief her body would not give him.

"By all means, let us have a serious conversation. As I was saying, Matthew volunteered to take my place, leaving me free to explore the castle unimpaired and enquire about the people's loyalties without raising suspicion."

"So... That is why you spent the whole evening watching me yesterday? Because you wanted to ascertain where my allegiance lay?"

There was no mistaking the bitterness in her voice. She was disappointed. She'd thought he was drawn to her as a woman, and now she was being told he had merely been on the lookout for proof of her treachery. It would be a sobering realization. Except that it was not quite what had motivated his scrutiny of her.

It was true that he had observed the others to ascertain where their loyalty lay, but he had watched her first and foremost because he'd been drawn to her. And he had not missed the looks she'd thrown him when she'd thought him Matthew's squire. She'd been equally smitten. At the time, he had congratulated himself, thinking that the revelation of his identity would be a pleasant surprise, since he appealed to her as a man. Of course, this had been before she'd had him bound and brought to her like a pagan offering, for her to use as she saw fit.

If she had been so quick to act on her interest for a man, would she not do the same thing the next time someone caught her eye? Was he married to a promiscuous woman, one who would make a fool out of him by taking scores of lovers?

Esyllt had claimed she merely wanted Lord Sheridan to walk in on them and change his mind about marrying her. But what if desire for him had been the main motivation for the scandalous encounter? What if she'd only used this as a ready excuse to justify her behavior? She could not be naïve enough to ignore how a man would react when a beautiful woman wrapped her legs around him. It had not taken much to convince her to surrender to his need. A man she had met only earlier that evening, whose name she didn't even know, had been in her bed and between her thighs moments after he had entered the room. She had welcomed him inside her body as readily as if they'd shared this intimacy a thousand times, she had been slick and hot for him, even though he had barely touched her. Such responsiveness was promising to a lover, but worrying to a husband.

Connor clenched his jaw when memories of the previous night assaulted him. Damn it, now was not the time to get hard. He needed to think clearly. This woman would make him lose his mind if he allowed her to.

He focused his mind back to what they were discussing.

"Yes, I thought Matthew's idea had some merit."

"Only because you are prejudiced and distrustful of Welsh people!"

"You're right, it would be silly of me to be suspicious of

them. After all, apart from being half-strangled in my sleep, trussed up like a fowl and brought to the lady of the castle so she could have her wicked way with me behind her husband's back, nothing of note happened to me since I arrived." He twisted his lips in a mocking smile.

"You were never in any real danger," she pointed out, refusing to be impressed, and once again he was struck by her courage. His lovely wife would be a formidable opponent.

"No, I know. Being alone with a half-naked woman is not what I would call dangerous. She was more intent on making love to me than piercing my heart." Fire ignited in his loins when he remembered how tightly her wet softness had wrapped around him. Ah, this had to stop! Why couldn't he focus on the conversation? "Still, I'm sure Matthew would think his precautions wise if he knew what happened between us this morning."

If...

That one word was enough to send hope coursing through Esyllt's veins.

"You mean he doesn't know?" Could it be that her humiliation had not been spread around the English retinue? She had been bracing herself for lewd comments all day, waiting for the moment when someone would ask her if all Welsh women were as hot-blooded and free with their favors as she was. Now she knew why no one had so much as looked at her with a suggestive smile.

"No one knows what happened in this room except you," Connor confirmed. "And me."

She shivered at the threat contained in those two words. He would never let her forget how she had opened her legs to him. As for her, she would forever remember the way he had made her body heat up and her inhibitions melt like wax in front of a flame.

It was all a disaster. Not only had she given him reason to

doubt her modesty moments after meeting him, but she was finding out that even before their marriage vows had been taken, her husband had been wary of her and her people's intentions. She could have been the most welcoming bride imaginable, he would still have observed her from a distance, and waited for her to prove him and his wretched brother right.

Deception, disappointment, distrust... Could there be worse ways to start a marriage?

"Why didn't you tell anyone about what I did?"

He cocked his head, as if displeased that she thought him capable of such treachery. "Would you rather I had? I can if you prefer. Usually, I share everything with Matthew, so I could—"

"No!" She was horrified by the prospect. He had just told her that, contrary to what she had feared, she was safe from humiliation. Why on earth would she want it any different? All the same, she did not understand why he had spared her when it was obvious he did not feel too kindly about his new wife.

By now, Esyllt was utterly confused. Connor had come to bed her but was talking to her instead. He was calm, as if it were not embarrassing for a man to be denied his marital rights, he was talking about their "coupling" without getting aroused and smiling as if her wantonness the night before pleased him when she knew it should not.

All in all, it was as if... She hesitated in formulating the thought, then could not avoid the conclusion any longer. He liked her spirit.

It was the most disconcerting thing of all.

"Why didn't you tell your brother what I did?" she repeated slowly.

He made a gesture with his hand. "You don't need to know why. But know that what happens between us in bed is nobody's concern. I will never speak about it to anyone. For that same reason, everyone will think that I bedded you tonight. Please do not say anything to shatter the illusion."

She would not, for it suited her fine to have everyone believe everything was going smoothly between her and Lord Sheridan. Now that she was married, she would do everything to let Gruffydd think she was going along with his plans.

It was her turn to pour herself a glass of wine. After a second's hesitation, she filled Connor's goblet again. The smile he gave made it clear he appreciated her efforts at behaving as a dutiful wife should in at least one respect.

"Why are you so bent on this union, since I am unsuitable in your eyes?"

His eyes gleamed. "A wife as beautiful as you are and as eager to be bedded is not what I would call unsuitable."

The words made her flush crimson. He thought her beautiful...

Yes. And wanton, she reminded herself sternly, he had just told her as much.

"Are you not afraid I will throw myself at every man who takes my fancy if you think me eager to be bedded ?" she challenged.

"Should I be?" This time Connor's eyes narrowed. He was not amused anymore.

Esyllt cursed herself. Why did she have to be so reckless all the time? On their first encounter she had given him the impression that she was a wanton, promiscuous woman, earlier tonight she had claimed to have killed her husband, and she had now all but announced her intentions to go and seduce every man who crossed her path. Quite an achievement.

"Of course you should not be worried. I shall be a faithful wife."

The snort he gave was not encouraging to say the least. "You will allow me to reserve judgment on that."

There was nothing else to say. She emptied her wine and watched him do the same.

"Now. My turn to ask questions," he said gruffly. "Why did you want *me* to change my mind about our union? Why did you not refuse to marry me outright instead of trying to rid yourself of me on our first meeting? It would have been easier. You are no innocent maid, but a widow of considerable means and a mother, you have no father or brother to force your hand, you could have remained mistress of Esgyrn Castle on your own."

Esyllt lowered her eyes. He was perceptive, much more than she had anticipated.

"It's not that simple. Rich as I am, I am still a woman. Do not tell me that where you come from women are allowed to dictate their lives and go against the wishes of men without finding themselves accountable for their actions?"

"They're not," he agreed with a faint smile.

"And in that unstable climate, a union with an English lord is highly desirable, a good guarantee of safety. I don't think I should need to tell you as much. All the local lords pressed me to accept your offer. I quickly saw I would not be able to withstand the pressure."

A mere month after Gwyn's death, Gruffydd had come knocking at her door, presenting his plans to her. That day, she had discovered her late husband's friend's true nature. He was cruel, greedy and dangerous. It had not taken her long to understand she had better go along with his plans and remarry. Had she been alone she might have had the strength to hold on a bit longer, but she had her daughter to worry about. She would not compromise Siân's safety.

Connor closed his hand around the hilt of his sword. "Well, married we now are, so I suggest we learn to make the best of the bargain." He arched a brow. "I have another question for you. Where is your daughter? I haven't seen her around."

"Siân?" She had, somewhat foolishly, hoped he wouldn't know about her. But of course he would have asked questions about the woman he intended to marry and been told she had a young daughter. "She is at my mother's."

His eyes narrowed. "I see. You didn't want her to meet the accursed English in general and me in particular. You were afraid for her safety."

"Yes." What was the point of lying, if he'd already guessed as much? But to her surprise, when she expected an outburst of rage, he nodded.

"You did well. There was no knowing what kind of man I would be. I would have done the same in your place. But I hope you will soon see that you can bring her back without worrying about the kind of treatment I would inflict on her. It must be hard for you to be away from her."

"It is." Esyllt didn't know what to say. Why was he being so understanding and considerate where her daughter was concerned, when he had been so devious and cruel with her the previous night?

He nodded again, as if all his questions had been satisfactorily answered. "Now, if you'll excuse me, I did not get much sleep last night and I'm about to collapse."

With those words, he sat on the edge of the bed to remove his boots as if it were the natural thing to do. Her heart skipped a beat.

"You are going to sleep here?" She had not imagined he would stay.

"Yes. I told you, I'm tired, I have no desire to be disturbed or worse, murdered by your men while I sleep," he said, as he started to remove his tunic. "I do not think they will dare to come and find me in their mistress' own bed, however."

"So I am to be your protector?" The idea that the warrior towering over her relied on her for his safety was so ludicrous that she could not help a note of amusement from creeping into her voice.

He smiled as if he had understood exactly why she was amused. "I suppose you are," he said, stretching as if to emphasize the difference in size between them. She gulped. Tall she may be, but he was so strong he could have lifted her one-handed. "How does it feel?"

"Odd," she admitted in a croak.

He disposed of his tunic and hose swiftly and then, looking at her all the while, grabbed the back of his undershirt to lift it above his head. Oh, Lord. She had only ever seen her first husband naked on a handful of occasions and now she was wondering if her memory was not failing her. The two men's bodies did not have much in common.

Gwyn's chest had been nowhere near as broad, his stomach had been rounded, his legs thin and bowed and his manhood... Well. Evidently, nature was quite discriminating when she handed out masculine attributes. There were the reeds of this world and the mighty oaks.

She swallowed hard.

"I take it that you *have* seen a naked man before?" Connor asked, a smile floating on his lips. He had not missed her reaction. "You are no maiden and you have borne a child."

"I have seen a man naked. But not... not you." She knew she sounded breathless. But how could she not? A magnificent, naked man was standing right in front of her. Had she extended her arm she could have touched him. It was enough to make her light-headed.

"Shall I assume from the way you are blushing that you like what you see?"

Oh, he could. But she was not about to admit it out loud.

"It seems to me you are going to assume as much anyway so do not let me stop you, my lord."

"A good, dutiful wife's response," he answered in a smirk. "I am pleased."

Without further comment, he went to the bed and slipped under the covers. Esyllt looked around, unsure what to do. Though she was in her own bedchamber, she felt like the intruder. Should she get undressed? Slip under the covers and lie down next to him? To her relief, Connor did not demand she join him. It was as if he had already forgotten her existence. She waited, while the night's silence wrapped around her.

A moment later, she understood he had fallen asleep.

Chapter Three

Unable to sleep with a stranger in her bed, even if he was her husband, even if he looked like a pagan god—or maybe *because* he looked like a pagan god—Esyllt wrapped herself into a blanket and went to the bay window to watch the starry night. What was she to do now? Who was this man she had married? Earlier that night she had told him to watch his back because she'd killed her first husband and here he was, naked, unprotected, in her bed, and so untroubled that he'd fallen asleep at a moment's notice.

The night before she had tried to put him off and make him renounce their union, and here he was, her legally wed husband for all to see.

Everything she'd tried had been a spectacular failure and she had no other plan, so what was she to do now?

Esyllt stared through the window and into the darkness below. Though she'd been married for nearly a decade, she had never spent the night in the same bed as a man, much less one as young and attractive as the one currently taking all the space on her mattress. She could not deny being rather breath-less at the idea of joining him, because that young and attractive man had every right to roll over to his side, take hold of her and impose his desire on her whether she wanted him to or not. He had said he would not, and he was currently asleep, but she could not be too cautious. If her arm brushed against his as she turned over, who knew what desire she might awaken in him.

A man was a man, and she had already seen that Connor Hunter was as virile as they came.

What would the next few weeks bring? How would she cope with being constantly on her guard? Would her new husband even stay at Castell Esgyrn? Perhaps in a few days he would return to England. Being married was one thing, living with his wife quite another. He might decide to return to his former life... his beloved brother... his mistresses...

When she tried to move her neck and felt naught but a stab of pain, Esyllt realized that she had fallen asleep on the hard stone seat with her head at an odd angle. Outside it was dark, even if the line above the horizon was slightly lighter. Dawn was still some time away.

Feeling chilled and stiff, she decided to risk lying in the bed a moment. After all, if she was careful, Connor might not notice she had joined him, and after a night spent on the cold bench in the bay window, she needed warmth and softness.

Silent as a shadow, she went to the side of the bed and watched him a moment. His beauty was even more glaring when his face was relaxed. In sleep he *was* just like a marble carving of a pagan god, one whose whole purpose was to lure mortal women to their doom. The idea that such a man was married to her, that she was not only allowed, but expected, to make love to him was nothing short of astounding. Pleasure had been the last thing Gruffydd had taken into account when choosing her husband, she knew, so it only made her feel all the luckier to be married to a man who appealed to her senses so.

When she approached the bed he did not even stir. He had not been lying when he'd claimed to be tired.

Esyllt could not resist the opportunity of taking a closer look at him while he was unaware of being observed. With the embers of the fire, she lit a tallow candle and tiptoed back to the bed. Holding it high, she illuminated the scene—and her heart skipped a beat. While she'd busied herself with the candle, the covers had slipped, revealing a long, muscular chest that seemed hewn out of stone.

Bathed in moonlight, her husband's body had been spectacular. In the light of the candle, it seemed too perfect to be real. One arm was flung over his head in perfect abandon, the pose highlighting its perfect shape and the elegance of his hand. His lips were slightly parted and the muscles on his stomach twisted and corded every time he took a breath. Esyllt could not take her eyes from the sight, she could barely blink or breathe. The golden light of the flame did full justice to his beauty, filling every dip and hollow with velvety shadows, shadows she wanted to touch and lick.

Her eyes followed the line of dark hair that started just above his navel and disappeared under the covers. It looked soft, impossibly enticing. Heat bloomed in Esyllt's veins and she bit back a moan of longing. Could she lean in and stroke it? Could she dip her head and kiss him while he was oblivious to his surroundings? Just when she opened her lips in anticipation for his taste, he moved and, jerked out of her contemplation, she almost dropped the candle. A drop of hot fat fell onto his naked torso.

It all happened in the blink of an eye.

All she saw was Connor rear up and grab her by the throat. The candle fell onto floor, plunging the world into darkness. Fortunately, the flame had been too feeble to set the rushes on fire, but the obscurity meant Connor would not see who she was.

"It's only me, Esyllt!" she cried out in panic, clawing at the hand holding her by the neck.

"I know it's you, I did not expect anyone else to try and crawl into bed with me," he growled, throwing her onto the mattress. A heartbeat later she was flat on her back, with her wrists pinned high above her head. Her eyes had adjusted to the darkness and she could see the ire flashing across Connor's face. "What's this, wife? Trying to kill your second husband in his sleep?"

Kill him? She'd actually considered kissing him! "I-I didn't—"

"Oh, so you didn't just try to stab me?" he hissed, trapping her under his hard body.

"No, I swear. It was only the c-candle. Some fat fell on you when I moved," Esyllt explained, fighting her mounting terror.

The man was formidable in his anger and strong as an ox. If he really thought she had been about to kill him, then there would be no quarter. She could understand why he would suspect foul play. Indeed, he would have been startled out of sleep, and he might well have mistaken the stab of sudden pain for the tip of a dagger piercing his flesh.

"What were you doing lurking in the dark?" he asked, relaxing his hold marginally. Perhaps he was starting to doubt he'd been in real danger.

"I-I was watching you." She was so afraid, so intent on having him believe her that she did not even think of lying. Besides, what else could she say?

He snorted, as if that were a ridiculous answer. "Why?"

"Because... You're beautiful."

The admission, so far removed from the one he was expecting, made Connor blink.

He had woken up to a sharp pain on his stomach and his wife bent over his sleeping form. Faced with what he had identified as a threat, his reaction had been instinctive. Had he been too hasty earlier in dismissing Esyllt's claim that she had killed her first husband and would not be above getting rid of him? What if she was truly intent on hurting him? Perhaps Matthew was right to be concerned over his safety now that they were in Wales.

But now, with his mind clear, he saw that he'd completely misread the situation. He was in no danger whatsoever, his wife had not tried to stab him, she thought him beautiful, that was all.

He released her wrists, wishing—not for the first time—that he slept less soundly at night. From as far back as he could remember, he'd slept with the sleep of the dead. It was why Esyllt's men had been able to abduct him from his bed so easily the night before. It was highly inconvenient and he feared it might cost him dearly one day.

As to her claim that she thought him beautiful, ludicrous as he had first thought it, he now believed her. Something about the way she had said the words rang too true. She was not lying, she was fascinated by him and, what was more, she was unable to hide it. He remembered the way she'd looked at him when he'd undressed and every time her eyes landed on him her mouth parted slightly, as if she could not believe her luck at being married to a man she found so attractive.

It was an involuntary reaction, and it would no doubt annoy her to know that he was aware of it, but he was.

Because it was the same for him. Every time he looked at her, he was taken aback by how drawn he was to her. He had chosen his wife for reasons as far removed from lust as could be conceived, without even knowing what color eyes she possessed.

But every time his gaze landed on her, his body gave an involuntary jolt of longing.

Like now.

He sighed. It seemed he did not even have to see her to be affected. It also happened in the dark, when her lush curves were pressed against him.

Now that he was reassured she had not tried to hurt him, he could feel his body respond to her proximity. Perhaps he should not be surprised. He was naked in bed, on top of a woman he found desirable. In the circumstances, it would be odd if his blood did not stir. He shifted slightly, not wanting her to notice the effect she had on him. He might not be able to stop himself from finding his wife desirable, but it was better not to let her know she had such power over him.

"So you find me beautiful," he drawled.

He kept his voice calm, so she could trust him to stay in control. Trapped under a trained warrior, utterly at his mercy, she could easily take fright. But killing or even hurting her was not what he wanted to do to her.

Quite the contrary.

"I do find you beautiful." She could not quite meet his eye but at least she was not stammering anymore. To ease her mind further and calm the raging in his blood, Connor slid off of her but he did not allow her to move away, instead keeping her tucked close against him.

"Is that supposed to reassure me?" he asked. "Am I safe for now? Will you let me live until I have lost my good looks?"

"I..." Apparently, she was nonplussed by the change in mood and didn't quite know how to answer. He decided to let her off.

"Well. Since you don't mean to kill me I guess I could go back to sleep. Unless you wanted to make the most of my beautiful body?" he drawled. "I would be amenable."

"No!" she instantly cried out, scrambling away. This time, he let her go. No sense in frightening her again by restraining her.

"I see that being beautiful will only get me into trouble without providing me with any advantages," Connor mocked. She was attracted to him, but not enough to do something about it. "Thus far it has earned an abduction and a trussing up in the middle of the night, and now it has caused me to be scalded with melted fat. A little soothing would not go amiss. You could lick the wound, at least."

Though it was dark, Esyllt would no doubt see his smile.

"Lick?" she repeated in a breath.

"The burn is here, just under my pectoral. It is not so low that you might be tempted to take me into your mouth."

At the words his cock protested vehemently.

I'm not so far! it seemed to scream. *I want to be licked as well!*

"Take you into my mouth? What do you mean?"

Esyllt sounded so bewildered Connor knew she had no idea what he was talking about. How was that possible? She'd been married for years, had she not? How could her husband never have mentioned such an act to her, even if he had not demanded that she perform it? Apparently, the Welshman had not been an adventurous husband. The fool. It was hard to believe he would not have wanted to make the most of his beautiful wife in every way. Helen had always denied him this delight, but at least she'd been aware it could be done, and he'd genuinely thought that all married women knew about it.

Well, Esyllt clearly didn't, if her furrowed brow was any indication.

Instead of answering, he arched a brow and glanced at his groin suggestively. It seemed it would be his responsibility to show her that there were many ways men and women could enjoy each other's bodies. When she blushed, he knew she had understood what he hadn't said out loud.

"You m-must be jesting?"

"I'm not. Some women like to pleasure their lovers in that way," he explained, doing his best not to imagine her on her knees at his feet, performing the act. Doing so would only make him even harder than he was. "And some men like it very much."

She seemed at a loss as to what to say, so she hid her embarrassment under a scoff. "By 'some men,' I'm guessing you mean you."

Yes. He did. In fact, he didn't know a single man who didn't. Even Matthew, who shared surprisingly little about his personal life with him, had alluded to the pleasure he'd gotten from a bold lover on occasion.

"Why don't you come over here and see? That would be one way to make me forget about the burn on my chest."

In truth, he hardly felt it anymore, but his shaft was definitely throbbing. He would like nothing more than for her to ease *that* burn.

Alas, it was not to be.

"Good night, husband."

"I take that for a no." Despite his aching groin, Connor could not help a chuckle at the ice in her tone. "Good night then, wife."

As had become her habit, Esyllt snuffed her candle and got undressed in the dark, so as to ensure Connor could not get any glimpse of her wearing only her shift. She slipped under the covers and was instantly hit by wonderful warmth. In spite of everything, it was hard to resist the impulse to snuggle up to the body stretched next to her. Her new husband was like a furnace, a welcome discovery, considering the temperature outside, and he ensured she was never cold at night.

But heat the bed was all he did.

They had been married for four days now and had yet to consummate their marriage. Although he joined her in her room every night, Connor had not tried to touch her once, and he avoided her during the day. They lived like strangers who slept in the same bed, like husband and wife who barely exchanged a word. It was all very weird, and the worst of it was, instead of being relieved that he left her alone, Esyllt resented it, which in turn annoyed her. Surely she shouldn't be pining after him thus? If he chose to spend his days with his men instead of with her, then it meant she was free to live her life the way she wanted, and if he had not bedded her yet, then it was for the best, given what had happened the night they'd met.

Nonetheless, it was hard to convince herself that was really what she thought.

In the morning, Connor usually woke before her. For all that he slept with the sleep of the dead, he was always up before dawn. Today, though, she opened her eyes to find him staring at her. The gleam in his eyes unnerved her. How long had he been staring at her thus? What was he thinking?

"Is anything the matter?" she asked, clutching at the covers. Was her shift revealing more of her breasts than she would have liked?

For a moment he looked on the verge of a confession, then he shook his head.

"Nothing is the matter, but I'm famished. Shall we go and break our fast together for once?"

Esyllt didn't see a way of refusing to go with him, and in truth she didn't want to. They might exchange more than a few perfunctory words if they ate together. It would be good to finally get to know him better. "Very well."

She didn't have time to avert her eyes before he got up. He had slept naked, as per usual, which meant he was now standing in front of her in his full glory and bathed by the first rays of the sun. How was she supposed not to be unsettled by such a sight? Connor, on the other hand, didn't seem embarrassed in the least. Esyllt focused on her hands. Never had her nails appeared so fascinating than they did right now.

"Look at me."

"I b-beg your pardon?"

"Look at me," he repeated, coming to stand at the side of the bed. "I'm your husband. I will not have you avert your eyes as if you could not bear the sight of me."

"I... You know that's not what I think." She had told him she found him beautiful, and she could not believe for a moment he had forgotten it.

"Then look at me."

Calling on all her inner resolve, she did as he bade her—and all but gaped. "You are..."

Hard was what she wanted to say, only she couldn't speak with the proof of his virility staring at her in the face. He had invaded her body once before, of course, and she had felt the strength of his arousal, but she had never *seen* him in such a state. On their wedding night he'd undressed in front of her, but his member had not been erect.

Now, it most definitely was, and the difference was staggering.

"Yes, I am hard," he said matter-of-factly. "I am a man, and it is morning, so there is nothing odd in that."

"Isn't there?" What on earth did he mean?

A corner of his mouth lifted up. The wretched man was amused by her ignorance, just like he'd been when he'd suggested she took his member in her mouth. He'd seemed to say it was something she should have known about, or even have done before. But now that she was seeing him in his full glory she had serious doubts about her ability to do such a thing. Not that she would ever want to, of course.

"Men tend to wake up hard," Connor explained.

Did they? "But... why?"

He raised both his hands, as if to indicate that was no reason for it, it was simply the way of things and then he cocked his head as if considering. "You know, I'm really starting to wonder why it is that someone like you doesn't know more about men's bodies and preferences."

Intense heat invaded Esyllt's cheeks, for there was no mistaking his meaning. He considered her a wanton who welcomed men to her bed as soon as they took her fancy, so he was surprised about her ignorance of men's anatomy and tastes where bedsport was concerned. But there was a simple explanation for it. She was nothing like the woman he took her for. She'd been married at a young age, before she could take an interest in men, and her marriage had not been one based on carnal urges. Gwyn had never spent a night in her bed, nor had he been in the habit of wandering around with no clothes on, and of course she'd had no reason to see any other man naked, much less welcome them into her bed. So it was little wonder she didn't know men woke up hard or that they liked being licked.

"Forgive me, but I am not used to seeing men naked, whether in the morning or at night."

She'd hoped he would say that he would refrain from exposing himself in the future, so as to spare her blushes, but of course he did no such thing. Instead, he smiled and leaned in toward her, so he could purr in her ear.

"Well, I guess I will have to walk around your chamber

naked more often, then, wife, so that you *do* get used to seeing me in all my glory."

With those words, he drew back and looked her straight in the eye. They were so close it would be easy for him to lean in for a kiss if he wanted. Was that what he intended to do? Though he'd arrived almost a week ago and he'd already entered her body, they had never kissed. But instead of placing his lips over hers, he took her hand and guided it to his straining member.

"Here. You've seen it. You've felt it inside you. You've been told that you can take it in your mouth. Now you can touch it."

Her fingers wrapped around a silky soft length forged of pure steel. Esyllt's eyes widened. It was unlike anything she had ever touched before, warm, iron-hard. Fascinating. It felt almost alive, about to burst. She forgot that she should be outraged, or at the very least, embarrassed.

"Does it hurt?" The question came out in a breath.

Something in Connor's eyes flashed. "Not in the way you mean. It doesn't hurt to be hard, but it hurts not to be able to release the tension in it. That is what intercourse, or 'coupling' as you call it, is made for."

Did that mean he was about to tumble her into bed? Had all this teasing been a way of telling her he was ready to bed her? Was he about to take her, not because he wanted her, but because he needed to, in his words, 'release the tension'?

The notion made her feel both dirty and unimportant.

"Can't release be achieved by other means?" she asked, letting go of his shaft as quickly if it had scalded her fingers.

He arched a brow in surprise. "You know about that?"

"I..." Not precisely. But she had heard talk of men bringing themselves pleasure, even if she wasn't quite sure how. She had wondered at the time if the same could be done for women but had never dared try to find out more. "Well, can it?"

"It can. Only, it is much less satisfactory. Rather like snatching a moment's rest on the hard floor of the great hall when what you crave is a good night's sleep in a comfortable bed." His lips stretched into a slow, sensual smile. "It serves a purpose, but doesn't give you half as much pleasure as a woman's soft body can."

Was it the voice? Was it the look in his eyes? Was it the evocative words? Esyllt didn't know what it was that made her insides melt like honey and her heart pound hard in her chest. In any case, it mattered not.

She shot to her feet before Connor tried to persuade her that she could give him relief he needed, or worse, that she offered it herself.

"Shall we? You were famished, remember?"

Chapter Four

It took Esyllt a while to recover from the intensity of the moment she and Connor had shared in her room, when she had felt his breath at her neck and his pulsing shaft in her hand. Fortunately, she could not get dressed as fast as her husband did, and she lingered purposefully over her toilette to give herself some time to compose herself.

By the time she joined him and Matthew in the great hall, she was confident neither of the men would see anything amiss.

"Good morning, Lady Sheridan," her brother-in-law greeted, standing up. "I trust you slept well."

She was certain Connor had asked him to be cordial, because he never spoke to her if he could help it, much less show her signs of deference. She decided to behave as if he were genuinely interested in her well-being. No point in antagonizing him further.

"I did, thank you. I hope you did too."

Pleasantries out of the way, they all sat to a lavish meal of bread, cheese, meat pies and gruel. While she ate, Esyllt looked at the two men sitting opposite each other.

One dark, one fair, one with piercing green irises, the other with velvety brown eyes, they could not have looked more different if they'd tried. Perhaps they did try. Their choice of clothes, their attitudes, the way they talked, everything set them apart. The only thing they shared was a powerful physique, but even that produced a different effect. Connor appeared relaxed, whereas Matthew seemed full of pent-up energy. The stealthy wild cat and the prancing hound, both equally fearsome, both equally compelling. You just couldn't avert your eyes from them, and she didn't try.

What sort of a lover was Matthew, she wondered? Tender or passionate? Did he tease his conquests, make them think they were about to explode, and then leave them wanting, like Connor had done? Or did he kiss them until they passed out in ecstasy? Did he expect his lovers to lick him? Did he demand it?

Esyllt shook her head as the shocking thoughts crossed her mind. She should not be wondering how her brother-in-law behaved in bed. Connor already thought her a wanton, she could not start becoming one.

She blushed and turned her attention back to her gruel. Soon, however, she was ogling the men again. It was impossible not to. They were simply too compelling. Inevitably, Connor caught her staring. He smiled and winked, as if he'd guessed why she could not tear her eyes from them, and did not mind.

She went red to the roots of her hair. So that was his game, he was trying to embarrass her, instead of reprimanding her. She wasn't sure which she preferred.

Matthew soon excused himself, explaining he'd already asked for his stallion to be saddled. Esyllt was not surprised to hear he wanted a ride. He'd never tried to hide his aversion for his new home. The more time he could spend outside of the castle walls, pretending to be in England, the better.

"I think your brother would prefer to go back to Sheridan Manor," she observed once the door closed on him.

"He would. But he is not going to leave without me. As long as he thinks I'm in danger, he will remain by my side." This was said with a side smile.

"You said he was your foster brother?" They had not discussed this any further since their wedding night and she was curious. Hadn't she wanted to make the most of the opportunity of a meal shared together to get to know him better?

Connor dipped his hands into the bowl of scented water next to him before leaning back into his chair. "He's my milk brother, really."

"Oh. But then how come he ended up being fostered by your parents?" It was not uncommon for noble families to foster sons of other noble families for a few years. But Matthew's mother could not have been well-born if she had fed the future Lord Sheridan.

"His mother, Rose, was a maid at Sheridan Manor but we are not sure who his father was. Unfortunately, we think it might well have been one of my parents' guests, a nobleman thinking he could use the servants for his pleasure while he visited them."

A dark shadow passed over Connor's face at the thought. Esyllt shivered, sharing his disapproval.

"That is awful." But all too common, unfortunately.

Connor nodded. "She fed me as a babe and Matthew and I grew up together, getting into all sorts of trouble, as real brothers do. When the poor woman died of a fever, we were both six. He had no family. I made my parents take him in and raise him as their own."

Esyllt stared. A child of six imposing his will on his parents... Such determination did not bode well for her wish for independence. Would she ever manage to stand up to such a man?

"Matthew was born the day before me, which was why his mother was chosen to nurse me," Connor added with a laugh. "He has never let me forget it and always acts the big brother."

This she did not doubt. The way he'd decided to play the role of her husband-to-be was proof of his protective nature.

"And you let him?" She wouldn't have thought her husband was one to be ordered around.

His green eyes gleamed. "I do, because it's easier that way. But only when it suits me."

And there she had it. Her husband could be docility itself, but only if and when it suited him. Otherwise, he would impose his will with implacable firmness. She shivered again, remembering how he had coaxed her into opening her legs for him the night before their wedding, all this without resorting to violence or threats.

"By the way," Connor said, helping himself to another slice of dried apple, "I never asked you, what does 'Esgyrn' mean?"

The change of topic was welcome. She'd heard enough about her husband's iron will for now.

"Castell Esgyrn means 'Bones Castle.'" At his raised eyebrow, she carried on explaining. "Legend has it that when they dug around for the foundations of the castle a century ago, they found the remains of two people in the ditch yonder. No one knows who they were or how they died."

"Mm. And what do you think? You must have a theory?"

Esyllt blushed. How had he guessed the mystery had fascinated her from the moment she had come to live here with Gwyn all those years ago? "I always imagined that they were two lovers dying together."

"Killed by a jealous husband walking in on them, you mean?"

"No!" She had never once in all those years imagined that they would be an adulterous pair. Trust him to immediately assume the worst. "Rather two young people who had to meet in secret because they could not be together."

"Ah." Connor bit into his dried apple but he couldn't hide the twinkle in his eyes. "My wife is a romantic."

What could she answer to that? Nothing, because she was. The only problem was, she had never had the luxury of being one. Two marriages arranged by other people had seen to that. Love was not something she could afford to think about, now less than ever.

"In any case, we'll never know who they truly were," she concluded.

Just then the castle steward entered the great hall, followed by Gruffydd, four of his men and Matthew, who came to stand beside Connor, as if he feared the Welshmen would lunge at him with their swords drawn before he'd had time to blink. Apparently, he'd changed his mind about going for a ride in favor of playing the protective big brother again. The thought both warmed and reassured her, because she knew Gruffydd was only waiting for the opportunity to strike, and she didn't want him to.

"*Bore da*," he started, using the Welsh greeting. Esyllt would not be surprised if he pretended not to be able to speak English, just to make a point.

"Good morning," Connor replied, standing up.

"And good morning to you too," Matthew said when the Welshman pointedly ignored him.

"As for you, I might have greeted you if I knew who you were," Gruffydd snarled, not in the least impressed. At least he'd reverted to English.

"You can call me Matthew. I'm his lordship's brother."

Though she should perhaps have sympathized with him,

since she'd suffered from the deception herself, Esyllt enjoyed the sight of Gruffydd's displeasure. He had been taken for a fool, but perhaps he did not deserve any better. After all, he had organized the match. If one person should have known who her groom was, it was him. The incident made her realize just how cynical he'd been, choosing a husband for her regardless of his personal qualities and not even bothering to meet him beforehand. If he'd been tricked, he had only himself to blame.

"Now, we have important matters to discuss," he said, facing Connor once more. "That is, if you truly *are* Lord Sheridan, of course."

"I am. You can safely address me with the respect you owe me and call me 'my lord'."

The rebuff was softened by a smile that would have ensnared a dragon, which was fortunate. Gruffydd had never looked more furious. Esyllt almost laughed out loud. There were some advantages to being married to a formidable man, it seemed, one who would not let anyone forget who was master of the situation. She would enjoy watching him tame Gruffydd.

"Leave us," the Welshman said, not even bothering to look at her.

Before she could answer, Connor raised a hand. "Lady Sheridan will attend the meeting if such is her wish. She will be a useful addition to the proceedings. After all, she's been the one looking after Esgyrn Castle since her husband's death. As such, she is the most appropriate person to bring me up to date with its working, wouldn't you agree? I will want to hear her opinion."

Esyllt's eyebrows shut upward. Was this another trick? Did her husband mean to expose her lack of knowledge in front of everyone and use it later on to impress on to her that she could not be involved in his decision making? If this were the case, he would be sorely disappointed because he was right, she *was* the best person to inform him of the castle's workings and she would be only too glad to prove it.

"With your permission, my lord, I will stay," she said, taking the arm he was offering. For the first time since she'd been told she was to remarry, a flicker of hope lit up in her chest. Perhaps this marriage would bring her some satisfaction. If she was allowed to help in the administration of their domain, she would not feel like a pretty ornament stripped of all power. As a trusted ally, she would be able to influence her husband's decisions and make sure to protect her Welsh tenants' interests from the worst of English greed. Not that she thought Connor an unreasonable man who would turn into a tyrant, but he himself was obeying his king's orders.

Gruffydd raised a hand in protest when she started to walk toward the door on her husband's arm. "Get back to whence you came and leave us men to—"

"If I hear you address my wife in such a disrespectful manner again, I will demand that you apologize for it on your knees," Connor snarled, coming to stand directly in front of Gruffydd. "Are we clear?"

He'd moved with the speed of an adder and looked barely less dangerous, ready to strike in her defense. Esyllt realized then that, no matter what he had subjected her to since his arrival, he'd always spared her from the worst of his temper. It was a welcome revelation. Even when he'd discovered her supposed wantonness or thought she'd been out to kill him, he had not spoken to her with half as much venom as he had just spoken to Gruffydd.

The Welshman, predictably, was beside himself with fury at being upbraided in front of his men. "But, she's a woman!"

"Thank you, yes, I had noticed. In the future there will be no need to point out the obvious to me. It will save us a lot of precious time." He glared at Gruffydd. "When you are ready, you can apologize to her. She is still waiting. If I have to remind you again, I will do so with the tip of my sword."

There was a pause. Then the older man surrendered.

"Forgive me, Es—Lady Sheridan. Please join us in the discussion."

Esyllt raised her head and afforded a gracious smile. "I will, thank you."

All together, they proceeded to the solar.

As he listened to Esyllt's report on what had transpired since her husband's death, Connor understood that his wife was as astute a negotiator and clever an administrator as he had hoped. He'd already had chance to see that the castle was running smoothly. By all accounts, everything that needed to be repaired had been repaired, the stockrooms were full, the tenants were happy and well-fed and his wife was aware of all that was happening on the domain, from the state of the portcullis to the due date of the cook's daughter's baby. It was an impressive achievement, especially in these troubled times. But even if she had not been so knowledgeable, he would have preferred to deal with her anyway. She was much more pleasant than gnarled old Gruffydd—and much easier on the eye.

The man really was insufferable, making it look as if his presence were indispensable when it was little more than an irritation. He had nothing to offer except pointless criticism.

"I think we have naught else to say," Matthew concluded a moment later, echoing his thoughts exactly.

"It's time to adjourn the meeting," Connor agreed. It was a mystery the men had come at all. As far as he could tell, nothing had been achieved.

One of the Welshmen, who so far had stayed silent,

allowing his lord to speak, could not help himself from delivering one last parting shot.

"You might be master of Castell Esgyrn now, but rest assured that we will never forget what happened the night you arrived."

Connor would have answered with his own pique, but before he could open his mouth, his attention was caught by Esyllt, who had gone bright red. What had caused this reaction, he wondered? It could have been anger at the man's presumption, of course, but somehow he doubted it. Then she bit her bottom lip and he had his answer.

Him.

Their first night together, when she had mistaken him for Lord Sheridan's squire and welcomed him in her bed, that was what she was thinking about, here, amongst all the men. His own body jerked in remembrance. Feeling her sheath wrapped around him had been one of the hottest moments of his life.

He sent her a fiery look and had the satisfaction of seeing her lower her eyes.

So he had been right, she was thinking of their night together.

Not for the first time, he marveled that he had found the strength to leave her bed when he had, and not stayed until he had reached his release. It had never been his intention to make love to her, simply to ascertain how far she was prepared to go, but once he had sunk into her silken depths and seen her eyes change colour with the pleasure it had brought her, he had almost thrown caution to the wind.

What harm would it do to possess her fully, he'd wondered? They were to be married in the morning anyway and she clearly wanted him. He could have pumped a few more times and brought about his release, and hers. It would not have taken long, he'd been close to bursting, and she'd been on the verge of climax. He'd seen it in her eyes, heard it in her breathing, felt it around his cock.

But in the end, reason had prevailed. He'd left her warmth, one of the most difficult things he had ever had to do.

"Rest assured that I will never forget that night either," he said, his eyes firmly on Esyllt.

His tone was so intimate that no one dared add anything, not even Gruffydd.

"I will take my leave now, if I may." The Welshman stood up. "I think all that needed to be said has been said. Lady Sheridan, will you see me and my men out?"

Though it was clear the man wanted an opportunity to speak to her alone, and in Welsh, Connor gave his agreement. Mayhap this gesture of goodwill that cost him little would go a long way into appeasing the man, and he could always ask Esyllt what they had discussed afterward. He felt sure she would tell him the truth, as she seemed no fonder of the man than he was himself.

Esyllt followed Gruffydd outside. As soon as they were out of hearing distance, he rounded on her, just as she had expected.

"Say what he might, Lord Sheridan played us for fools, asking his brother to impersonate him!"

"He did, but I don't see why you should object. If anyone should be angry, surely it should be me," she replied, not in the least inclined to sympathize with his recriminations. What did *he* have to complain about? She was the one who'd paid the price of the brothers' deception and she was still hot from remembering how Connor had seduced her into agreeing to let him inside her body.

"Why should you complain?" Gruffydd snarled, oblivious to her inner turmoil.

Why? She blinked. Had he really asked her that question? "Because I am the one who married him, who now has to live with him!" she answered, unable to believe she actually had to spell it out. Was the man really so lost to all common decency that he thought she wouldn't mind being introduced to one man and then told a moment later she was actually to marry another?

Gruffydd shrugged, as if her qualms were worth less than his humiliation. "What's his game, I wonder, first hiding behind his brother, and now acting as if he'd lived here all along?"

Really, the man was not to be believed. How obtuse could one be? The workings of Connor's mind were not so difficult to understand, not to her anyway. "He was probably suspicious of the welcome he would get and is now trying to establish his authority before it's too late, and I cannot say I blame him."

"Oh?"

She stared at him in disbelief. He really was that obtuse.

"Of course not. Have you considered what he's doing? His king might have conquered the land and extracted a treaty saying so out of the reluctant lords, but he is not here physically to keep everyone under control, is he? Though he is officially amongst the victors, Lord Sheridan has been sent into hostile land, surrounded by a very small retinue, to try and maintain an enemy's authority, a difficult challenge at best, an impossible task at worst. I say it takes a great deal of courage to do what he's doing."

It could well cost him his life. It *would* cost him his life if Gruffydd had anything to say about it. The notion sent a shiver down her spine.

"Do you?" Gruffydd's eyes narrowed. He hadn't liked hearing her take an Englishman's defense. But for the first time since she'd been told she was to marry an English lord, Esyllt had put herself in Connor's shoes, and it did not make for a comfortable situation. It was as she'd said. His supposed superiority over them was little protection. It only made the local lords eager to get rid of him.

"Yes, I do. And have you seen the way you talk to him?" she carried on. "It will not be long before he suspects that you wish him ill."

"If he doesn't suspect it already, then he really is as foolish and arrogant as the others. I have every reason to wish him ill, and so have you. So stop fawning over him and remember where your duty is."

Chapter Five

"You will no doubt be relieved to know that I'm leaving."

"Leaving?" Esyllt's heart started to pump erratically in her chest. Connor was leaving? And she was supposed to be relieved? She was not. In the last week she'd thought they had come to some sort of understanding. Was she wrong? Had all her efforts at conciliation come to nothing? He had still not bedded her, but he had come to her every night, and since the meeting with Gruffydd, he had even started to seek her out during the day.

And now he was leaving?

Far from being relieved, she was filled with dismay at the idea. Only a few days ago she would have been delighted to see him go but today... well, today she was not.

"Matthew and I are going to Sheridan Manor. There are some matters for us to attend to as we left in haste. We will be gone a few weeks, possibly even a couple of months, I do not know. In any case, it doesn't matter, I imagine that the longer we are gone, the better. Our presence here has not been greeted with what I would call enthusiasm."

No, it had not. And yet... It was not as bad as all that. She had started to see that the servants had thawed toward their new master. Because of the language barrier, they could not talk to him, but it seemed they were no longer avoiding him. It was a progress of sorts. As for her, she had made peace with the idea of being married again, because against all odds, her new husband was not the monster she had feared he would be.

"You might get a warmer welcome if you didn't come back surrounded by so many fierce-looking knights," she could not help but retort.

"Oh, so it's my fault, is it?" He sounded amused. "Well, I'll be sure to return with only a small retinue next time. It's just as well. The men who actually want to come live here are few anyway, and I would hate to force anyone to settle in such a hostile country."

Well, she had deserved that, she supposed. "That is not quite what I meant."

"I know," he soothed. "And I agree with you. Patience and persuasion can sometimes achieve what brute force can't."

She could only nod.

The next morning, as promised, Connor was gone. She watched him ride out of the gate with a heavy heart.

For seven long weeks Esyllt reverted to the life she'd been living since Gwyn had died. The irony was not lost on her. Married or widowed, she ended up being the sole one in charge of Castell Esgyrn. But whereas she hadn't minded at first, she now did, because in a short week, she had seen what it would be like to have a reliable ally in what was a monumental task.

The only good thing about Connor's absence was that she had gotten her daughter back. With the English gone, she had called for Siân's return. Her pleasure at being reunited with the little girl and being able to assure her she would like her stepfather gave her the patience to wait for his return.

When the snow started to melt, she found herself looking forward to seeing him again. How much longer would he stay away? Would he even want to come back to Wales? He'd said few of his men wanted to live here, and she couldn't blame them. Life here could be dangerous for the invaders. Entire towns were burnt without second thoughts, houses were razed to the ground for no reason at all, and people were killed as a matter of course. She would understand if he preferred to stay in the safety of his own home without the bother of the wife he'd only married to appease his king.

But the day the last patch of snow in the shade of the lists surrendered, Connor came back.

The retinue of Englishmen, much smaller than on the day of their wedding, passed through the gates on lathered horses. It was obvious they had been riding hard all day. Absurdly, the realization sent Esyllt's nerves into a tangle. It looked as if he had pushed his men so that they could reach Castell Esgyrn before nightfall, instead of postponing their reunion for another day. She couldn't understand why he would have done such a thing. After an absence of almost two months, another evening would have made no difference.

"My lady."

Connor jumped down from the saddle and walked up to her, all tall, dark and brooding. In his chainmail and spurred boots, he looked even more formidable than in her memory, which was saying something.

To her surprise, once he'd stopped in front of her, he wrapped a hand around her waist, drew her to him and kissed her full on the mouth, leaving her slightly breathless—and thoroughly confused. It was not an intimate kiss, per se, but they had never shared such intimacy before, especially not in front of other people. Matthew, who, inevitably, was part of the retinue, seemed just as surprised as she was, and not best pleased.

"What is this, my lord?" Esyllt couldn't help but ask.

"Can't I kiss my own wife?" He kept her close while he spoke.

"You can, but I do not see why you would want to," she replied with some spirit. "You leave me for weeks on end, you do not send so much as a word in all this time and now you are behaving as if we were passionate lovers." It made no sense.

"Mm, not quite. Passionate lovers do more than give each other such tame kisses, you know," he whispered in her ear. "If we were passionate lovers, I would have lifted you into my arms and marched you to your chamber before you could even take in a breath. And once I had kicked the door closed and thrown you on the bed, I would have fallen on you like a starved wolf devouring his prey, all this before I even removed my hauberk. You would this very moment be spreading your legs for me, and crying my name."

Esyllt whimpered at the reaction his shocking words provoked inside her. Suddenly she wished he would do just that, sweep her into his arms and bring her to bed where he would feast on her. Well, she would not give him the satisfaction of knowing he had succeeded in filling her mind with lewd images.

"The point is, I do not understand you."

How could she? The man was a mass of contradictions. He was wary of what she might do to him, yet he slept in her bed. He was her husband and an Englishman, yet he trusted her to administer Castell Esgyrn in his stead. He had left her a week after their wedding but upon his return he had kissed her as naturally as if he had been pleased to be reunited with her. He described shocking acts to her and talked of devouring her, but he had yet to bed her properly.

"There is nothing to understand," he answered breezily, keeping her tight against his mail-clad chest. "We are married. It is natural that I should greet you after an absence of six weeks, don't you think?"

"Seven weeks," she rectified before thinking.

"Ah. So you kept count?" he asked, eyes gleaming. "I hadn't dared hope as much."

"I..."

Esyllt could have kicked herself for falling into his trap. She had not meant to sound as if she'd been languishing in his absence, yet that was exactly what she had done. Though she hated to admit it to herself, time had dragged on without him. She had missed him every day. Obviously, she was a mass of contradictions as well, for how could she feel that way toward someone she had known for such a short time? How could she miss a husband she had never wanted to marry? How could she feel comfortable in the arms of a man she had every reason to be wary of? After what he had done to her on the night of his arrival, she should hate him and consider herself well rid of him.

But instead, she had woken up every morning hoping that this would be the day he would finally come back.

Most of all, she had missed his warm presence at night. Sleeping with someone was a new, pleasurable experience, and even if she had been too shy to do what she wanted to do—press herself against his long body—she had made sure that a part of their bodies touched before she fell asleep. Though she kept her back to him at all times, she liked to feel she was not alone in bed. A toe brushing against his leg or, more daringly, the swell of her buttocks resting against his lean hip, she had been unable to resist the urge to snuggle up to him. One night, the one before his departure, she had woken up in his arms. Whether he had reached out to her in his sleep, or she had been the one nestling herself into his arms, she did not know. Either way, she had been unable to move away, and she had drifted back to sleep with her nose pressed against his neck.

They had only spent seven days together, and yet she had the impression that they had known each other their whole lives. How could that be when they were total strangers, from different countries, who had not desired this union?

She moved away from Connor, realizing that everyone was waiting for him to proceed to the great hall before attending to their own needs. Even Matthew was silent, as if witnessing something extraordinary.

Wishing to re-establish herself in the role of mistress of the place, and in control, Esyllt reverted back to polite civility.

"Will you and your men have a cup of ale, my lord? I wager you have earned it."

Connor smiled at his wife's reaction. He was not fooled by the attempt at detachment. She was looking at him with composure and behaving like a chatelaine ought, but there was a flush to her cheeks that made her turmoil clear. Earlier, her body had relaxed in his arms, as if she craved the embrace without even realizing it. Her lips had softened under his, betraying a desire to be kissed she would never have admitted to. It mattered not if she did or not. He knew the truth.

She was pleased to see him, to be held and to be kissed.

How right he had been to demand an extra effort from the exhausted men and horses. When Esgyrn Castle had appeared into view at the edge of the forest, and he'd understood that he could reach it before nightfall if they increased the speed, he had given the order to push on.

And when he'd seen her walk into the bailey, tall and regal in a dark gown that made her skin glow, the impulse to kiss her had been so impervious that he had not even tried to fight it. Unexpectedly, he had missed her too, and now that she was in front of him, he did not wonder why. Just like it had on the night they had met, everything about her drew her to him. She smelled divine, and after being stuck with a retinue of men who hadn't bathed for a sennight, all he wanted to do was bury his face in her sweet-smelling neck and breathe in deeply.

Leaving Matthew to oversee the men and horses, he followed her into the great hall where a welcome fire was blazing. Though the days were getting warmer at last, with the sun sunk below the horizon, it was growing chilly.

He accepted the cup she was handing him with a nod. "Everything all right here?"

"Of course." Her eyes narrowed at the question. "To ensure I took care of the domain adequately, is that why you came back so quickly?"

His lips quivered at the use of the word "quickly". He knew full well she was remonstrating because she had thought his absence too long. Hadn't she counted the days until they were reunited in the same way he had?

"No. I trust you to have managed Esgyrn Caslte well in my absence," was all he said. "And now, after a few hard days on the road, I wish for a hearty meal, a warm bath, and a good sleep, in that precise order."

"I'll see to it that you get it all, my lord," Esyllt said, appearing every inch like the meek, dutiful wife he knew she was not.

Finally, sated and refreshed after an excellent meal and a sweet-scented bath, Connor joined Esyllt in her bedchamber. That she had not been sure whether he would come to her or not was obvious from the way she blinked when she saw him in the door frame. As luck would have it, he had caught her just at the right time. She had not had time to put on her dressing gown yet and the linen shift she was wearing was almost transparent. Her hair fell in loose strands over her back and her skin was glowing from her recent ablutions. If ever there had been a sight to rouse a man's blood, this was it. His blood certainly responded.

"My l-lord," she stammered. "I thought you would want to sleep in your bed tonight if you're tired."

"I don't. I will sleep here, like I did before I left."

Nothing could have made him admit it, but he was dying to touch her. He had almost added that after his bath, and before his sleep, he needed a wild romp between the sheets with his wife but he knew that was not the way to go about it. Eventually he would bed her, but he would have to wait, not pounce on her the night of his return like a sailor jumping on the first whore he saw upon reaching shore. Some finesse was required here.

"Tell me about your first husband," he asked instead, surprising her—and himself with the demand.

"Why?"

"You do not need to know why to answer me. I know he was older than you, but I don't know much more." He couldn't have said why he wanted to know, so it was better to invoke his right as a husband to have his wishes obeyed. Esyllt didn't seem impressed but she answered nonetheless.

"At the death of my parents, I was seventeen. Gwyn married me. He had been one of my father's closest friends and they had arranged the union between them when Father lay on his deathbed." She let out a laugh that held no humor. "Believe it or not, he had wanted to prevent an unscrupulous English lord from claiming me, or rather Castell Esgyrn and my extensive domains, for himself. It seems he was right to fear such an eventuality, for that is exactly what happened."

Fear... The word sat ill with Connor.

"I am English, and I am a lord," he agreed, crossing his arms over his chest. "It doesn't necessarily follow that you will be ill-used.",

"No, but in the wrong hands my domain might."

"My hands are perfectly capable," he snapped. "I thought you'd have realized that by now."

Oh, oh. And now she had angered the beast, Esyllt thought with a sinking heart. In truth, she was not surprised, for, if she had not exactly tried to rouse Connor's ire, she'd been rather confrontational since he'd arrived.

"Land!" he spat. "Is that all that matters to you? Do you prefer a husband who treats you well or one who merely ensures that your land remains in Welsh hands? Are you saying that you are less valuable than an expanse of grass-covered mud?"

Esyllt blinked. This was not something she had ever wondered about. Did she really place the integrity of a piece of land above her own peace of mind and possible happiness?

No. But this would only be a relevant question if she were free to choose her husband. As she was not, she'd had to forget her peace of mind and happiness in favor of what could be guaranteed, namely the safety of the people relying on her. As to her husband treating her well, Connor was a hypocrite for even suggesting that her agreeing to marry Gwyn had been a bad decision. *He* had never played humiliating games with her, he'd only wanted to protect her.

"You need not make it sound as if you were a model of solicitude. Or have you forgotten what you did to me the night before our wedding?" He had enjoyed getting the upper hand and showing her who was master. That was not something to be proud of.

"Hardly." The corner of his lip curled. "It was quite memorable."

Esyllt forced herself to ignore the flash of heat that wicked smile provoked in her body. "So I have to assume this is your idea of good treatment? Proving that you are stronger than me and could have me under you in bed at any time? I cannot say I care for it!"

"I was only in your bed because you had brought me there yourself," he retorted. "Had your men not brought me up to your room tied up like a sucking pig ready for roasting, I would never have behaved so crudely. It was never my intention to force you to reveal your true nature before our wedding but you forced my hand, not the other way around."

"My true nature!" Esyllt almost choked on the words. "What is that supposed to mean?"

"You are a brazen, lustful woman. Do not think I have forgotten the way you came to straddle me on the chair or how you rubbed yourself against me once you had allowed me to lie on top of you in bed." Connor gave a groan and she remembered her furious writhing. Indeed she had behaved like the veriest wanton. "I don't think that a woman who provokes a man thus is new to it and she cannot pretend to be shocked when the man responds to her advances. I was lying between your spread legs, for Christ's sake, and I was there with your full agreement. In taking you, I treated you exactly as you wanted to be treated."

There was nothing she could answer to that. If he really thought she'd gotten what she'd wanted all along then there was no way to make him change his mind.

Still, Esyllt's body combusted in hot shame, because he was wrong in at least one way. She was not a wanton, a brazen lustful woman who went around teasing men. She had been the first one surprised by her reaction. That night her senses had taken over, something that had never happened to her, and she had, for a wild moment, not been herself. The feel of Connor's body over hers, of his manhood poised at her entrance, hard and ready to push in, had utterly undone her. It had been like nothing she had ever experienced, irresistible. It was as if her body had been made to welcome his and his to fill her, as if they fit together as perfectly as a walnut kernel fit inside its shell.

It had been delicious, beautiful even.

And he had spoilt it all by withdrawing from her in disgust.

As if that was not enough, he was now using what had happened to insult her.

It was not to be borne.

Pain and shame overwhelmed her. She had wanted him to come to her that night? Perhaps, but now she wanted him gone.

"You can sleep here, my lord, and get the sleep you asked for. But you shall do it without me. I will not impose my true, brazen, lustful nature on you a moment longer," she said, fighting back tears. Would that he had stayed in England if he'd only come back to make her feel so wretched! "Your bedchamber is empty. I will go there."

"Wife." Connor caught her by the arm before she could leave the room.

"My name is not 'wife'," she snapped, wondering what possessed her to provoke him so when he was already angry. Probably her own anger. She was almost suffocating with it. "It's Esyllt. I suggest you start using it. And I am amazed that you would want to be reminded that you are bound to me, if you think me little more than a whore." The word had difficulty passing her lips but she forced it through. Wasn't that what he thought?

The green eyes flashed but she was past heeding his warning. "Wait, I never said that. Do not put words into my mouth, *ever!*"

"What should I put instead?"

He growled and, before she knew what was happening, Esyllt was flat on her back on the bed, pinned under him. Again. And the shift she was wearing did little to prevent her from feeling how hard he was. Again. She swallowed.

What would he do now?

Connor could barely breathe for anger and desire combined. His little wife wanted to provoke him as soon as he'd come back? That was a dangerous game to play while wearing nothing more than a thin shift. She was pushing him when he'd been trying his damndest not to impose his desire on her? She would soon see he had a snapping point, as patient as he liked to think himself.

And she wanted to know what she should put into his mouth? The answer was simple.

Her.

He would devour her, get his fill of her, until she screamed his name and was too weak to even think of provoking him further.

"Open your legs."

Her eyes widened. "I—"

"Open. Or I will do it for you."

For a dreadful moment he feared she would not comply. But despite the threat he'd just uttered, he didn't want to force her. It never came to that. Slowly, her gaze still locked with his, she eased her thighs apart. As she was only wearing her shift, it was easy to expose her to his gaze—and mouth. The hem was lifted in a hurry and her maddening scent hit his nostrils. Under the floral bouquet he had smelled in her hair, he detected a headier, spicier scent. Arousal spiked through his spine, causing his eyes to close.

He started to salivate in anticipation of the softness he would feel against his mouth. He extended his tongue and groaned. This was it, finally, the first taste of his infuriating Welsh wife, the woman who had haunted his nights while at Sheridan Manor. How many times had he brought about his release while imagining this moment? More than he was comfortable admitting.

"No!" Esyllt closed her legs—or tried to. Connor placed his hands on her thighs to prevent her from doing so. Now that she had surrendered, he would not allow her to retreat.

"Yes," he said ruthlessly, pinning her in place. "I told you I would give you what you deserved, and this is it. Open for me."

He waited, knowing she would not be able to resist.

When she did, he gave her everything he'd dreamed of giving her. His mouth to kiss her wet folds, his teeth to nibble at her hidden pearl, his fingers to squeeze with her intimate muscles, and then finally his tongue to soothe when she spasmed so fiercely he thought she was going to pass out. The whole thing was beautiful, perfect. She squirmed, she bucked, and surrendered in a long agonized rasp. Her release coated his lips and he knew he was perilously close to coming himself. For a moment, he considered tearing at his braies and plunging into her but then sanity prevailed. He had only meant to make a point, not to get carried away. Tonight was not the night to consummate their marriage. He refused to do it like this, after an argument, while he was half-crazed with lust.

At last the world quietened and his groin stopped throbbing.

With regret, Connor removed his fingers from her softness. Desperate to prolong the moment, he put them into his mouth and sucked. A mistake. His desire, momentarily mastered, leapt to life again. He nipped it in the bud, determined to be sensible.

Slowly he crept up Esyllt's sated body, leaving her legs spread open and her womanhood exposed, and came to speak into her ear.

"Every time you feel like putting words in my mouth, remember that the only thing I will ever allow you to put there is your delectable little pussy. It is not only women who can use their mouths to pleasure their lover."

Esyllt gave a squeal and hid her crimson face in her hands. Connor growled and closed his eyes. This had been a close cut. Smelling her arousal, seeing her writhe for him, hearing her moans, tasting her release, had almost pushed him beyond what he was capable of enduring. Had he not called on all his inner strength, he would have taken her in a frenzied assault he would only have regretted later. Forcing her to accept pleasure was one thing, showing her a side of him he wasn't sure he liked, quite another.

Still fully dressed, he lay on his back and stared at the ceiling. Even exhausted by the long ride, he knew it would be a long time before he could will himself to sleep.

Chapter Six

The deep voices talking in English could only belong to two men. Esyllt stilled before she entered the solar. She had no intention of seeing Connor right now. After what had happened last night, she wasn't sure how to face him, least of all in the presence of his brother, who would no doubt see straight through her embarrassment and enjoy every minute of it. The traces of what her husband had done to her were surely etched on her face for all to see. He had buried his head between her legs and what was worse, or better, or at least, more shocking, was that he had seemed to enjoy it as much as she had. Though she had been the one being given pleasure, he had sounded as if he was the one benefiting from it.

How were they to behave after sharing such intimacy? It had been bad enough when he had made her hold his manhood. But this was a thousand times more unsettling.

Oblivious to the fact that someone was behind the door, the men carried on their conversation. Unable to stop herself, she listened.

"So you really intend to stay in Wales?" Matthew didn't sound pleased with this development, which didn't surprise her.

It wasn't hard to guess he only wanted one thing, to go back to England as soon as possible.

"Aye, for a little while at least. I mean to make this marriage work and gain the people of Esgyrn Castle's respect."

"Well then, you're a braver man than I am."

"I am. But we've known this all along, haven't we?"

While the men laughed, Esyllt considered. Her husband had come back, as promised, and he'd just announced that he wanted to take his responsibilities seriously. She had no time to wonder whether this decision made her happy or not, because what she heard next froze the blood in her veins.

"There is only one problem. If I am to remain here, then you will have to go and get Jane for me. I cannot be without her for so long." There was a pause, during which her heart almost failed her. "And, Matthew... My wife need not know about it just yet. There will be ample time to introduce her when she arrives."

The closing of the door indicated that her brother-in-law had left, thankfully using the exit at the other end of the room. It would not do for her to be caught eavesdropping.

A moment later, she heard the sound of boots in the bailey below, heading toward the stables. Clearly, not a moment was to be wasted to go and get this precious Jane. Red hot fury washed through Esyllt, replacing the hurt she'd felt at hearing that in England there was a woman her husband could not be without. How could she have been so naïve? Of course Connor had a mistress, perhaps even more than one. He had not married her to find love or build a family but to further advance his king's political ambitions, and he did not love her. In the circumstances, it was not to be marveled at that he should wish to carry on with his life as if nothing had changed.

Had he not all but told her the previous evening that he considered her a wanton creature governed by lust? Hardly a suitable attribute for a wife, as everyone knew. Wives were there for the breeding of legitimate children and, if they were competent enough, the management of the domain. Passion and tenderness were reserved for mistresses, women who had actually been chosen for their allure.

Although... Esyllt frowned. Had Connor not pleasured her in a selfless manner last night, forgetting his own needs, behaving as if he could not resist the desire she inspired in him?

No, he had stamped his authority over her, nothing more. That he had chosen to do it in such an unusual manner did not change the intention. She would not be grateful for an act that only proved his high-handedness.

Before she could think on the wisdom of her actions, Esyllt stormed into the solar. She would not have known how to behave in front of the decadent lover, but she had no problem facing the secretive adulterer. Fury helped overcome any lingering embarrassment over what they had done the night before. Now she understood why he was so knowledgeable about brazen, lustful women, how he knew about the scandalous ways men and women pleasured each other. Because he had a leman who opened her legs to him whenever he lay over her, a mistress with whom to enjoy shocking, decadent lovemaking, the likes of which he had introduced her to only the night before.

And now he wanted that woman, Jane, by his side, here at Castell Esgyrn.

Did he really think she would accept that?

She came to stand in front of him, feeling ten feet tall because she had right on her side. "Husband," she said as coldly as her boiling rage would allow.

"Wife," he replied cautiously. Evidently, he had picked up on her mood. Not that it was difficult, she imagined, because she could feel herself trembling with indignation. Her face would most likely be a picture of ire. "How are you this—"

"Your beloved Matthew is as we speak on his horse, riding back to Sheridan Manor, from what I understand. My, that was quick, considering he only arrived from England last night," she spat, ignoring the question. "He left without even saying good-bye. I cannot say I will miss him, but I see why you would think that your wife should not be informed of the arrival of your whore in her castle!"

Connor ran a hand over his face. It was clear he had wished to avoid this conversation. Well, too bad, they were having it.

"You were there," he said warily.

"Of course I was there. This is my home, why shouldn't I be?" She straightened her spine, wishing she were even taller, more imposing, so she could look him squarely in the eye, as a man would, and intimidate him into contrition. "Who is this Jane? As if I need to ask."

"Indeed, you do not. You need not concern yourself with her," was his blunt answer.

Her husband was a daunting man when he chose to be and evidently he had decided that fixing her with his amazing eyes would be enough to deter further discussion on a subject he was loath to discuss. He thought that impressing his phys-ical superiority upon her would quell any rebellion on her part.

It was not. By now she'd seen enough of him to guess he would never actually strike her. The only hurt he would cause would be with his words and deeds.

"Oh, but I do need to concern myself with her. Any woman my husband chooses to bring under my roof is my concern. If you cannot see that, then you really are—"

"Enough!" He raised his hand. "I promise to introduce her to you in due time. I was going to wait but since you insist, it shall be as you wish. Matthew will be back with her before the end of the month, I expect, and then you two will meet."

His impudence was not to be believed. That was all he had to say? That the two of them would meet in due time? What for? Surely he didn't expect them to create a bond over gossip about Connor's behavior in bed? Was he considering the three of them sharing a bed?

Esyllt gritted her teeth. If he didn't see how insensitive he was being on his own, there was little chance she would manage to make him see how inappropriate his comments were. Better not to make a scene and leave with her dignity intact.

"Very well. I see that I have no choice over whom to welcome to my own castle. I hope you will at least let me choose whom to welcome into my bed," she replied, taking a step back. If he forced her to share a bed with his mistress, make her watch them together, she would leave, and not worry about the consequences of her actions. "You will oblige me by staying in your own bedchamber tonight. If you do not, you will only have to watch me go to yours before you can tumble me into bed and use me to satisfy your perverse urges. Heed my words, what happened last night will never be allowed to happen again."

Without waiting for an answer, Esyllt exited the room.

A fortnight later, as planned, Mathew was back with Jane. Connor welcomed them both in his solar, where he offered them a drink.

"How do you hope to keep her from your wife?" Matthew whispered, while Jane focused her attention on the litter of puppies tumbling about by the hearth.

"There is no need for me to do that," Connor replied. "I fully intend to introduce the two of them today."

The pursed lips made it clear his brother didn't think it such a good idea. Nevertheless, he did not comment. "What is going on between you and your wife?" he asked instead. "I have seen the way you look at her, and how she looks at you at times. Yet... You are supposed to hate each other, are you not?"

"Not hate each other," Connor corrected immediately. That had never been the intention, rather what he had feared might happen, given the fact that she was Welsh and he English. But they did not hate each other. For certain, there were misunderstandings and issues between them, they had not yet consummated their union and Esyllt had made some veiled threats about killing him, but fortunately, he could not say that they hated each other.

Small consolation, perhaps, but consolation nonetheless.

He slapped his brother on the shoulder. "Stay here a while, then join me with Jane in the great hall. I will go get Esyllt from the chapel."

With one last nod in Matthew's direction, Connor went down the spiral staircase. It was best to get this over with quickly. He and his wife had barely spoken in the past two weeks, and he had not slept in her bed at night. The people at Esgyrn Castle might not have seen anything amiss, but he guessed that Esyllt would have thought of nothing else than the impending arrival of his "whore" during that time.

It was time to disabuse her. He might even enjoy seeing her squirm when she realized how wrong she'd been to assume the worst of him.

Luck was on his side. She was making her way out of the chapel when he spotted her. He would have hated to drag her away from the comfort she found in the sacred place. As she was already in the bailey, however, he had no qualms about coming to find her.

"A word with you, if you please."

When she didn't move, he took her by the arm and led her to the great hall, in preparation for the encounter.

"What is it, my lord?" Esyllt asked, her tone frosty.

"Jane has arrived," Connor told her, letting go of her elbow. He watched as she stiffened, then he hesitated, not knowing how to word his request. Perhaps he should have waited a bit before organizing the encounter, or gone about it in a different way. But it was too late now. Jane and Matthew were on their way to meet them. He had to speak now. "Please, be kind to her."

Kind! Esyllt barely refrained a scoff of outrage. Her husband was asking her to be kind to the woman he had dared bring under her roof! He really had some gall.

She had gone to the chapel that morning, hoping to find the calm she needed to bring some order to her thoughts. The past weeks had been hard on her, and she could not quite understand why. Why was she so upset about the distance that had settled between her and Connor? Wasn't it better for them to live separate lives? After all, that was what she had wanted. At the time of their wedding she would have liked nothing more than to be assured she wouldn't have to endure her English husband's presence for more than a few days at a time. Now the idea that they were to live as strangers bothered her, and she did not like it.

Her time of reflection had done little to appease the whirring in her mind and she had barely come out of the chapel than Connor had come to demand she be kind to his mistress. It was as if he was determined to make her hate him when she had resisted the urge to do so for months. And he might finally have succeeded.

"I will do what I—" she started, only to be interrupted by the opening of the door behind her.

"Father, *there* you are! I was looking at the puppies and then you were gone!"

A dark-haired little girl bounded into the room and threw herself into Connor's arms. He caught her in mid-air and proceeded to cover her face with kisses. Esyllt watched in amazement as the child dissolved into a fit of giggles under the onslaught. She had never seen a man do such a thing before. None of the men she knew would have gathered their child into such an embrace, never mind in front of witnesses. The look in his eyes when he looked at his daughter was another surprise.

There was so much emotion there, as if the little girl was his whole world. All traces of doubt, anger and calculation had vanished, to be replaced by pure happiness and love. Her heart gave a jolt of delight. Connor Hunter was capable of loving as fiercely as she was. Up until then she had not been certain of it. She was now—and it made all the difference.

He placed the little girl back onto her feet and looked straight at her. There was an unusual earnestness in his green eyes, as if he was urging her to heed his earliest request to be kind.

"Jane, this my—" He cleared his throat. "This is Lady Sheridan."

Esyllt could tell he was uncomfortable with calling her his wife. Of course, Jane's mother had been his wife once. With a measure of shock, she realized that she had never wondered if he had been married before. Because it had never been mentioned, even when she had told him about her previous marriage, she had assumed he had not. Evidently, she'd been wrong.

As to him having a daughter, it was the last thing she had expected.

Yes, because he had never alluded to it, even when they had discussed Siân's whereabouts. It would have been the perfect moment to mention he had a daughter too, if he'd thought it a good idea for her to know. But he had not.

Why not? Why had he kept the existence of this child a secret? Because she was illegitimate? *Had* he been married to Jane's mother?

So many questions... Her head was fair swimming with them.

She looked at the little girl more closely. Jane looked remarkably like Connor, which was to say she was a stunningly beautiful child. She had his dark hair and green eyes but her features, so stern and masculine in Connor, were softened in the heart-shaped face tiled up to her.

"My lady." Jane dropped a wobbly curtsey. "I am very glad to make your acquaintance. Uncle Matthew told me everything about you on the way here."

"Did he really?" Esyllt did her best not to snort. What had Matthew been telling his niece? Beware of the Welsh, in all probability.

"He did. But he never said you were so beautiful!"

The little girl's words were so guileless, she looked so awestruck and adorable that Esyllt could not help a laugh. She instantly knew that she and her stepdaughter would get on well.

"I would be surprised if he had," she answered warmly. "I do not think your uncle Matthew has had time to notice my supposed beauty. He's been very busy since his arrival at Castell Esgyrn." Too busy being prejudiced.

"It doesn't take long to see that you are beautiful!" Jane sounded almost affronted at the idea. "Father, you agree with me, don't you? You think her ladyship is beautiful?"

"Yes, I do." Connor gave a cough.

As angry as she had been only a moment ago, Esyllt was now enjoying herself immensely. She had dreaded meeting a woman who would act as mistress of the place by day and play the whore to her husband by night, and instead she was meeting a sweet child who was ready to love her.

"I'm very happy to welcome you here, Jane, and I know someone who will be even happier to have you here at Castell Esgyrn. I have a daughter who is seven years old, just like you must be," she said, judging that both girls would be of an age.

Green eyes lit up with excitement. "You do? But Uncle Matthew and Father never told me about that, either!" she said, scowling in the two men's direction. Esyllt wondered about that. Connor, at least, knew about Siân's existence. Why had he kept it a secret from his own daughter? "Where is she? When can I meet her?"

"She is in her chamber at the moment, practicing her letters with her tutor."

Jane's face fell at that. "Oh. Maybe I should wait to go to her, then."

Esyllt barely repressed a laugh. Her stepdaughter, like every child she knew, was not a lover of lessons. "Mayhap she can be excused for once. I think she would prefer to meet a new friend than write a series of perfect Ws." Her daughter would be ecstatic at Jane's arrival at Castell Esgyrn, that was certain.

"It is the most difficult letter for me too." The little girl grimaced in commiseration.

"Matthew," Connor called, turning to the corner where his brother was waiting with unusual discretion. "Take Jane to see Siân, then leave, taking the tutor with you. The two of them can get acquainted in private, if my wife agrees."

Esyllt nodded. Perhaps it was for the best if their daughters found out about one another away from prying eyes. A stronger bond would form that way. *If*, of course, they found a common ground. That was not guaranteed. In any case, Esyllt congratulated herself for insisting her daughter learn English from the moment she'd been born. She now spoke it without any accent, unlike her, who had learned it much later in life. Teaching her child the invaders' language had not been a popular decision amongst her friends, but Esyllt had always been of the opinion that one had better be armed to face people who could turn against you when the mood took them. Despising them or hoping they would ignore you did no good. The English were here to stay, only a fool would refuse to accept it.

"Thank you, Father, thank you, my lady." Jane darted out the door, followed by her smiling uncle. Esyllt arched a brow. Her dour brother-in-law was also a child lover, it seemed. Who would have thought?

Connor turned to his wife, gratitude swelling in his chest. "Thank you for your welcome of Jane."

He had not mentioned Siân to his daughter before today but his reasons were commendable, he thought. He had not wanted to raise her hopes before everything was finalized, and then he had wanted to see how they would get on. A girl her own age, living under the same roof, and more than just a friend, was what Jane needed to heal.

Having a stepsister could well be a lifesaver for her, which was why he was here.

Left to his own devices, Connor would never have married again but his daughter needed a female presence in her life. Even more pointedly, she needed another child to play with. He had finally surrendered to the king's entreaty that he marry a Welsh woman purely based on that consideration. Jane's needs came before his own wishes. He had decided to marry Esyllt when he had been told about her little girl. The other potential candidates had been young, childless virgins or older women with grown sons, neither of which had been what he needed.

"Please," Esyllt protested. "What else did you want me to do? She is a lovely little girl. I would never treat her in any other way than kindly." She made a grimace and he braced himself for the accusation he was sure was coming. "Why did you not say she was your daughter when I accused you of wanting to bring another women to Castell Esgyrn? How could you do such a cruel thing? You allowed me to assume she was your—"

"Yes, I did," he cut in, ruffling his hair with his hand, feeling less than proud of himself. "But perhaps you deserved it for the way you immediately assumed the worst of me. Tell me, do you really think I would be insensitive enough to introduce such a woman under your roof, mere weeks into our marriage?"

She appeared thoroughly chastened by the rebuke, which did little to ease his guilt. It had been cruel to let her torture herself for a week over the idea of him bringing his mistress to Esgyrn Castle, there was no denying it.

"Why did you not say anything? You could have upbraided me in the most stringent terms, and gotten your revenge that way," she insisted. "Made me pay for thinking the worst of you."

His mouth twisted. He could have. Most of the men he knew would have done just that, maybe even hit her for daring to speak to him in the way she had. But Connor had never condoned violence against women. "You seemed so certain I was a heartless lecher... I didn't have the heart to shatter your preconceptions about me."

She did not let this provocation pass, as he knew she would. Teasing his wife was quickly becoming a favorite pastime of his. "No. I can see why you preferred to make me feel like an ogre in front of the poor child."

An ogre indeed. He barely repressed a scoff. There was nothing monstrous about the woman in front of him. "Jane thinks nothing of the sort. Or do you not recall she called you beautiful?"

Connor was making light of it, but he had been surprised by his daughter's reaction to his new wife, and the easy affection Esyllt had shown Jane. Considering she had been convinced she was about to meet her husband's mistress, she had recovered from her shock with remarkable alacrity.

"Your brother is not the only one reluctant to pass on relevant information it seems. You failed to mention you had a daughter or had been married, something anyone would agree is worthy of note. Is that because Jane is the product of..." He threw her such a withering look that she did not dare finish her question. But he would not bear to hear that she thought his little girl illegitimate even if, in truth, he understood why she might think it. He had not mentioned a first wife, so she would wonder who Jane's mother had been.

"She is not a bastard," he said through gritted teeth. "Her mother and I were married when she was conceived."

"So you are a widower, then. When did you think to inform me of that fact? Didn't you think I had the right to know?"

"What difference would it have made for you to know I was a widower or had a child?"

His wife did not seem to think that this was a reasonable question. "None, admittedly, but still, I would have liked to know!"

"Why? We both know our union was never based on anything other than very pragmatic considerations. Our pasts or personalities didn't have any role to play in the decision. In your case, you weren't even the one choosing me."

Icy silence filled the room and Connor regretted his words. What was wrong with him? Why had he felt the need to remind her she had been used as a pawn in a man's game? As a woman, she'd had even less choice than him.

"I thank you for the reminder," Esyllt hissed. "But I hadn't forgotten that fact."

"Forgive me. That was not kind of me."

"No. It wasn't."

Just when he thought she would storm out of the room, she asked. "How did your wife die?"

Her voice was calm, her anger under control once more. Nevertheless, he found it hard to answer that question, because, if he suspected Esyllt had not really killed her husband, as she claimed, he certainly felt responsible for Helen's death. Matthew had tried to tell him many a time that it wasn't the case, but he still wasn't convinced he was blameless in the whole affair. He might never believe it and carry the guilt to his grave.

"A fever," he said tersely. That was no lie, but it was not the whole truth either. Still, it was the best he could offer for now. Esyllt, bless her, seemed to sense it and did not press him.

"Jane seems a lovely girl."

"She is." Instantly the anxious man was replaced by the proud father. "Thank you again for welcoming her so warmly. She has been through a lot lately."

Yes, she had, the poor mite.

"Please, it is not a problem. And if you happen to have other sweet little daughters hidden away, legitimate or not, I will welcome them with equal warmth, as long as they call me beautiful, like Jane did." Esyllt gave him a shy smile as she spoke.

In that moment, Connor wondered if he had not fallen just a tiny bit in love with his wife.

Chapter Seven

"So... Your husband is back."

"Yes."

Esyllt didn't know what to tell her friend. Branwen had heard her complain about her union with a stranger many times in the past few weeks, but today, she didn't feel like ranting about Connor. The day before, when he had introduced her to his daughter, had made her look at him in a different light. The way he had kissed the little girl had moved her deeply. Then, later that evening, there had been Siân's joy at meeting a stepsister her own age. She had been beside herself with joy and declared them the best of friends.

It was difficult to speak ill of the man who had given her daughter such a gift.

And, of course, there was the small matter of what he had done to her on the night of his return... Not that she would ever mention that to anyone, even her best friend, but it meant that she didn't know quite what to think of her husband anymore.

"I don't envy you," Branwen observed. "Being married to a domineering Englishman has to be what every Welsh woman dreads."

"He's not domineering, exactly."

No. That was not the word she would have used to describe him. With Gruffydd, perhaps, but not with her. With her he could be devious, stern, even manipulative at times, but never domineering. It was one of the things she liked the most about him. Whatever their differences, he dealt with her as an equal who could, and would defend herself, and what was even more important, she was never afraid of retribution.

So no, her virile warrior of a husband was not domineering.

Just then, as if he'd sensed she was talking about him, Connor strode into view. Crossing the bailey, he made his way to the stables with fluid steps that gave the impression he was about to break into a run.

"There he is," Esyllt said, struck anew by his masculine presence.

"*He*'s your husband!" For all that they had discussed him at length, Branwen had never seen him before and her shock was evident. "But... I thought you said he was a monster!"

Esyllt gave a sigh. She had said that, when Gruffydd had informed her of her impending marriage, because that had been what she'd feared at the time. She had then repeated it while he was in England, when she had wanted to hang on to the pretense that she was better off without him. As a consequence, her friend could be forgiven for thinking the worst of Connor.

"Yes, well," she said with a cough, not knowing how to rectify this impression without appearing like a lovestruck fool.

"He doesn't look like a monster from where I'm standing, not even near."

"No," Esyllt agreed. He did not. In fact he looked nothing short of stunning. A groom brought his stallion to him, and he started to examine the animal as if in search of an injury. His touch was gentle, his gestures slow and careful. For a long moment he ran his hands over the horse's legs, then, apparently satisfied, gave him a tap on the rump.

Esyllt's buttocks tingled as if he'd just patted her there and heat crept to the place between her legs, the place where he had placed his mouth only the other day. *Arglwydd Mawr*, was she ever going to forget the sensations he had awoken in her with his tongue? To think they had not even yet shared a real kiss, only a swift brushing of the lips...

With difficulty, she tore her gaze from her husband and made to lead Branwen into the solar where she had asked refreshments to be brought earlier. After reminiscing about the scandalous encounter with Connor, she was in sore need of a drink. But her friend did not move and instead kept looking in his direction. She was fascinated, which was all too easily understandable. Anyone would be.

Esyllt waited, hoping he would not see the two of them leering at him. They were hidden in the shadow of the tower but you never knew.

"And who is that?" Branwen asked as a second man emerged from the stables.

"That's his brother Matthew."

"Brother! They look nothing like each other. Are we to question the late Lady Sheridan's morality?" she asked in a mischievous giggle.

Esyllt laughed in turn, relieved at the break in tension. "No. Matthew is his milk brother, actually. But I've never seen two men share a closer bond than these two." The laughter died in her throat when she thought back to the trick they had played on the night before their wedding.

Indeed. The two men did everything together. Had they ever shared a woman, she now wondered? It was not impossible.

At that moment Matthew turned to face the tower.

Branwen sucked in a breath, clearly as struck as Esyllt had been the night of his arrival.

"My word. I might have to change my opinion of Englishmen."

"Don't. This one *is* an ogre," Esyllt warned. "He might be one of the most good-looking men you've ever seen but he despises the Welsh. I'm not sure he doesn't despise all women, come to that." She made a face. Since his arrival, he had not had a kind word for her. The only compliment he had paid her had been when he'd posed as her betrothed. Oh, how he must have enjoyed duping her. "The man is as stubborn as they come and seems determined to make my life uncomfortable."

As if to prove the truth of her words, it wasn't long before he spotted them. He must have a sixth sense where she was concerned. A smirk on his lips, he walked toward them while Connor vaulted on top of his stallion.

"Plotting again, Lady Sheridan?" Matthew always made a point of using her title and making it sound as if she had usurped it.

"No. I'm afraid the Welsh language is far too primitive to discuss anything as subtle as political upheaval," she answered, as Connor started to ride toward them. My... He was at one with the strong animal, and just as elegant. She could not tear her eyes from him, even as she carried on talking to Matthew. "All we can do is talk about the awful weather plaguing our country or compare our respective skin diseases. Be assured that all the plotting that is conducted against England is conducted in English."

Connor laughed as he brought his horse to a halt by her side. It was a warm, appreciative laugh that reached a place deep inside her. He might not like to be challenged, but he seemed to like it when she challenged others. It was a start.

"Well, Matthew, that is all good information for you,

desperate as you are to further your knowledge of all things Welsh." He tilted his head to her. "Thank you, wife, that puts us back in our place. We shall leave you and your friend so you can discuss your revolting bodies and ungodly weather in peace."

Matthew bowed, looking none too pleased. It was not hard to imagine that, usually, the two brothers were on the same side and he had not like being mocked.

Branwen let out a little nervous cough. Never one at ease with confrontation, especially with men, her friend tried to soothe the sting of her rejection. "Forgive Esyllt, she's—"

"Who?" Matthew cut in, contempt curling his lips.

"Me!" Esyllt cried, goaded beyond endurance. "Believe it or not, my name is not Lady Sheridan." She knew the wretched man thought she was only allowed to exist in relation to Connor, an Englishman. "It is Esyllt ferch Llewelyn."

"Of course it is," Matthew said on a laugh. She glared at him. Difficult as he might be, at least her husband would never dare do anything so hurtful as to mock her just for having a Welsh name. "And how on earth are we supposed to say that?"

"With your mouth, like everyone else. And if you can't, then I suggest you keep it shut."

With this sally, she stormed in the direction of the solar.

Later that afternoon, shortly after Branwen had left, Esyllt received Gruffydd's visit. She braced herself for a difficult moment. The old man's behavior, never what she would have called pleasant, was quickly becoming unbearable.

"How are things going with the Englishman?" he asked, looking around with an eagle eye. "Has everyone turned against him yet?"

"No, and that might well never happen, for he is a fair and

measured master. The people here at Castell Esgyrn have nothing bad to say about him. He has not given them any cause for complaints, quite the contrary."

This answer, for all its honesty, was not to his liking. "We had better start giving them cause for complaints, then, hadn't we?"

"What do you mean?"

He shrugged. "Rumors can ruin a man. A few chosen words falling into the right ears, and someone who was admired can become the most reviled man in the country. Lechery, murder, everything would be believable coming from an Englishman. No one would question what they hear. Besides, as he cannot understand what the servants would say, or even realize they were talking about him, he would be unable to set things right. 'Tis perfect."

"You would stoop so low?" Esyllt was both incensed and disgusted.

"I would do whatever is necessary to make the accursed English think twice about coming here and stealing what's ours."

He meant to lie and paint Connor as a lecherous, dangerous tyrant, a murderer. He could try, but she would have no part in it. "I will not spread slander against my husband," she said with decision.

If Connor was to be hated or despised, let it be for something he had done, not because an evil man was working in the shadows to besmirch his name.

Gruffydd had made her marry him, and in doing so, he had placed her in a position of strength. She was no longer a pawn in his game. She was a married woman now, mistress of her own castle, with men ready to do her bidding. She was not powerless anymore. He could not make her do his dirty work.

"I'm not sure it would work anyway," she said more

amenably, thinking it safer not to antagonize him too much. Perhaps he could be made to see reason. After all, if what he wanted were better conditions for the local Welsh people, this could be achieved through peaceful means. "I told you, his actions have made clear to all that he is not to be feared in any way. The fact that he turned out to be so reasonable in his dealings with our people could be used to our advantage. He could perhaps win around some of his more powerful friends to our way of thinking. It would be a more long term, profitable solution, as I'm sure you'll agree. If you get rid of him, he will only be replaced by another, less amenable lord."

Gruffydd was not interested in her arguments. He grabbed her by the elbow and drew her to him. "Stop trying to justify the unjustifiable. You will heed my instructions or, I swear I—"

"Are you threatening my wife?"

Connor appeared as if out of nowhere. His voice was calm, but there was no mistaking the intent in his voice or in his eyes. He was glaring at Gruffydd, certain he'd interrupted an argument. Though he didn't understand Welsh, he would have picked up on the aggression in the man's voice and her defensive position.

"Your wife!" Gruffydd scoffed. "You need not behave as if you doted on the woman. You only married her because I arranged it."

"That doesn't make her less my wife than if I had arranged the union myself." Connor was still calm but the undertone in his voice was now icy. Esyllt shivered. In a moment he might well start making threats or even draw out his sword.

"Do not pride yourself on the fact. I could have married her myself. God knows I thought about it often enough."

Esyllt sensed Connor had turned to face her, but she could not look at him. She was too busy staring at the Welshman in open-mouthed astonishment. This was the first time she had heard about a possible union between the two of them. Was it true he'd considered making her his wife, or was he making it up to earn himself some legitimacy over the Englishman? Perhaps. In any case, the idea of her being married to the old goat sent shivers up her spine. Welsh as he was, he would prove an awful husband.

As if guessing she needed some support to stop herself from crumbling, Connor placed a hand on the small of her back. She barely refrained from sagging against him in thanks. Never had any show of unity been more appreciated.

"You might have almost married her but you did not," he said, putting an end to the loathsome matter. "*I* did. And now she's my wife. You had better remember it."

Esyllt shivered again. He sounded fierce, proprietary, but not in a worrying way, rather as if he were proud to call her his, and would do anything to protect her.

Gruffydd, who was not a fool for all his bluster, did not miss the veiled threat and stayed silent. Despite the frosty atmosphere, something warm bloomed inside Esyllt. Whatever their disagreements in private, in public Connor would stand by her whenever the need arose. The hand on her back slid lower, spreading the warmth even further.

"I believe the two of you were finished?" His tone made it clear it was not a question.

She nodded, eager to escape the Welshman's oppressive presence. "Yes, we were."

With luck, that would be the last she saw of the man.

Chapter Eight

"Are you waiting until my brother has sired an heir on you to kill him?"

Shock caused Esyllt to swivel round. Matthew was leaning against the wall, his arms crossed over his chest. A smirk was floating on his lips. How had she thought that he would leave her alone after the confrontation with Branwen the day before?

"K-kill him?" she stammered.

"Don't look so shocked, lady. Connor told me what you did to your first husband. I wasn't overly surprised, I must say. Except for one thing, that you actually told him." He tilted his head in what could have passed as respect if she hadn't known he despised her.

"Oh, you think I should have let him think I was a meek, harmless woman?" she snapped. The man grated on her nerves and she didn't see why she should spare him from her ire, or tell him the truth about Gwyn's death.

"It would have been wiser, though I am not sure how long the pretense would have held. You don't have a meek bone in your body, that much is clear, and I'm not sure you're harmless."

He nodded as if pondering the matter. "So what will you do to him? Dispose of him once he has given you the son you need to replace him?"

"You are a fool if you think I will discuss this with you."

But the question made Esyllt think. Evidently, and despite their closeness, Connor had not told his brother that they had yet to consummate their marriage properly. Neither of their scandalous encounters could have led to a pregnancy, but Matthew seemed to believe that she was in a position to fall with child, an assumption she didn't want to contradict. He would only use it against her, attributing Connor's failure to consummate the marriage to a fault on her part.

"Fortunately for him, my brother seems incapable of fathering anything other than girls, so you might have to wait a while until you are rid of him."

Girls.

Esyllt's heart sank. Jane was the only child he had brought home. She had jested about him bringing his other children to her, not thinking he would actually have any. Now she knew different. Just how many by-blows did Connor have, scattered along the width and breadth of England? She gritted her teeth. This was not a discussion she was prepared to have, least of all with a man who would enjoy her discomfiture. He wanted to hurt her. Why else would he have brought up such a painful topic?

"If you will excuse me, I have other things to do than stay here and listen to your insults." She made to walk past him, fully expecting him to try and stop her. It did not surprise her therefore when he took hold of her arm. "Kindly let me pass," she demanded, doing her best not to flare up. Who did he think he was? She was in her own castle, and Connor's wife, not his. He had no right to detain her.

"My brother is being too soft on you. Your womanly charms

cloud his judgment. It is understandable, I suppose, since you are uncommonly pretty." Matthew leaned in closer. "But I will not make the same mistake. You do not sleep in my bed and therefore are not in a position to lull me into submission with your wiles."

Connor, submissive! She actually snorted. The man was the epitome of the dominant male. How could his brother doubt it?

"I do no such thing!" Was everyone determined to consider her a fast woman using her body to gain what she wanted? Could they not see she would have no idea where to start, even supposing such an idea had crossed her mind?

"I will be watching you, Lady Sheridan. Very closely. You are bound to make a mistake sooner or later."

Esyllt felt tears sting her eyes but didn't want to let him suspect him how much his insults had hurt her. She straightened her spine. "I asked you to release me, I believe."

"You are—"

"Matthew. If you do not unhand my wife on the instant, I will make you wish you had stayed in England."

Esyllt turned in time to see Connor amble into the room. The look on his face was calm but deadly. It was just like it had been with Gruffydd the previous day. How was he always at hand to offer his help? Was it mere coincidence or was he actually spying on her because he was as suspicious of her as his brother? She had never wondered about it before but in that moment she did not care. The important thing was that she would be free from Matthew's venom.

With obvious reluctance, her brother-in-law released her and took a step backward.

"Forgive me, Brother. But I don't trust her."

"I know you don't." The smile floating on Connor's lips proved he had heard the same thing over and over again. "But you are not to manhandle her for all that. She is not only a woman but also my wife. Violence will not solve anything."

Esyllt worked hard at hiding her surprise. He was taking her defense against a man he had grown up with, a man he loved and respected. That was unexpected. Something flashed in his eyes. She wondered if it was amusement.

"I'm glad to see that you do not believe in resorting to violence to tame your enemies," she said when it became clear he was expecting an answer from her.

"I did not quite say that. But you are not my enemy."

"Am I not?"

His lips quivered, and she realized that she had been right. He *was* amused. "Even if you were, you are a woman. That places you safely out of my reach. And you are my wife. What-ever our disagreements, I will not allow anyone to disrespect you, even my own brother." His gaze flicked toward Matthew, who did not seem best pleased at this declaration.

She, however, appreciated it at full value.

"Thank you, my lord."

Esyllt was more confused than ever. He had taken her defense against Gruffydd the day before, but that was under-standable. He would have enjoyed using this opportunity to put a man he felt no love toward back in his place. But this interven-tion was less easily explained. Aside from his daughter, Matthew was the person Connor cared for most in this world. Why would he place her above him?

Matthew seemed to ask himself the same question. He appeared shocked, as if up until then Connor had never disagreed with him. This small victory over a man she disliked pleased her.

"You know," he said, looking at her and Connor in quick succession. "You both have green eyes. You cannot see it of course but I, who is looking at you at the same time, can see it all too well."

"What are you blabbering on about?" Connor snapped, clearly as nonplussed as she was by the unexpected comment.

"Yours are clear, almost transparent, and Lady Sheridan's are a deep emerald, but make no mistake, they are both green."

With those enigmatic words, he left.

"Does he often say things like that?" Esyllt asked her husband. "He seemed to think there was a point to his declaration."

"He certainly did, even if I can't for the life of me see what it could be. And no, he is usually very pragmatic, not at all the type of man to start referring to a lady's eyes as 'deep emerald'."

"Why did you take my defense against him?" she couldn't help but ask when silence descended between them. "He didn't seem to like it."

Connor let out what sounded suspiciously like a chuckle, as if the notion pleased him. "He did not. But why would you complain that I did? I did not hear you complain when I defended you against Gruffydd yesterday."

"I'm not complaining, and you know very well that was different. You don't like Gruffydd."

"Are you suggesting that you think I will fulfil my role as a husband only when it suits me, with people I don't like?"

"No, and you know full well what I mean!" Esyllt shook her head in irritation. Would they ever be able to have a discussion without him trying to confuse her? "I get the impression that you wanted to help me less than you wanted to put him back in his place."

"Perhaps I did, and can you blame me? The man is every inch the intractable Welshman I was told to expect, without any of the charm that could entail. I can respect a man wanting to protect his people, a man who values his freedom above everything else, but that old goat cares less about his country than he does about his own privileges."

His mouth twitched and Esyllt knew he had indeed enjoyed putting Gruffydd back in his place. And no, she could not blame him for it because she thought the same thing. Hadn't she called Gruffydd an old goat in her mind many a time?

"Tell me. Is he telling the truth? Were you two really betrothed?" Connor asked, coming to stand right in front of her.

"No, not to my knowledge." Esyllt had almost forgotten the outrageous claim. And she didn't like being reminded of it.

"You sound mighty relieved, I must say."

"That's because I am."

"So an Englishman, a stranger, is preferable to your old Welsh friend as a husband. Be sure that I appreciate the compliment at its full value." Connor gave a little bow.

"It's not a compliment," she said weakly, unsettled by the light flashing in his eyes. His "transparent eyes", as Matthew had rather aptly called them.

"Indeed it is not. Saying that you chose to marry me rather than a self-centred, hot-headed brute is hardly flattering."

"And not true either. I had no say in this decision, as you reminded me only the other day. I did not choose you for any qualities you might possess."

Connor barked a laugh when she had expected him to flare up. "Oh no, I will not fall into that trap, my lady. I will not presume to tell you what you should think of me. I will leave you to decide on your own what my qualities might be."

"A hazardous decision, as I may not find any."

Esyllt wondered what was urging her to tease him so, and then she understood. She was enjoying herself. As was her husband, if the twisted lips and glittering eyes were any indication. As unlikely as it was, they were deriving equal pleasure from their verbal jousting.

"I will take that risk. I'm fairly confident that you will find at least one or two redeeming qualities about me. If not, then so be it."

"So be it. We are married now."

Or were they? Technically, the marriage had not been consummated yet. To her relief, he did not point that out. Instead, he drew her into his arms. The move was so unexpected that she did nothing to stop him. For a moment he just held her tight and she focused on the beating of her heart.

"No need to sound so glum, dear wife. Being married is not a death sentence. For you, at least," he murmured in her ear. "I know that I am at your mercy, my little Welsh murderess. I might wake up one morning and find myself tied to the bed with you poised over me, ready to strike, with a candle or with a dagger. If only you agreed to shed your clothes while you do so, I believe I would die a happy man. I might even try to persuade you to delay the execution until I'd had my fill of you."

Esyllt felt herself grow red to the roots of her hair. His smell was so enticing, his voice so seductive, his words so provocative... It was all too much. She could feel herself becoming soft and pliable, and her will melting way.

She took a step away from him before she could beg him to kiss her, properly this time.

What was happening? Only a moment ago they'd been enjoying some banter and before she knew it, Connor had reverted to talking in the velvety tones of a lover. He was accusing her of wanting to kill him, but he was doing so in a sensual purr, all the while talking into her ear. He was not jesting with her anymore, he was seducing her.

What was she to do? How was she to deal with a man capable of such ambivalence? He was supposed to hate her, not seek her company, he was supposed to enjoy watching her struggle with her enemies, not help her out. And she... She wasn't supposed to be attracted to him, this man who had been forced upon her, who had taken pleasure in humiliating her the very night they'd met, who had still not made their marriage valid and could spurn her at any moment because of it.

What was she doing, being rooted to the spot in front of him? Bantering with him?

She should walk away, not look at him like a prey too transfixed to move in front of its predator.

Behind them a servant coughed. He was hovering by the door, a couple of logs cradled in his arms, not knowing whether he should enter and disturb them or retreat and come back another time. Seeing the confusion on his face gave Esyllt the jolt she needed.

"I will ride into the village and see Branwen," she muttered. "I know she went to the fair the other week. I daresay she will have news to share."

The way Connor tilted his head indicated he'd guessed this was just an excuse. They both knew she had seen her friend the day before. Any news of the fair would have been imparted then. "I dare say she will," he said nonetheless. "Something about having found the people there ridden with boils no doubt. It is bad news, but at least it means that you will be able to converse in Welsh."

Esyllt almost laughed out loud. He remembered what she'd told Matthew in her fit of rage yesterday. This touched her soul as surely as his seduction had stirred her senses. "Yes. Not to mention that the weather has been awful of late. That should give us plenty to talk about."

"Ride away, then, wife." He took her hand and kissed it in a gallant gesture. "As long as you come back to me."

~

"You can't run! I'll only catch you. And then you'll be sorry!"

While Esyllt wondered who Connor was threatening with retaliation, Jane and Siân rushed past her, giggling like the two little imps they were. She smiled at the shriek of delight they gave when another roar from Connor reached them. Relief swept through her. A game, that was all. No retribution was coming. She rounded the corner of the keep—and found herself all but catapulted into Connor's arms.

They almost fell to the floor together, but he steadied her with two hands around her waist, something a less strapping man would have been unable to do.

"Careful here, little wife."

"What are you doing?" she rasped. The feel of his hands on her body, although it had prevented her from falling flat on her face, had sent her senses all aflutter.

"I was running after the girls. They wanted a game of hide and seek."

"And you agreed?" She was incredulous.

"Why, yes, why wouldn't I?" He smiled. That smile reduced her already shaky limbs to jelly. "Surely you don't believe me so dim-witted so as to not understand how to play the game?"

"I do not think you dim-witted," she replied, half-amused at the teasing, half-mortified by her inability to hide her turmoil from her voice. She sounded just as affected as she felt. "But perhaps unwilling to join in such childish games."

"Well." He was still holding her, which didn't help her hold on to a sense of composure. "I guess I am a man full of surprises."

"You certainly are." A warrior running after two little girls just for the pleasure of hearing them giggle... It was unexpected to say the least.

"I hope to provide you with many more surprises in the

weeks to come. It might be that it helps you make peace with this marriage."

There was no need. She already had made her peace with it. Hearing that Gruffydd had considered her for a bride had only confirmed it.

"I think you should go and get the girls," she said in a whisper. "Otherwise you could lose them."

"Oh, I think I already have. They could be halfway to the village by now." He made a grimace. "I fear it will take me all afternoon to find them."

"I'm sorry I detained you."

"I'm not." His lips quivered. "And it seems to me that I am the one detaining you." To illustrate his point, his hands tightened around her waist, and he leaned in, his head stopping only inches from her face.

Esyllt bit her lip as realization hit. Here, in the bailey, in full view of everyone, he was going to kiss her.

Finally.

The perfunctory kiss in the church when they'd exchanged vows hardly counted, as did the chaste one given upon his return from England. And the scandalous nibbling at her private parts was an entirely different thing, of course.

She moaned in anticipation, longing to experience a real kiss at last.

Connor almost groaned out loud when Esyllt moaned.

In all his life, the urge to kiss a woman had never crashed over him with such force. It coursed through his whole body, from the top of his skull to the tip of his toes, but he fought it, unsure what Esyllt's reaction would be if he took her mouth here, in the bailey, for all to see. Because this kiss would be nothing short of scandalous, he already knew it. Everything within him was burning. Never during the weeks of negotiations, when her name had been one amongst dozens of others, had he imagined that he would be attracted with such force to the wife he was choosing with such detachment.

He wasn't even sure why she appealed to him so.

She was beautiful, but also confrontational enough to test his temper to the limit. With another woman, that would have been enough to dampen his ardor, but with her, it only exacerbated it. He was attracted to her outside the bedroom as much as he was aroused inside of it. It was an unexpected development. Back in February when he had seen her on that dais, he had congratulated himself on having chosen a bride who stirred his senses with her beauty. He had not suspected he would actually have found a wife who also piqued his interest with her sharp wit and utter lack of fear.

His first union had been neither happy nor unhappy, it had simply been. His wife's death had struck him hard, but not because he had loved her. He had been struck by the loss but his heart had remained intact. Helen had been a quiet woman who had failed to provoke any emotion in him, and barely enough desire to produce children. Bedding her had been as close to a chore as sleeping with a woman could be, and every discussion he'd had with her had ended with him wishing he could be somewhere else.

In short, she'd been the exact opposite of Esyllt.

His hands tightened around her waist. Despite the odd circumstances of their union, he enjoyed being married to her. Because his first marriage had been so uninspiring, he had not balked at the idea of marrying a stranger. His first wife had not been a life companion. There had been no reason to imagine that his second would be any different. But Esyllt was not just his wife, she was a woman in her own right, with abilities and a fiery personality. A very desirable woman who set his loins on fire. He liked to have her in his arms every time he could justify holding her, and he was itching to be allowed back into her bed.

Although they had never really made love, he felt more of a sensual connection with her than he had with any woman he'd ever bedded. The night he had licked her to orgasm had given him more pleasure than all his encounters with Helen combined. She had just lain passively under him and never once made a noise, though he'd tried his best to see to her pleasure.

Whatever satisfaction he'd gotten as a married man had not been gained in the marital bed but in his daughters' company. As for his masculine urges, they had been fulfilled in a perfunctory manner with whatever willing woman was at hand. He had not consciously decided to take mistresses, and he was not particularly proud of the fact that he had made the most of the advances he'd received over the years, but it had seemed the only way not to die of boredom and frustration.

Now, everything was different.

With a wife like Esyllt, he would not be bored or frustrated. The urge to take another woman in his arms would not plague him. She would not lie under him rigidly when he bedded her, she would squirm and writhe and moan and beg. She would pleasure him in turn, he was sure of it, and ride him until he couldn't think straight. God, the mere thought of everything they could do together made him hard. Yes, the little Welsh hellion would be a reckless lover.

He could not forget the way she had arched her back, rubbed herself against him and moaned, how she had been overwhelmed by his touch, by her desire for him, even while fighting it, even when she'd had no idea who he was.

Before she noticed how hard he had become, he drew away.

Waiting until she was ready before taking her to bed was the only satisfactory solution, but he was only human, and holding her close was just too much of a temptation.

As if she'd seen his inner struggle, she took a step back herself.

"It's so good to have children running around Castell Esgyrn," she said rather breathlessly. "Siân has always been somewhat quiet, but I can foresee this will soon change. I'm glad."

Children. Yes, that was an innocuous topic of conversation, one that might help put lewd images out of his mind and allow his body to cool.

"With Jane around, she might not be as quiet," he agreed. It was good to see his own daughter happy as well. God knew she deserved it.

"All we need now is for Matthew to bring his by-blows here."

Connor smiled. "No danger of that. To my knowledge, he has none. In fact, I have never seen him with a woman."

Esyllt could not hide her shock at that piece of information. Matthew, leading a chaste life, or as near as? She found it impossible to believe. "Really?"

"Yes. That is not to say he doesn't meet any, of course, but he has never introduced anyone to me or even mentioned anyone special."

That was surprising. Whatever she thought of his gruff manners toward her, there was no denying that a man as well-favored as he was would appeal to the ladies. Why, she had been struck by his appearance herself, until his golden good looks had been eclipsed by her husband's brooding intensity. Even Branwen, who never remarked on men's appearance, had commented on it.

And now she was told that he was, if not exactly a monk, at least discreet enough to hide his conquests from the brother with whom he shared everything. It was unexpected to say the least.

"And do *you* have by-blows?" she asked, heart in her throat at her own daring. But since Connor had not thought it relevant to inform her that he was a widower, she had no choice but to ask directly if she wanted to know—and she dearly did.

There might be dark secrets lurking everywhere with this man who was still a near stranger.

Green eyes pinned her in place. He had not liked the question or what it implied, but after a while seemed to conclude that it was only fair of her to ask the question and that he owed her an answer. His expression softened. "No. I do not."

His sincerity could not be doubted. Esyllt nodded in relief. But then... "Wait. I'm sure Matthew said you—"

"What the hell did he tell you?" Connor cut in with a snarl.

She recoiled at the violence of the outburst and did not have the courage to reveal what his brother had said. "N-nothing," she stammered.

But it was not nothing. Matthew had definitely told her that Connor could only father *girls*. Plural. Perhaps she had read too much into it. Perhaps he'd only meant to unnerve her by alluding to possible illegitimate offspring, or even lied outright. She wouldn't put it past him. Stirring trouble between his brother and his unsuitable Welsh wife would have been Matthew's intention all along and she would allow him to win.

"It's nothing," she repeated, cursing herself for having spoilt the moment. They had been physically and emotionally close, they had almost kissed, they had rejoiced in their daughters' happiness. Why couldn't she have left it at that?

Something flashed in Connor's eyes. Anger? Wariness?

"As long as it *is* nothing. I will not have you casting aspersions on my character—or Matthew's. We do not go around taking our pleasure with women and then leave them to deal on their own with the bastards we have fathered, do you hear?"

His voice had acquired a rough edge Esyllt had never heard before. Apparently the topic of children was a sensitive one with the Hunter men. She gulped, now convinced that there was indeed a dark secret somewhere. Nevertheless, she knew she would never have the courage to ask now, or perhaps ever.

"I have to go and find the girls," he told her, eyes still glittering.

"Yes."

Good luck to him. The two giggling friends were probably safety holed away in a dark corner by now. It would take him forever to unearth them.

When Connor left, Esyllt realized that she had completely forgotten why she had been making her way to the great hall, so she stayed where she was. Her legs were too weak to support her anyway.

A moment later she heard Siân's shriek, betraying the fact that the girls had been found out. The sound pierced at her heart. Her daughter had never sounded happier, or more care-free. A rush of gratitude toward Connor washed through her. *He* had done that, by bringing Jane to Castell Esgyrn and being the benevolent, mischievous father figure her child had never had.

And then it struck her.

If she let him, he could also be the fiery, sensual husband she had never had.

The rest of the day was spent in a haze. The scene in the bailey kept playing in her mind. The moment she had thought Connor would kiss her, the anger in his eyes when she had mentioned possible children, her daughter's shrieks of laughter. Everything melted in a confused mess. What did she feel for him? What did she want to do now? Was it even her choice to make?

Before going to bed, as was her custom, she went to say good night to Siân. More than ever, she needed to see that her daughter was safe and well before settling for the night. It might bring peace to her soul.

The door opened just as Esyllt was reaching out for the handle. She froze. Connor stood in the frame, gilded in the light of the candle she was holding. As he was one step above her, she had to tilt her head to meet his gaze. Intimidated by his looming presence, she flattened herself against the stone wall.

"I came to say good night to Siân," she said unnecessarily. Why else would she be here? Her daughter was the only one sleeping in that room. Or... Was she? She frowned. "What are you doing here?"

"I came to say good night to Jane."

"Jane? But she... She's not sleeping here."

Connor sighed. "I know she was given her own room, but she insisted she would sleep with her new best friend from now on. I did not have the heart to refuse her, so I agreed. I found the two girls asleep in each other's arms just now."

Esyllt did not know what to answer. She bit her bottom lip.

"You disapprove," Connor said, misinterpreting her reaction.

"No, of course not." She did not disapprove, but she was unsettled all the same. The notion of the two children sleeping in each other's arms had brought an image to her mind of her and Connor lying entwined in bed together. It was not an image made to help her keep hold of her composure. "If that's what they want, I see no reason to deny them."

"Thank you." He sounded so sincere, so grateful, that she could not help but wonder why it was so important to him.

"Let me go and see Siân."

He smiled. "I fear she's already asleep, exhausted by all the running."

She smiled back. "I can imagine. But I like to see her settled before I go to bed. I sleep better that way."

He nodded as if he understood the sentiment and moved to let her through. The door frame was so narrow and Connor so big that she had to brush past him to get in. The contact of his chest against her breasts made her heartbeat go faster and her nipples harden. Without thinking about it, she stopped in front of him. The flame of the candle she held sent shadows over the left side of his face while placing the right into sharp relief, as if to illustrate the fact that her husband was a man of many facets. A fierce knight eating from the palms of seven-year-old children. A warrior and an enemy who had never caused her a moment of alarm, a husband who had not yet bedded her, a fiery lover who was keeping his urges in check, and a man who would be the perfect protector the day he came to trust her.

Right now he was watching her with an enigmatic look on his face. Would she ever understand the workings of his mind? He was tender when she expected him to be angry, whimsical when other men would take offense. Yet he did not lack passion or fire. None of it made sense.

"Will you sleep with me tonight?" She looked at him from under her lashes. "I mean, in my bed. I m-mean—"

"Do you want me to?" he asked softly, putting an end to her stammering.

"Yes," she admitted in a low voice. "Even if we had a disagreement earlier in the bailey."

He ran a hand through his hair in a gesture she hesitated to identify. Then he averted his gaze and she could not fool herself any longer. He was embarrassed. Connor Hunter, Lord Sheridan, the mighty Englishman, was embarrassed. And... Was he about to *apologize* to her?

She stilled, waiting.

"It wasn't really a disagreement, and I'm sorry about my reaction. I was angry but it wasn't your fault." He gave a sigh. "I shouldn't have reacted that way. It is only natural that you should want to know if the man you married has other children."

She decided to put him out of his misery. "I swear I was not suggesting... I do not think for a moment that you would be so dishonorable as to abandon any child you might have fathered or that you had imposed yourself on unwilling women, only—" It was her turn to be embarrassed.

And his turn to interrupt her.

"Yes. I know. Please. I'm sorry. Do you think we could just forget the whole thing? I don't think it reflects too well on either of us."

Esyllt frowned at the odd comment. It could have sounded like a rebuke if he had not berated himself as well as her. But one thing was clear, children were a touchy subject where he was concerned, she could not ignore it any longer. "Of course. Let us put the whole thing behind us."

"Thank you. I will be waiting in your bedchamber. Come and find me when you've finished with the girls."

He made it sound so evocative that for a moment she wondered if he would not bed her tonight, like a husband should. The prospect sent her heart aflutter. Was that the real reason she had asked he resumed his sleeping in her bed? Because she wanted him to finally consummate their marriage? It wouldn't surprise her if she had.

Well, in any case, now was not the time to think about it.

Without a word, she stepped into the room.

The sight meeting her eyes made her heart melt. Jane had her arms around Siân, and her face buried in her hair. Her daughter was holding her tight, and a smile was floating on her lips. It was such a touching picture that Esyllt felt tears well up in her eyes. It seemed that Wales and England could be at peace with one another. There was no question of domination here, just pure love. After blowing a kiss to each of the little girls, she retreated to the staircase.

On the way to her bedchamber, her heart began to beat

unbearably fast. What if Connor really was expecting an invitation to do more than sleep? She had banished him from her bed after his return from England and he had respected her wishes when another husband might well have asserted his authority over his wife. It seemed obvious that he was waiting for her to be comfortable with the idea of them becoming intimate before he attempted anything. Whether it was because he did not want to force a woman who had made her opinion clear about bedding him or for a reason she was ignorant of wasn't clear. Still, she was grateful, all the more so that she knew he was aroused by her proximity and ready to make her his.

You do not live next to a man without noticing certain things about his body.

Only today when he had taken her into his arms, she had felt how hard he was.

She flushed. What would she do if he pressed his advances on her? If he decided that her request that he join her meant that she was finally ready to accept his touch, then he would have no reason to hold back. And she wasn't sure she would have the will to resist.

In the end, she could have spared herself all the worry because when she entered the room, Connor was already asleep.

Esyllt knew from the disappointment crashing through her that she had indeed been ready to accept his touch and would have welcomed him if he had reached out for her. But it seemed that passive acceptance would not be enough.

If she wanted him to finally make love to her, she was going to have to beg for it.

Chapter Nine

"Father, did you know that Siân means Jane in Welsh?" Jane asked, taking her stepsister's hand in hers.

Connor saw Esyllt blush. *Now* he understood her reaction when he'd announced his daughter's name. She had seemed caught out. At the time he had attributed the flush to the realization that the mysterious Jane was not, contrary to what she'd thought, his mistress. Now he knew different.

"No, I did not know, for no one told me," he answered, looking at his wife pointedly. She blushed again, and he felt his lip curl. Teasing that delicious color out of her had become his favorite pastime. It made her glow.

"Siân said she would teach me to speak Welsh. That way we can have secrets just between the two of us. Isn't that great?" the little girl said, oblivious to the direction his mind had taken.

Connor clenched his jaw, all thoughts of his wife's beauty instantly forgotten. He knew very well what Jane was really saying, and why the idea of a secret language appealed to her so. How had he not seen this coming? To her, Siân would be much more than a friend, or even a stepsister. That was what he had wanted, but he hoped it would not end up causing her more pain.

"Your plan has a flaw in it, little niece. You are forgetting that Lady Sheridan speaks Welsh, as do all the people in this castle," Matthew pointed out, earning himself a grateful glance. His brother had come to his rescue without prompting, as per usual. Unsurprisingly, Matthew had guessed what was playing on his mind and he had drawn Jane's attention away from him to give him time to recover.

"It will be a secret from Father and you, that is the important thing," Jane said with the air of someone talking to a simpleton. Then she turned to Esyllt with an angelic smile. "My lady, will you promise to keep anything you hear Siân and me say a secret from my uncle and father?"

"I do," his wife answered solemnly. Indeed, who could have resisted that smile? Not him. "Though I do not believe there should be secrets in a marriage."

Connor could not help it. He arched a brow. This comment had been meant for him, that made no doubt. Was she saying she believed he was hiding something from her? He cleared his throat. He was not, not precisely...

"That's not a problem," Jane told Esyllt, looking suddenly much older than her seven years. "You and Uncle Matthew are not married, are you?"

"No, we're not, and I bet he's mighty glad of it."

"Then he's a fool, for you are the most beautiful woman I have ever seen. I cannot wait for you to give me another sister."

Another sister.

Connor felt his insides wither.

Another sister.

There was no prize guessing what Jane meant. After such a short time she already considered Siân as her sister. Esyllt's heart melted when the two little girls clasped hands. To think she had worried about her daughter's well-being while she'd waited for her groom to arrive. But having a new family might well be the making of her. She turned to throw Connor a grateful glance, but something about the way he was clenching his jaw froze the smile on her lips. He looked... He looked like he had never looked before.

Like a man in pain.

His eyes were also shinier than usual. Was he about to cry? From the way Matthew was gesticulating to keep his niece's attention focused on him, Esyllt understood that she was not wrong. Something was amiss, and he didn't want Jane to realize it.

"Come, girls, I know that the cook is making apple and walnut tarts today. The smell almost had me swooning when I walked past the kitchen earlier, and I think you two might be able to charm one out of her for me."

Jane gave a scoff. "If we manage to get one, we'll share it between us, be sure of it! You won't get a crumb."

"We'll see about that. Let's try and get that tart first, shall we?"

Esyllt shook her head in disbelief. Whenever the children were present, Matthew was a different man, cheerful and carefree. She'd often thought that his only redeeming feature was the unconditional love he bore his brother. Now she would have to add the feelings he harbored toward his niece to the list. He doted on the little girl, who adored him in turn. As if that was not enough, he had also taken to Siân, who regarded him as the uncle she'd never had. All that made it impossible for Esyllt to hate him, as she felt sure she should.

But perhaps she should not be surprised, for it was just as she had suspected. With people he trusted, he was all charm and smiles. The girls adored her, his men respected him, Connor considered him as a real brother, the servants had nothing to say about his behavior. It was only with her that he insisted on showing his boorish side.

"Come, I'll race you to the kitchen!"

The three of them disappeared in a chorus of laughter.

"My lord, are you quite all right?" Esyllt asked once she and Connor were alone.

Their eyes met, and she had the sensation someone had punched her in the stomach. He was glowering at her. For a moment she could not understand what she might have said, or done to provoke his anger, then she realized it was not really aimed at her. He simply hated that she'd seen his moment of weakness. Up until then he had always been the one in control, the one who could make her recoil or grow weak at the knees.

But now...

Now he was the one ill-at-ease and she felt as if she had the upper hand.

Ignoring her question, he stood up and helped himself to a cup of ale from the pitcher on the trestle table. When he came back to face her, he was his usual commanding self once more. She knew then that he would not reveal what had happened, and that she would not force him.

"Let us go to the village today and meet the people." He was as composed as if he had not been on the verge of a collapse moments ago. "It is time for my new tenants to be introduced to their lord, and for me to see what the feeling toward the English is."

Esyllt gave him a slanted look. "I can already tell you what that feeling is. Wariness in the main, fear mingled with suspicion for the rest, and of course the occasional burst of hatred." No, unfortunately, she had no illusion about the welcome the English lord of Castell Esgyrn would get.

He heard the news with equanimity, as she could have

guessed. "Well then. It is lucky I've never been a man to turn down a challenge."

"It is indeed, for you will have your hands full. Not to mention that you don't speak their language." She didn't mean to make him feel bad but, undoubtedly, that was a complication.

"No, I don't. But if I remember correctly, I am married to someone who does." The smile that followed the words would have reduced any woman to a quivering mess, Esyllt told herself to justify the weakening in her knees. It was not that she was too easily swayed, it was simply that he was too irresistible for words. "Will you come with me and face the hordes of enemies baying for my blood?"

"Yes." The word was out of her mouth before she could think.

In truth, she was impressed to see that her English husband wanted to introduce himself to his new tenants rather than stay hidden away behind the castle walls like a mighty lord, was brave enough to confront people he knew would not give him the best welcome and wanted to earn their approval. That he'd asked her to accompany him was the proof that, just like he'd told Gruffydd, he wanted to include her in the managing of the estate. She knew he was not taking her along just because she spoke Welsh.

He took her hand and kissed the fingers in a gallant gesture that had now become familiar. "Come. With a lady like you at my side, I cannot fail to win every heart."

Alas, it was not to be. As far as Esyllt could tell, no heart had been won that day.

As they left the village, her ears were still ringing from the shouting they'd had to endure and her body was still trembling from indignation and fear combined. Connor did not seem overly affected by the reception he'd gotten, however. Cantering by her side, he seemed as relaxed as he had been when they had set off that morning.

"What did you say? Suspicion at best, hostility at worst? I think I know which category the men we just saw belong to," he said, bringing his horse back down to a trot. "Perhaps the next village will not be as bad."

"I wouldn't count on it," she mumbled.

"Your honesty does you credit, wife, and I fear you may be right." He flashed his teeth, not in the least worried. "In the end it was probably a good thing that my sword broke. I should perhaps thank the blacksmith who forged it, for I'm not sure what would have happened otherwise."

Esyllt could not believe he was talking so blithely about what had been one of the worst moments of her life.

Morgan, the cooper, had attacked Connor with an axe. An axe! She had scarcely been able to credit it, and the violence of the ensuing confrontation had deeply shocked her. It was one thing watching men practice swordplay in the bailey to hone their skill, but this had been different. There was no doubt the Welshman, who was a notorious drunkard, had aimed to kill his lord in the most gruesome manner imaginable.

Even though Connor had done his best not to hurt the man, faced with such a weapon, he'd had no other choice but to defend himself. His skill as a knight had been enough to ensure he came to no harm against a drunken novice but, as he was parrying a particularly vicious blow from Morgan, his sword had broken clean in half. Cries of protest had instantly filled the village square. One could not wield an axe against an unharmed opponent, they all agreed to that at least. The villagers had all rushed to Morgan in case he decided to forget all sense of honor and carried on anyway. It was one thing meeting a knight in combat, quite another hacking at a defenseless man.

"Morgan will have been relieved with this outcome, even if he would never admit it," she observed, doing her best to hide how distraught she had been to see Connor face a madman brandishing an axe. "He'd probably started to realize that he would never best you, addled though his mind was by drink."

"My wife is a connoisseur of swordplay, then." Connor arched an eyebrow. "I'm impressed."

"I know a good swordsman when I see one, so I know you did not fight as hard as you could have." It had quickly become clear, even to the untrained villagers, that her husband was doing nothing more than prevent Morgan from hurting him, allowing him to vent his rage without posing a threat to his life.

"Of course I didn't. If I had, he would have found himself with the tip of my sword through the heart in no time."

The bloody image made her grimace.

"Why did you hold back? You could have bested him a dozen times over and, in truth, he deserved it. He was the one who attacked you."

She had been thoroughly disgusted and ashamed by the man's behavior. How were the English supposed to want to treat her countrymen like equals when they behaved with such crudeness and exhibited such lack of judgment? It had been clear that Connor had come in a spirit of conciliation and yet he had been met with nothing but hostility. Before he'd even had the chance to explain what plans he had for the village, Morgan had launched himself at him.

"Would you have rather I humiliated him in front of the whole village? That would not have been the wise thing to do," Connor said. "I think he would have preferred I cut his hand clean off. He would never have lived it down if I had sent him sprawling to the dirt with his friends, and perhaps his enemies, watching."

"Yes... Of course, you're right."

Esyllt sighed. Indeed it was better that way. She was certain the Welshman would never have provoked Connor if he had suspected him of being such an accomplished knight. Just before he'd run at him, axe in hand, she'd heard him tell his friends he would teach the pretty boy a lesson. Pretty boy! She had almost laughed out loud. For all his beauty and smooth manners, her husband was all man, as Morgan had found out to his cost.

But perhaps all was not lost.

When they had left, she could tell the tide had started to turn in favor of Connor. Faced with his skill and determination not to kill or even hurt a man who had struck first and would have deserved to be taught a lesson no one would forget, the villagers had reluctantly given him the respect he had hoped to earn.

It might not be as hard as she had first feared to make them see they had been lucky to be placed under the protection of a man like him, English though he may be. They might come to accept their new master as easily as the servants at Castell Esgyrn had, as easily as she had made her peace with the idea of being married to him.

Because she was now not only accepting of the idea, but proud to be his wife.

During the fight she had wanted him to win, not Morgan, and when his sword had broken, her heart had almost stopped beating. For a dreadful moment she had feared for his life and the distress this had provoked inside her had been so acute she knew she was going to have to examine her feelings soon. Perhaps pride was not the only feeling Connor elicited inside her.

"But how could your sword break so?" she asked, as they came to halt by the river. After the long ride, the horses needed a drink and she was glad of the respite herself.

He merely shrugged. "Who knows? It is rare but it happens. One can never rule out a defect in the making of a sword or indeed of any object. Oh, well, better now than in the midst of battle, I say."

Yes. Cold invaded her. Indeed.

"So, do you think—"

Connor abruptly stopped and frowned, looking into the distance. A group of small grey and chestnut horses had just crested the hill and was thundering toward them.

"Welsh ponies," Esyllt murmured, echoing his thoughts. These were not English knights mounted on destriers, but possibly rowdy villagers running after them, in search of trouble. "We must hide," she cried, looking at his empty scabbard. Evidently, she worried he would be unable to defend himself if they were attacked.

Before he could point out that he was not a man to cower and hide, she drew him to the other side of the oak tree. At its foot was a shallow ditch. She all but pushed him down into it then came to lie next to him, covering their mercifully dark clothes with dried leaves.

Smiling to himself, Connor allowed Esyllt to do as she saw fit. If the men were really from the village and bent on trouble, then he agreed he would be better off out of the way. He was unarmed, after all. And even if the riders turned out to be mere travelers, their arrival could still spell trouble. He was not worried about himself, but he would not be able to defend Esyllt without a weapon if they decided to try their luck with a beautiful woman.

More to the point, it warmed something inside of him to see her jump to his defense and want to protect him from harm.

And being pressed against a warm, beautiful woman was not exactly unpleasant. So he dutifully lay on the ground when she gave him a shove that would have failed to move a kitten.

"Stay still," she whispered. "Let them ride past. They won't see us hidden where we are."

"I daresay they won't. We are buried in dried leaves. I'm grateful they are not soggy with rain, at least."

"I'm sorry, I panicked," Esyllt murmured in his ear, sounding contrite. She must have realized how ridiculous it was for the lord and lady of the castle to lie on the forest floor under a pile of leaves. He smiled. Not ridiculous exactly. Endearing rather. "I don't think you're a coward, only it—"

"I know." He could not quite hide the laugh in his voice. "You thought that I was only one man. I'm sure I cannot fault you for that observation, however much it hurts my vanity."

He felt her tremble against him and thought for a moment she was beside herself with fear, then he understood she was fighting a giggle.

A moment later the forest filled with the noise of snorting horses and laughing men. Welshmen. It soon became clear that they were merely travelers pausing to water their horses, not angry villagers who had set off in pursuit of their English master with the intention of hacking him to pieces. Still, now that they were hidden, they had better remain where they were. It would be awkward to be seen coming from a ditch together, covered in leaves, and draw unnecessary attention to themselves.

With his wife pressed tight against him, Connor closed his eyes. It felt good to have her in his arms. Allowing everything to disappear from his mind, he reveled in her touch while the men caroused in the distance.

And then the noises around them changed. Laughter stopped. He guessed that the men had seen their two horses and realized someone else was out there in the forest.

Connor's eyes snapped open. "What are they saying?" he asked Esyllt. "Can you hear?"

"They are wondering where the horses have come from and where the riders are," she whispered back.

He nodded. He had suspected as much. "Are they suspicious?" Were the men about to pounce?

"No. They seem to think..." She stopped.

"To think?" The two words made it clear she had better finish her sentence. He needed to be ready in case the men decided to look for them.

"They have guessed from their build and saddles that they belong to a man and a woman. They seem to think that two lovers have gone into the woods to..."

"Gone for a tryst, you mean," he supplied when she faltered again.

"Yes."

He barely repressed a snort, utterly charmed by her embarrassment.

Then coarse laughter reached their ears and Connor stiffened. Why was he amused? This was serious. If the men thought a woman was this moment naked and in close proximity, they might well think to dispose of her vulnerable lover and take his place between her legs. By the sound of things, there were at least five or six of them. With such odds, it would not be long before he was overpowered.

"Are they considering coming to find the hapless pair and make the most of the woman's charms?" he growled in her ear.

"No," Esyllt breathed, sounding as appalled by the prospect as he felt. "But I fear they are considering taking the horses with them."

Of course. How had he not thought of that? His stallion alone would be worth a fortune, an irresistible temptation to poor people.

Should he go to the men before it was too late and impress them with his status and physique?

Before he could make a decision, Esyllt pressed her palm over his chest. She had read his intentions and was telling him not to move. "They won't. One of them has pointed out that a man in possession of such a mount is probably an important knight, able to hold his own against untrained opponents. They will not risk his wrath now or retribution later. They know Storm will be too easily recognized when you start looking for him."

"Good." The travelers had shown themselves to be sensible and honest. The rest of his fears were allayed. Such men would not hurt Esyllt, even if they saw her. He relaxed again.

A moment later a thunder of hooves was heard. The men were gone.

Chapter Ten

Though it was now safe to move, Esyllt stayed right where she was, wrapped in Connor's arms. It felt too good to be held against his strong, warm body. She could have remained there until nightfall, with her leg draped over his thighs, her arm curled over his chest, her head in the crook of his neck.

It struck her that if they were discovered in such an intimate position, then they would for sure be taken for two reckless lovers sneaking out for a tryst in the woods, not two respectably married people.

Well, it mattered not. She knew what they were to each other.

She could have told herself that she was too frightened to do anything in case the men came back but she knew it was something other than fear that had her in its grip. Connor was so close to her that with every breath she took she inhaled his spicy leather scent, a scent that sent her back to the night before their wedding when he had teased her and proven to her that she desired him. Suddenly his warmth, his sheer physicality overwhelmed her.

She gulped.

Being close to a man like him, in his prime, was totally different to being close to her late husband had been. She had felt affection for Gwyn, even a sort of tenderness, but his proximity had never made her breath catch in her throat, her heart flutter in her chest, her body go limp with desire. Why was she so affected by Connor, an Englishman she should despise, when Gwyn, the husband she had respected, had never managed to stir any emotions within her?

She tried to move her head so that her lips would not brush against the skin of his neck but he tightened his hold around her, just enough to keep her in place. Apparently, he had no intention of getting up just yet.

On the contrary. He moved slowly, until he was poised over her, caging her under his strong body. Eyes fluttering, she tried to fight the array of sensations assaulting her senses.

"I think they're gone," Connor said, speaking in her ear.

She nodded, unable to answer.

He moved slightly, so he could look her in the eye. All the blood drained from Esyllt's veins. Looking at such a handsome man whilst being so close to him was intoxicating. For a long moment, they remained glued to each other, with their faces only inches apart, breathing in the same air. Somehow, this was even more intimate than when he had entered her flesh, or pleasured her with his mouth. There was nothing scandalous about it, but it was more than the joining of two bodies overcome with lust, it was the union of two souls.

There also was a light in his eyes she could not quite account for. Was he embarrassed? Moved? Aroused? Yes, that might be what it was, he was feeling the same as she did, aroused by her proximity. Was he finally going to kiss her?

"Thank you," he said eventually.

"W-why are you thanking me?" she stammered.

"You could have called out to your countrymen just now."

"Why? What would I have said to them?"

He shrugged. "Anything. It would have been impossible for me to understand a word. I would have been unable to defend myself, and disposed of without even knowing what my supposed crime was. The men weren't to know we are husband and wife, and I am obviously not Welsh. You could have accused me of assaulting you or of having robbed you of your riches or anything else." A corner of his mouth lifted. "A perfect solution, don't you think? Then you would have been widowed but your hands would have been clean."

"Do you think I have so little honor?" she flared up.

The green eyes softened when she had expected them to flare in turn. "I do think that you are a woman of uncommon determination. And you did not desire our union."

"No." The word left a strange taste in Esyllt's mouth. She had not at first, but now things had changed. Could he not see it?

"Need I remind you what you did to Lord Sheridan's supposed squire to make him break your betrothal?" he purred. "How far you were prepared to go?"

No, he did not. She remembered it all too well. For a long moment she was unable to protest, or even speak. She simply stared at him, fascinated, the way she imagined a vole would stare at the hawk about to trap it into its claws.

"You think I want you dead?"

"You said you'd killed your first husband. Compared to that, handing your second husband to others to be dealt with would probably weigh little on your conscience."

"It's not the same," she managed to say.

"Is it not? You never told me what the poor man did to deserve his fate. But I'll admit to being curious."

He leaned in closer. Oh, God, he was not going to kiss

her, he was going to *kill* her. It was the only reason why he would ask such a question, the reason why he had trapped her under him, in this forest where no one would come to her aid and her body would never be found. Hers would be another skeleton found in a ditch, and in years from now, people might name their castle after her. The irrational thought whirled through her mind, causing her to suffocate in panic. Connor had not married her for love, but to obey his king. He had needed a match with a Welsh woman, but he didn't need the wife that went with it. From the moment she had signed the wedding papers, her lands had been handed over to him. She had now outlived her purpose, so why would he spare her?

"Please don't hurt me," she croaked.

She was utterly at his mercy, already on the ground, already half dead with fright. She would never survive this.

"Hurt you?" Connor's eyes clouded over at her plea. "Tell me, when have I hurt you?" He brushed a finger along her cheek and frowned. "Are you afraid of me? Please Esyllt, don't be. I would never hurt you, I swear."

It was the first time he had used her name. The way he said it, so perfectly, told her that he must have asked someone to help him with the unusual pronunciation, perhaps Jane or Siân. Dear God, she was a fool, and her overheated imagination had gotten the better of her for a moment. Of course he was not about to kill her, just because they were away from the castle! If he wanted her dead he would not have waited so long.

They slept in the same bed, the opportunity to hurt or kill her had been there from the start.

"I'm not afraid of you," she said in a whisper.

"You just said 'don't hurt me'."

"I'm sorry, I panicked again." She knew she all too easily did that, and it was a habit that was hard to break. "You asked about my husband, and you had this strange look in your eyes... I could not make sense of it."

He stilled, then leaned in to speak with his mouth at her temple. The feel of his lips against her skin was delicious, and the heat of his breath stirred her senses. This was not a threatening embrace, far from it. "That might be because I was about to kiss you."

With those words he placed a finger against her mouth. Her heart almost stopped. What she had seen flashing in his eyes was desire, not hatred. How could she have mistaken the two? There was a brief caress and then the finger pressed against her bottom lip slid inside her mouth, stopping when it bumped against her teeth. It was as shocking as if Connor had caressed her intimate folds and slipped the finger inside her heated flesh instead of between her lips. Esyllt moaned and fought the urge to open her mouth further.

"Will you let me?" he breathed, evidently pleased by her reaction. "Will you let me kiss you, Esyllt?"

"You don't need to ask. You are my husband."

He had certainly not asked her permission to kiss her *there* the other day. Surely, he didn't think this would be an even more forbidden act?

He shook his head, not satisfied with the logic of her answer. "I have never kissed a woman who did not want me. I am not going to start with my own wife." He took his finger from her mouth and let it slide along her throat, stopping just at the swell of her breasts. "So will you let me kiss you?"

"Why do you want to kiss me?"

"For the same reason you want to kiss me." With those words he brought his lips within touching distance of her. "Kiss me, Esyllt. I'm your husband. You don't need to ask for permission."

She could not resist. He was right. She wanted to kiss him

but she couldn't have explained why. Weren't they supposed to be wary of each other? No, not anymore. The time to be wary had long passed.

The time to be bold had come.

The gap between them was bridged without her knowing who had moved first. Did it matter? No, as they wanted the same thing. And she instantly knew this would be a kiss like no other.

Connor's lips were soft, as soft as the rest of him was hard, and though his intent was clear, she didn't feel forced in any way. His tongue probed at her lips instead of invading her, coaxing them open. She obeyed the sensual command and allowed him to explore at his leisure and take them both to unexpected heights of pleasure. She had been shocked when he had made her body explode with his kisses on her womanhood, but she had not been surprised. It made sense that such a sensitive part of her anatomy should create mind-blowing sensations when properly touched. But the lips... How could a kiss' heat spread through her every nerve ending in that way?

Deciding she would never find the answer to that question, she settled for enjoying the moment. As if he'd guessed her intentions, Connor growled into her mouth, the sound deeply erotic. Then there was another rumble, one that made the ground tremble under her back. Esyllt almost groaned in frustration.

No, not again! Not now!

Connor was on his feet before Esyllt could move because it was clear from the beat of the hooves that it was only one rider this time, so he had no qualms about being seen. Whoever this was, whatever their intention, he could handle them, even unharmed. The kiss with Esyllt had infused him with strength, and he felt ready to face a dozen men, so one would be no threat whatsoever. He would not hide anymore, he would defend and claim her as his to whoever dared approach.

But the rider didn't stop. It was simply a lonely traveler cantering along the path, oblivious to their presence. He didn't slow down, or even glance in their direction when he rode past the clearing. They weren't in any danger. Connor turned in time to see Esyllt get up and brush the dried leaves from her skirts. She looked flushed and was unable to meet his eye.

She was also unutterably beautiful, and more precious to him than ever.

He walked up to her, remembering the look in her eyes when he had come over her earlier. Up until then, he had never thought she might actually be afraid of him. She was always so brazen. But she had been like a rabbit in front of a fox about to tear it to shreds, pale and frightened. And all because of him.

The sight had torn at his insides. He never wanted to cause her another moment's worry in his life.

"Esyllt, I—"

"I think we should go," she said, moving before he could reach her.

"No, not yet."

She shook her head and carried on looking at the ground, at her shoes, anywhere but at him. "Please, don't say anything. I couldn't..."

He did not allow her to walk away but he did not touch her. As she was already mortified, he did not want to add to her distress. But why was she so disturbed to have kissed him? Married people had every right to do this and more. When the rider had interrupted them, he had been about to lift her skirts and stroke her intimately. Whether he would have done so simply to give her pleasure or to prepare her for his possession, he wasn't sure, but what was certain was that he had been about to take the kiss to the next level.

What else could he have done? He wanted her, had wanted her for days. It was time they started acting like husband and wife. Would she have agreed to the intimacy? Unfortunately, he could not be sure. The day he had pleasured her with his mouth, he had not given her any choice, he had devoured her like a man demented with need. He might have frightened her by his vehemence.

And even if she felt desire for him, after what had happened the night of his arrival at Esgyrn Castle, he feared she might not allow herself to follow her desire. Because of him, of what he had done to her, of how dirty he had made her feel then, of how he had teased her, calling her a wanton, lustful woman, and denying her the release she craved after taking possession of her body.

Guilt assaulted him. She did not deserve to be made to feel like that.

"We're married," he told her softly. "There is no shame in us kissing."

No, Esyllt privately admitted, there was no shame in kissing, but what about the heat burning a path down her whole body? The inexplicable urge to grind her hips against Connor, to feel him thrust inside her? Surely kissing someone should be just that, kissing? It should not transform you into a lewd creature, wild enough to forget everything around you, and make you behave so shamefully?

Had the rider not interrupted them, she would have bared her body; she would have begged Connor to make love to her here out in the open, amongst the leaves in the ditch. Even worse, had he refused, she might well have pushed him flat on his back, so that she could ride him like she rode her horse.

Dear God... What would he have thought if she had done such a scandalous thing? It was something she had heard two maids discuss once, and which had shocked her. Now the notion did not shock her as much as send her nerves into a wild tangle. After the way she had behaved the night they'd met, when she had sat on him with her bare legs and then allowed him to come to her bed and possess her, he would really think her depraved beyond all hope.

How far are you prepared to go? he'd asked her.

Quite far, apparently. Much further than she would have liked, much further than a lady should go. Too far.

Her English husband did not trust her because she was Welsh. That was bad enough. She did not want him to think her a wanton as well.

"Please, let's just go, night is already falling." She made to walk to the horses, but he was in front of her before she could take more than one step, blocking her path.

"No."

Her heart skipped a beat. Was he about to tumble her to the ground and show her that he would not countenance being teased one moment and refused the next? He would have felt her response to his kiss, known she was melting for him, so why would he not want to make the most of it?

"No?" she repeated, hoping to be wrong. By now, she had understood that they would consummate their marriage before too long, but she didn't want it to happen like that.

"Not before you have looked me in the eye and told me that you are not ashamed of what happened."

Esyllt hesitated but knew there would be no swaying him. At long last, she lifted her eyes to him. He was staring at her almost sternly. "I-I am not ashamed of what happened."

"And *mean* it," he specified with a smile.

This she couldn't do, for she most definitely *was* ashamed, whatever he said.

"Esyllt," Connor said more firmly. "Forgive me, this is all my fault. I should not have... well... I'm sorry."

Her eyes widened at his fumbled apologies. None of the men she knew would ever apologize to a woman, especially not unprompted. "You should not have what?"

"I should not have kissed you just now. It is clear you did not want it."

Oh, but she had wanted it! Too much, that was the problem. Esyllt would hold the memory of that first kiss close to her heart forever. It had been perfect, as if they could ignore all that had happened between them for a moment. There had been no distrust, no doubt, no resentment. They had been just a man and a woman who wanted one another.

"I did want it. But 'tis now over and we should…"

They should what? Go before she asked to kiss him again? To forget about it? To leave before it was dark? But how could she leave in such a state?

"My hair," she said, fingering the ribbon that had held her tresses in place. It had slid down and was not holding anything anymore. She could not get back to the castle like this and face everyone's comments or worse, Matthew's hawkish stare. He would no doubt ascribe some dark motives to a tryst in the woods with her husband.

He would remind her that he was watching her, he would accuse her of having led her husband right into the heart of the forest so that Welsh rebels could jump on him, or something equally ridiculous. He would ruin one of the most incredible moments of her life with his foul suspicions.

"What about your hair?" Connor asked slowly.

"I cannot be seen in such a state of disarray. It will look as if we had…"

She didn't finish, and mercifully, he didn't pass any comment, because they *had* rolled around on the ground and shared a passionate kiss. "Shall I braid it for you?" he asked instead.

"You?"

Esyllt almost laughed, all the tension in her body releasing in one exhale. This man, tall and broad, this warrior who dressed in chain mail and wielded swords as easily as she handled embroidering needles, was offering to do what her delicate lady-in-waiting usually did. The idea was too ludicrous by half. Then the laughter got stuck in her throat when she imagined him running his fingers through her hair. It would feel nothing like Seren's perfunctory touch. It would make her want him to touch other parts of her.

Just like that, the tension between them was back.

"Yes, me," Connor said, his voice deep. "You are forgetting I have a daughter. I cannot recall how many times I have been requested to impersonate a lady-in-waiting and adorn Jane's hair. I have picked up one or two things along the way, you'll be pleased to know."

Her heart melted at the thought of him playing with his little girl's hair. "I am sure that you make a very poor lady-in-waiting."

He did not even flinch. "I would. I have yet to find a dress that can fit me."

And just like that, she started laughing. It was not the first time Connor had displayed a propensity for mischief, but usually it expressed itself with Jane, Matthew, or one of his men, not her. But she needed to laugh right now, or she would end up throwing herself into his arms.

"Well, be that as it may, I have no intention of having my hair pulled when you cannot control your strength!"

He did not protest, or laugh. Instead he leaned toward her.

"I have absolute mastery over my strength, Esyllt, and I can control my fingers very well. Don't you remember? I thought you had quite liked my caresses. And my intimate kisses."

Her mouth fell open at the provocative words. Was he really reminding her of all he had done to her in bed? "You…"

"Yes, me. Your husband, the only man who has the right to give you such pleasure. I shall do it as often as you need me to." Oh, now, he was just being cruel, by alluding to what they could do together. "So what say you. Are you ready to risk it? Shall I braid your hair, lady wife?"

She swallowed hard and then nodded, utterly under his spell. By now, she would have agreed to almost anything.

"Sit down."

To Connor's surprise, Esyllt obeyed without a word. She settled on the log he had indicated and waited for him to start seeing to her coiffure. He placed himself behind her, readying himself.

As soon as he buried his fingers into her hair, Connor understood that he had grossly underestimated the difficulty of the task. Not only was his wife's hair nothing like his daughter's but he was not usually distracted by lewd thoughts when he braided Jane's hair. His body didn't burn from the inside, his shaft didn't pulse with need.

To add to his confusion, Esyllt sat rigidly on the piece of wood, as if she would bolt at any moment, when surely she should be melting under his touch. Seeing her fight the desire she felt for him was an unusual and unwelcome feeling. Connor was used to having women fawn over him. They wanted his body, his fortune, the prestige of an association with him—or all of this at once. As a consequence, they acted as if the sun had been created to shine over him alone.

He had never enjoyed such blatant seduction ploys, but to have a woman look at him with diffidence was no better. It was downright unpleasant, all the more so that Esyllt had no reason to fight her desire for him.

They were already married, and he knew her motives were

pure, as she had nothing to gain by giving herself to him. Status, she had already had, as Lady Sheridan. His domains and possessions meant nothing to her, as they were in England, and prestige she did not care for. As to his body, she had every right to it already... and she wanted it, that made no doubt in his mind. But unlike the other women who were ready to do anything to find themselves under him, she did all she could to avoid finding herself in that position.

Rather than try to attract him, she did her best to keep him at bay. She wasn't using her charms as a weapon; she seemed almost afraid of them. He hated this diffidence, but it also inflamed him.

It was a refreshing challenge to have to make a woman give in to him rather than find a way of refusing her advances without offending her, to make her understand that there was no shame in admitting what she felt for him. They were husband and wife, so they could indulge their senses as much as they wanted.

His other lovers had feigned attraction and used desire to stir him into proposal.

Esyllt felt desire for him and yet she resisted the attraction.

It made no sense.

Still, the result was the same. He was irresistibly drawn. This woman he had not chosen for her personal qualities intrigued him, provoked his lust, infuriated him, and made him laugh all at once. Despite the trick she had played on him the night before their wedding, he was attracted to her like he had never been attracted to anyone. Perhaps it was because of the trick she had played. After all, it wasn't everyday a beautiful woman had you bound in ropes so she could sit on your lap then dragged you into bed and silently begged to be fucked.

Even his most determined conquests had not been so bold. It had been arousing as hell to be at Esyllt's mercy, all the more so that she had been unaware of his identity at the time. What he had seen in her eyes had been pure, honest desire, not calculation, and it had been for *him*, for the man he was, not for the lord who could offer her protection and wealth.

Since she had found out his real name she had not dared show her inner feelings or carnal side and he longed to see it again. When he had pleasured her intimately, she had not demanded a more complete possession. When he had kissed her just now, she had recoiled from the possibility of more, instead of pushing him onto the ground and have her way with him.

And now here he was, tamely braiding her hair, when what he wanted was to bury his fingers in it while he rode her hard.

"Here," he said in a breath. "As good as the most seasoned lady-in-waiting, I would say."

Esyllt tentatively patted at her coiffure. He groaned inwardly. God's teeth, if that innocent gesture stirred his blood, he really was in deeper than he'd thought. Something would have to be done about how he felt, and soon.

"I cannot see anything so I guess I will just have to take your word for it."

"You will. Don't worry, you look as lovely as ever."

She blushed, as if she had never heard the word applied to her before and did not quite know what to make of it. He would have to ensure he complimented her more often, so that she got used to it, just like he was making sure she got used to his body by walking around naked when he got up in the morning. As he'd informed her, men woke up hard. What he had never told her, however, was that usually the erection went down almost immediately. His was kept alive for much longer by the way she looked at him.

He was starting to wonder how long he could keep pretending that he didn't see the desire in her eyes, or didn't want to act on it.

"Let's go then."

But just as she took her first step, her skirts got caught in a holly bush.

"Allow me." Connor knelt at her feet to disentangle the dress from the foliage keeping it captive. He smiled to himself when he saw the way the leaves had sunk their teeth in the delicate material, as if to keep her with them. He could understand the urge. "Holly reminds me of you, dear wife."

As if to illustrate the similarities between her and the plant, she glared at him. "Does it?"

"Yes. Your hair is just as shiny as the newly unfurled leaves and your eyes are the same vibrant green."

He saw in those beautiful eyes the surprise he had hoped to provoke. She had obviously feared he would compare her to the prickliness of the bush.

"It's a beautiful color," she finally conceded. "But I doubt 'tis what other people see when they look at holly."

"I care not what other people see. I'm your husband, and therefore I like to think that I see things in you they might not."

"Oh. So now you're saying that no one else but you could consider me beautiful. I'm flattered."

Connor burst out laughing. It was not what he'd been saying at all and she knew it. "I think I shall keep my compliments to myself in the future, if they displease you that much."

"Compliments? I don't know how it is in England, but here in Wales compliments make the person receiving them feel good."

He raised his hands in surrender. "I'm beaten. Next time I shall praise your beauty in a more conventional manner, comparing your hair to the sun, and your eyes to sparkling gems. Would that be better?"

Esyllt didn't answer because, in truth, she had liked the unconventional compliment, much more personal than the ones she was used to receiving. But after their passionate kiss, she didn't know how to deal with Connor.

"I believe we were on our way to the horses?" she said pointedly.

"We were."

The horses nickered at their approach. Esyllt looked at her mare and then at her heavy dress. There wasn't a log in sight that could serve as a mounting block.

"Once again, you will allow me," Connor whispered, not resisting the urge to speak with his lips against the delicate shell of her ear.

When she nodded her agreement, he took her by the waist and turned her to face him. This was not the best way to hand her over the horse, not by any means, which made him realize he had asked permission for something else. As to what it was, he was not quite sure. A kiss? A simple embrace?

Esyllt seemed at a loss also. "I-I meant—"

"I know. Forgive me."

Turning her once more, he gave her a leg up, then helped arrange her skirts around her when she was sat in the saddle.

He vaulted onto Storm's back, and they set off at a brisk trot, intent on reaching Esgyrn Castle before it was full dark.

"I will have to go to the village by the coast soon," Esyllt announced out of the blue. Connor guessed she was trying to act as if nothing licentious had happened in the woods, probably a sensible idea. It would not do to dismount in the bailey with a bulge in his braies. "It is time we elected a new reeve."

"We will send word that we'll go together three days hence, so that they can select a few candidates to present to us," he ruled. "From now on I will preside over the election, with your help, of course."

She looked at him from under her lashes. "Very well. I'm

glad to see you taking your role as master of Castell Esgyrn and husband seriously."

"Oh, believe me, I take my role as your husband very seriously, and mean to fulfil it to the best of my abilities." Aye, he did, and in all senses of the word. Not least of all in bed. "I want to make you proud, make you trust me."

Make you moan, make you come.

The image of her squirming under him had him hard as a poker in the blink of an eye. Damn it all! Only a moment ago he'd been thinking he didn't want to arrive at the castle with an erection the size of his arm.

Connor launched his stallion into a gallop.

Chapter Eleven

"Have you seen your brother?"

Esyllt stormed toward Matthew, feeling like a pagan goddess ready to unleash her wrath. She could not remember ever being so irate and he was the perfect target for her fury. The resentment of the last few months built up until it could do nothing but erupt in his face.

The arrogant Englishman had it coming anyway. It might as well be now, when she needed something to take the edge off her ire. After a day of difficult negotiations on her own and a ride in the driving rain, she was not in the mood to even try to spare him. He'd been nothing but condescending or downright insulting toward her since he'd arrived.

"Where is he?"

"What do you want with him?"

Matthew made a grimace but she was too far gone to notice that he looked ill at ease when she had expected him to snap back, claiming that Connor did what he wanted and was not accountable to a Welsh schemer, be she his own wife.

"I'll tell you what I want with him, shall I? We were supposed to go to the village today and elect the new reeve together. He promised he would be there, he even sent word ahead to say so. Everyone was waiting for him there. And did he come? No. Did he give any explanation to me or anyone as to why he was absent? No. It was humiliating! What sort of a message do you think it will have sent?"

That the new, proud, arrogant English lord could not bestir himself to come and see his poor Welsh tenants, that was what. She could have cried in frustration and hurt combined. To think that only the other day she had thought him reasonable and involved in his domain's affairs, ready to give their marriage and his new responsibilities a try.

The last two days had been perfect, and the last two nights even more so, even if they had not made love or even kissed. Sensing she needed time to adjust to the new accord between them, Connor had merely drawn her into his arms before falling asleep and held her tight against his warmth. It had been all she'd needed.

And now she was forced to see that it had all been an illusion. He cared nothing for her or her people.

Matthew let out a sigh. "Connor is in his room."

"Oh, is he?" It had not even crossed Esyllt's mind that he would still be in the castle. Her husband was many things but he was not lazy. What was he doing in his room at this time? When she had not seen him by her side upon waking up, she had not for a moment thought he had gone to his own room. He never did that. Why had he hidden there today of all days? Well, there was only one way to find out. "Methinks it's time to wake him up."

She picked up her wet skirts and rushed past Matthew.

"My lady, wait!"

Esyllt didn't turn around or even slow down, for suddenly an awful premonition seized her. Evidently, Matthew was aware of what Connor was up to in that room and he didn't want her to see it. Why? An image of her husband lying in bed with another woman tore through her mind and almost sent her to her knees. Had he let her go all alone to the village so that he could spend the day in bed with a mistress?

No. Surely he wouldn't have dared!

But why not? He had known she would be out of the castle and busy with the election of the reeve and it had been months since their wedding, months during which he had not been able to indulge his masculine urges with her. Why would he not do like every virile man she knew and find a willing woman for a wild romp?

Followed by Matthew who, despite his obvious anguish, was doing his best to heed his brother's instructions and not bodily restrain her, she climbed the spiral staircase and opened the door to Connor's bedchamber. She had to know the truth if it killed her.

Her first thought was that her worst fears were confirmed. The bed was all in disarray and her husband lay sprawled on his stomach, wearing only his hose. It took her a moment to realize that he was alone in the bed, however, and asleep, rather than labouring over a woman. It was only a small consolation. His conquest could have just left, leaving him too spent to move.

She rounded on Matthew. "Where is she?"

"Who?"

"Don't play the innocent with me, you know perfectly well who I'm talking about. Forgive me if I don't know my husband's leman by name." Were there more than one? Was that why he was confused?

Matthew sighed and ran a hand through his hair. "Connor did not spend the day in a woman's arms. God knows I would have preferred him to." This was such a shocking thing to tell a man's wife that Esyllt instantly believed him. Disapproving of her as he may be, her brother-in-law would not have dared tell her to her face that he regretted her husband had not spent the day rutting away with another woman.

No. She was now certain of it, Connor had spent the day alone.

"Then... What happened? Is he prone to spending days lying in bed thus?"

"No." Matthew gave another sigh. Esyllt saw his eyes flicker toward the floor next to the bed. Now that her anger had dissipated somewhat, she saw a cup and a jug next to a puddle of dark liquid she assumed to be wine.

"I see," she said frostily. "He decided to drink himself into a stupor instead of coming with me to the village as planned. Well, I cannot say I'm impressed."

She didn't know whether to be relieved to see that he was not with a woman or horrified by what she was seeing. Was her husband a drunkard? She had never suspected it, certainly since their wedding he had not given her any indication that he might like drinking to excess. But there was no mistaking the tableau in front of her.

"Listen," Matthew said, sounding like his usual unbearable self once more. "You don't know Connor. You cannot judge him on what you—"

"You mean that he *is* a drunkard and that this is nothing you have not seen before, that I should expect such behavior in the future?" How was that supposed to reassure her?

"No. And if only you listened to me, I might tell you what I mean." He was now exasperated, but Esyllt did not see why she should try to be more patient. She was annoyed as well. Just *what* was happening here?

As if guessing she was about to lose her mind, Connor stirred. He gave a groan and turned to face them, confusion etched all over his face. Esyllt threw him a look as cold as she could muster.

"Awake, husband? Do not tell me we disturbed you?" she sneered. "I'm sorry, we didn't think anyone would object to hearing people move about and talk. It is, after all, well past the nooning hour."

He rubbed the back of his neck and looked at her with eyes that had lost some of their usual spark. She frowned. In this moment he did not look like a man befuddled by drink, but rather like a...

She blinked. Had he been crying? The answer hit her with the force of a clap of thunder.

Yes, he had.

Her anger disappeared in the blink of an eye and she took an involuntary step forward. It seemed that for the second time in just a few weeks, she had jumped to the wrong conclusion. Just like she had when she'd first heard of Jane, she had been quick to accuse him of duplicity when it seemed he had a genuine reason for acting the way he had.

"My lord? Are you well?" she asked tentatively. "What is it?"

"Do you want me to talk to her, Brother?" Matthew asked from behind her. For once, Esyllt did not bristle. It did not sound as if he was interfering where he had no reason to, rather it was obvious he was trying to help his brother out of a difficult situation, an intention that found favour with her.

"No, I will do it, thank you." Connor's voice sounded rough but he looked determined—and sober—enough to do it. Esyllt braced herself, wondering if she wanted to know what the matter was after all.

"Please don't be too harsh on him," Matthew said, looking at her squarely.

Her eyes widened. What was going on here? Before she could say anything he left the room, closing the door behind him.

"What's the matter?" Esyllt croaked, coming forward. She was now truly worried. What terrible secret was her husband hiding from her? Was he ill and trying to drown his fear at the prospect? Her insides twisted in fear. No! Not him as well! He was a picture of strength and health such as Gwyn had never been, surely he could not be at death's door? "Are you unwell?"

There was such dread in her voice that Connor instantly reassured her, using the word she had not dared use. "No. I'm not dying."

Slowly, the blood returned to her veins. If he was not about to die, then she could start breathing again. Still, something was definitely wrong. He had not shaved, his jaw was shadowed by a dark stubble that should have made him appear unkempt. But all it did was draw attention to his manly face and offer a contrast to his green eyes.

"I'm sorry I did not come with you to the reeve's election. It was my intention to go, as you know, but at the last moment I could not. I had not realized what day it would be when I sent word to the village."

Oh God, the reeve's election. Lost to her worry, she'd had forgotten all about that. She shook her head. "It's not a problem. But will you tell me what's wrong?"

By now, she had understood that it was not a whim or a mark of disinterest on his part. The fact that he had apologized for it immediately and unprompted was enough to tell her he had a serious motive for letting her go on her own.

"Today is the feast of St Philip and James," he started. She waited. Was that supposed to mean anything to her? Because it did not. "Last year on that day my wife died, whilst giving birth to my baby girl."

Esyllt froze. He'd lost a child? She'd had no idea, and she could not imagine suffering a worst loss.

"Oh, God, I'm so sorry..." She sat on the bed and took his hand in hers. It was warm and big. So big. So strong. And yet in that moment he appeared so fragile. Her heart broke for him. "I didn't know."

"I know you didn't, even if I think you suspected something. What did Matthew tell you about them?" he asked softly. "My girls?"

Of course... The day of the hide and seek game, when she had revealed his brother's taunt. She remembered Connor's outbursts of anger at the mere mention of children, how he had flared up despite being a measured man. Now she knew why the topic was a sensitive one. Because he had lost a child, and a wife, in traumatic circumstances. No wonder he had not welcomed any probing on her part.

"He said that you could only father girls, that I would never be able to give you an heir. I know he was trying to rile me, but at the time I thought Jane was an only child, that's why I wondered if you had—"

She did not finish her sentence. Not only did she not want to remind him of her clumsy accusations regarding illegitimate children, but he had gone deathly pale. He ran a hand over his face like a man trying to chase a nightmarish vision. That he was reliving the moment he'd been handed his dead baby was obvious.

"I fathered three girls," he said in a voice she had never heard before. "Two of them are dead. Jane's twin sister, Elspeth, died six months ago, of a fever. She fought bravely for a week, we all hoped she would make it, but in the end..." His voice caught in his throat and he fell back on the bed, hiding his face with his bent arm.

"Oh, Lord, I'm sorry," Esyllt whispered, feeling sick to her stomach. To lose a baby at birth was awful, but a little girl he had seen grow and learned to love was unthinkable. How had he not gone mad with grief? Even as the question crossed her mind, she knew the answer.

Because of Jane.

He'd had to stay strong for his surviving child. There had been no other choice, her father was all she had left from her loving family.

Connor gave her hand a squeeze. "That's the real reason I accepted the king's orders. I could have made my peace with never marrying again, in fact I think I would have preferred it at the time, but Jane was too young. She needs a stepmother, and a sister. I chose you because I was told about Siân. Jane would be so glad to have a stepsister her own age. I thought..." He paused. "She will never forget Elspeth, of course, but I hoped it might help her get over the worst of the grief. And Siân has proven to be the support she needed not to collapse, and more. I will never thank her enough for that. Between you, you and Siân have given me my daughter back. I had not heard her laugh in months when Matthew brought her to Esgyrn Castle."

The lump in Esyllt's throat almost prevented her from talking but she made the effort. "I'm glad we could help."

Now she understood everything. The way Jane insisted on sleeping with Siân, their limbs entwined together, her protectiveness about her new friend, the look on Connor's face when his daughter had mentioned a secret language between the two of them. She had heard that twins sometimes shared such a connection. It seemed that Jane was trying to recreate with Siân what she'd had with Elspeth.

Her heart squeezed in compassion.

It was what she had thought all along. This man had a secret wound. He was not the ruthless, uncaring man she had feared he would be when Gruffydd had forced her into this union. She had been attracted to him from the first, before she'd known who he was. But then, after his awful deception, she'd thought it wiser to steel herself against her treacherous feelings. It had been much safer to think him as detached as he strove to appear.

But now she knew she would not be able to rely on that anymore, because he was not detached or remote, quite the opposite. His indefectible love for a man who was not his real brother proved it, as did his devotion to his daughter and his attitude toward Siân—and toward her.

The story he'd just revealed made her heart bleed. To lose an innocent soul, the light of your life, did not bear thinking about. To make matters worse, he had to live with the living, breathing image of the little girl he had lost. He had to witness the suffering of his daughter every day, see her miss her twin like you would miss a part of yourself.

"I'm so sorry. I cannot imagine what you must have suffered."

"No, I know. I was hoping to be healing, but when I realized this morning what day it was I just... crumpled. I left the bed before you could wake up. It was cowardly of me but I could not think of anything else to do."

She shook her head slowly. "I wish I could help."

"You have. By listening to me."

They were still holding hands. Connor raised hers to his lips and kissed it. Their gazes locked for a moment. Esyllt's breath caught in her throat at the emotion she saw on his face. This day would mark a turning point in their relationship, she knew it. She had finally unlocked the mystery that was her husband. All that was needed now for them to start their marriage in earnest was for him to know who she really was.

It was time she told him what had happened with Gwyn, what no one but she knew.

"I too have a confession to make." He had confided his pain to her, unveiled the heavy secret weighing on his heart.

Suddenly, she wanted to do the same and prove that she trusted him.

"I will listen, but only if you're certain you want to make it."

"I am." Connor waited while she gathered the courage to speak out. "I did kill my husband, like I told you the day of our wedding." Her eyes filled with tears as the memory of that night assaulted her. "But it was not cold-blooded murder. I did it at his request. And now I... I cannot live with myself."

Connor stared at Esyllt. She thought she had made an extraordinary revelation but he had guessed long ago there would be more to this story than she had claimed. This loving, generous woman was no murderess, whatever she said.

"You don't have to tell me if you don't want to."

"But I do." She wiped the tears from her eyes and took in a deep breath. "Last winter he was injured during a hunt. A stupid accident, but the wound became infected and his whole leg soon started to turn black. He suffered agony day and night, and there was no hope of a cure. He was already an old man, and he had been sickly for some time, ever since the birth of our daughter. We didn't know what to do. I was beside myself with worry."

Connor waited. Eventually, he would hear what had happened. There was no hurry. After months of marriage, he and his wife were finally getting to know one another. He would not rush things.

"One day he called me to his bedchamber and asked me to help him. He wanted to die. He asked me to find a way to... make it happen." Esyllt closed her eyes, and another tear fell on her cheek. He reached out to wipe it away and cradled her cheek in his palm.

"I'm sorry. This must have been so hard to hear."

She nodded. "I refused, but he begged me for days. I could see his suffering, hear his cries of agony at night. Unable to stand it any longer, I went to see a wise woman. I asked her for some brew that would... put an end to it all. Still, I hesitated. One particularly bad evening I prepared it, following her instructions, and I told Gwyn about it when he called me to his side. As soon as I had spoken, he had a kitchen scullion brought up. He asked if she had seen me prepare anything that day. When she said that she had, he asked her to bring the potion to him."

"Hadn't you placed it in a safe place?" It seemed incredible she would have left such a lethal drink lying around.

"Yes, of course, but he ordered the girl to find it on pain of dismissal, knowing full well I would not allow him to punish her so drastically when she could not find it. I was forced to reveal to her where I had hidden the vial." A sob escaped her lips. This confession was costing her, but he would be there for her. He gave the hand he was still holding a squeeze. "Once she had brought it to him, he kissed me one last time and ordered me out of the room. His squire found him dead in the morning, the empty vial on the bed by his side."

She lowered her head, the weight of the guilt heavy on her shoulders. Connor gave her a moment to collect herself before speaking.

"Esyllt, listen to me. You didn't murder your husband, or even kill him." He lifted her chin so that she could meet his eye. "He chose to drink the potion, he killed himself because he could not bear to live anymore. I am sure he wouldn't want you to torture yourself for helping him, for doing what he'd begged you to do, many times. He was dying a painful, slow death and he knew it. You gave him the means to put an end to his suffering, at his request, that is not the same at all as killing him."

"Deep down, I know it. I just can't seem to accept it." She stared into his eyes and he felt his chest tighten. Dear God, she was so beautiful. So vulnerable.

"Why did you tell me you had killed your first husband the day of her wedding?" he asked, lifting her chin slightly.

"I-I wanted you to be wary of me. I thought that if you were scared of what I might do it would be my best defence against the revenge you would inflict on me in retaliation for what I had made you go through the night before, when I thought you were your squire." She shrugged. "How silly of me. How could a man like you ever be afraid of me?"

Her words hit him hard. She'd been afraid of retaliation, and he'd never seen it, never thought to reassure her.

"Oh, Esyllt, there was no need to try and protect yourself. I never intended to make you pay for anything, much less hurt you." He gave her cheek a tender stroke. Hurt a woman? *This* woman? Never! "In any case, your plan did not work."

"No, of course not. How could you have taken any threat I represented seriously? You're a knight in your prime, and I'm just a woman."

Just a woman. He could not help a smile. Did she have any idea of the power she had over him? Apparently not.

"I mean that warning me to stay away from you was not enough to make me wary of what you might do, or unwilling to be with you." He leaned in, ever so slightly. "Surely you saw that?"

"I don't know," she breathed, when his thumb started to brush her skin in small, rhythmic strokes. Her cheek was so soft he could not repress a groan.

"We were interrupted yesterday." As he spoke, his loins caught fire. Interrupted during the best, most sensual kiss of his life. "But we are alone now and I don't think anyone will come riding past."

"No."

"So, will you let me undress you, Esyllt?" he rasped, almost mad with the need to see her body. "I need to see you."

"Yes." She sounded dazed.

"Then stand up."

As soon as she did, he placed himself behind her, so he could unlace her bodice. In that position, all he could think about was how delicate she was compared to him. When he touched the front of her gown, he frowned.

"Your clothes are wet."

"It... It rained rather heavily on the ride back from the village."

Yes, the village, where he'd sent her alone. Connor clenched his teeth. As if he didn't feel guilty enough about that, now he was told she'd had to endure foul weather while on horseback. "Will you—"

"I have forgiven you already," she breathed. "Please, don't stop. I'm cold."

A growl escaped Connor's throat. "Not to worry, soon you'll be burning."

The wet gown was disposed of, then the shift, which, mercifully was only very slightly damp.

Facing her once again, he slid his hands along her arms to come and encircle her waist, then squeezed her buttocks gently, forcing her to mold herself against him. She gave a whimper, as if no one had touched that part of her body before. In all probability, no one had. Her late husband, if he'd looked after her adequately during the day, had apparently not made the most of having a woman like her in his bed at night. Connor swore he would not make the same mistake.

The time to consummate their marriage had come.

With much less delicacy than he had used with her, he disposed of his hose. Thank Christ he had not been wearing much, for he could not wait to feel her against him. Once he was naked, he sat on the edge of the bed and pulled her toward him, not even trying to hide the proof of his desire for her. Though she blushed, she did not seem worried or afraid or even surprised. Good. Perhaps the lessons in handling male nudity had not been in vain.

"Please, let me kiss you here," he begged, brushing his cheek against a nipple made hard by the cold. Esyllt inhaled, proving he'd been right to suppose that the stubble on his jaw would create pleasurable sensations within her.

"Yes."

He suckled her a long moment, one breast then the other, reveling in the feel of her softness in his mouth as well as the moans escaping her lips. Then, slowly, he lay back, coaxing her forward until she was draped over him. Her whole body was in contact with his, from forehead to toe.

So smooth, so arousing.

"Still cold, wife?" he breathed against her neck. Dear God, she not only felt good, she smelled divine as well.

"Was I cold?" she breathed back. "I can't remember."

Connor knew he was going to lose his mind. Finally he was about to possess his wife, the woman who had inflamed his desire for weeks. And what a woman she was! Stretched over his body, with her face buried against the crook of his neck, she fit against him perfectly, as if she'd been created to be there.

Bringing his hands to the back of her thighs, he coaxed her legs apart so that she was straddling him. The provocative position made him groan out loud. Would he take her like this and watch pleasure erupt on her face while she rode him? Would he turn her to her side and enter her from behind while he nibbled at her neck or make her support herself on her hands and knees so he could massage her breasts while he thrust inside her with all the strength of his desire?

No.

All this would have to wait. He wasn't sure how experienced she was in the art of lovemaking. In fact, based on what he'd seen and heard so far, he was confident her elderly husband would have taken her only in the most traditional manner, and the last thing he wanted right now, when he was moments away from bliss, was to startle her. They had the rest of their lives to experiment together.

"Please, I need you," he rasped in her ear.

"Me too." The words were little more than a sigh.

Unable to wait a moment longer, he gave a jerk of his hips and rolled her onto her back, placing her under him. There. Perfect. Her legs were already spread wide and he assured himself with a light finger that she was ready for him. To his relief, he found her slick with longing. Nothing stood in his way now. Thank the Lord she was not a virgin, for this first possession would be quick. He was ready to burst. Not to worry, they had all night to quench their thirst for each other, he would make sure she got her pleasure time and time again. For now he just needed to be inside her.

He looked deep into Esyllt's eyes—and found them huge. Huge with fright, not hazy with longing.

"Christ, Esyllt, you're afraid of me again!" He recoiled in horror. Was she disgusted by his unkempt state? It would be little wonder if she was. He would smell of drink, his stubble would feel rough on her tender skin. All his desire vanished at the sight of her fear. "Forgive me I should have waited for a better moment to—"

"Please, no... It's not that. Yes, I guess I am afraid, but it's not what you think. I'm not afraid of you."

His heartbeat eased marginally. If she wasn't afraid of him, then he could handle it. "Then, what are you afraid of?"

Esyllt hesitated and, seeing that Connor was genuinely worried, forced herself to explain. She could tell he had not expected her to refuse him at the last moment, and in truth, she didn't want to refuse him. It was only... well, that she was also scared.

She decided to be honest. They had just bared their souls to each other, she could not go back to secrecy now.

"I'm afraid of myself. Of my reaction. I don't understand what is happening to me and it scares me. I've never been like this, I swear, but when you touch me I seem to become another woman, a wanton, lustful one, just like you said. I'm sorry, I know it displeases you, and it shames me to admit as much, but I cannot seem to help myself."

It was shocking, decadent.

It made her want to squirm, to force him to place his hand on her, to reach between his legs and stroke his erect member, maybe, yes, maybe even take it in her mouth, just like he had alluded to.

What power did Connor have over her? How could he reduce her to this wild creature just by stroking her? Or maybe the fault lay with her, maybe he was right and there was something wrong with her. Maybe she really was depraved. Utterly dismayed, she hid her face in the crook of his neck as his words came back to taunt her.

I haven't forgotten the way you straddled me or how desperately you rubbed yourself against me.

I treated you exactly how you wanted to be treated.

Your true nature.

How could she persuade him that she was not like this, that her reaction that night had surprised and frightened her in equal measure? How could she argue that she was not a lust-crazed creature when the same thing was happening right now? He would never believe her. Why would he? She had been startlingly forward with him that first night. His first impression of her had been of a woman so lost to common decency that she had spent the evening before her wedding eyeing up her husband's squire in lust, then had him taken to her bedchamber in the middle of the night so she could make love to him.

There would be no changing this impression now, least of all when she was naked and spread open beneath him.

All she could do was try to make him understand that it did not make her any less respectable in other ways.

"I don't know what's happening to me but I swear I'm not the wanton you think I am." She felt close to tears at the idea that he might be disgusted by her now that they had finally reached an understanding. "With my first husband it was never like this, and I know you will not believe me but I—"

"Hush, I know, sweetheart," Connor interrupted her. He didn't sound repulsed or even shocked. Her breathing eased a bit. Maybe he did believe her. "Listen to me. You want me, you desire me, there is nothing wrong with that. It shouldn't scare you, and it definitely doesn't scare or disgust me. That you did not feel it with your first husband doesn't mean that you should not feel it with me. I did not feel desire for my late wife, the Lord may forgive me, but I do with you. We have this heat between us, and I will not allow anything or anyone to tell you that it is wrong."

Hope surged within her. "So, it's normal?" Oh, if only it could be!

"Yes. Your body is responding to my touch, as mine is responding to yours. I'm aroused. I want you just as much as you want me. Feel this." He took her hand and placed it on his hardness. Esyllt barely repressed a gasp. It was even harder than the morning he had made her hold him, the undeniable proof of his desire. "It is good that we have this heat between us, for we will spend the rest of our lives together, and in that time I will come countless times to your bed. I would hate it if you endured it like a chore. It is much better if we both get pleasure out of our coupling, don't you think?"

He nudged at her nose with his, the tender gesture at odds with the shocking words.

"Yes, but..." She bit her lip and let go of his manhood. There was still something she needed to ask.

"But what?" Connor encouraged.

"As much as I want you, I dread you taking me. Last time you did, it was almost unbearable. I felt as if I would explode and then... I did not." She found it hard to explain herself, because what she was saying made little sense. "It... it started well but in the end it was almost painful and I don't know if I can bear to feel like this ever again."

"Oh no, sweetheart, this is all my fault. It is not supposed to happen that way, you are supposed to 'explode' as you say, but I teased you that first night and stopped it from happening. I'm sorry." Connor crushed her in his embrace, sounding filled with remorse. "I took my revenge on you that way, to my everlasting shame, I denied you the release you needed to make you pay for wanting to fool Lord Sheridan. I promise I will never do that again. Tonight it will be different. You will get the pleasure you deserve when I take you, more than once if I can control myself."

His hand reached to the place between her legs. Esyllt gasped when he cupped her intimately.

"Do you trust me?" The low, sensual voice matched the slow, teasing strokes of his fingers. Her body was ready for him, warm and slick already. How could she not trust him when he was making her feel so good?

"Yes."

"Do you remember how it felt when I used my mouth on you?"

"Yes." How could she forget such a thing?

"It will be the same this time, you will experience the same release. Only it will be even better, with me inside you." He gave her a tender kiss. "Let me make amends for denying you your pleasure that first night."

A finger slid inside her. Esyllt whimpered. Oh, God, there it was, the sweet agony, the desperate need clawing at her. She could not face it, whatever he said.

"No, I can't..." She grabbed his wrist but he did not stop.

"You can. Would it help if I kissed your breasts?"

"Yes," she panted. Anything to distract her from the pressure building inside her. The green eyes caught fire, as if the idea aroused him as much as it aroused her, quite a feat, because she was on fire.

"Then let me do that."

Esyllt moaned when his lips, hot and demanding, closed around her nipple and drew it deep into his mouth. As he started to suckle her, his finger slid inside her heat again, then another joined it. She couldn't think, couldn't understand what he was doing. Her whole body was burning, the tension in her muscles reached an almost unbearable point. It was just like that first night, unbearable.

"It's happening again," she whimpered.

"I know. Let go, Esyllt, give your pleasure to me."

The order was all it took. Esyllt fell. Everything stopped functioning at the same time and all the liquid poured out of her body.

Before she could make sense of what had happened, Connor surged inside of her, hard and fierce, stoking her desire anew. She opened her eyes. He was above her, just like that first night, *in* her. Only this time he wasn't slow, he wasn't careful, he wasn't teasing. The look in his eyes stole her breath away.

He was on the verge of losing control.

"Come again," he ordered gruffly. "You need to come again for me, I won't stop until you do."

Even if she had wanted to, she could not have resisted the

waves crashing over her. This time it did not worry or frighten her. She surrendered to the pleasure and it wasn't long before her body shattered, pulsing around his shaft.

Another few thrusts and he stilled, emptying himself deep inside her, so deep she felt the warmth spread all over her.

Perfection.

Connor fell by her side, his breathing as ragged as her own. Although she had not been the one exerting herself, Esyllt was utterly spent. She could barely open her eyes or move. A hand landed on her breast and she did not resist the torpor stealing over her. Moments later, she was asleep.

Esyllt woke up in the middle of the night, completely engulfed in Connor's arms. Her nose was pressed against his chest, and she was almost buried under the covers. Warm... so warm. So safe. She moved and gave a sigh.

"Awake, sweetheart?" he asked instantly. Had he even slept?

"Yes."

His hand came to her face and he brushed away a lock of hair from her brow. "Tired?"

"No."

He gave a grunt and came to position himself above her. "Afraid?"

"No." She smiled in the darkness and opened her legs to him.

"More?" The word was little more than a groan in her ear.

"Yes."

An owl cried into the night.

Chapter Twelve

How was she going to face everyone?

As she placed her feet onto the rush-covered floor of the bedchamber, Esyllt wondered how she was going to handle everyone's scrutiny, Matthew's in particular. He had asked her not to be too harsh toward Connor the day before and he would see immediately that she had not been, quite the opposite. It seemed to her that what had happened last night in Connor's bed had left an indelible trace on her. She would appear different, she was sure of it, and he would no doubt tease her about it.

And the servants? What would they say behind her back? Had they heard her cries of rapture? It didn't bear thinking about but she could not see how they wouldn't have. And what if they had seen Connor leave the room at dawn, looking disheveled and sated, what if they'd noticed the shadows under his eyes, betraying his lack of sleep, what if they'd heard them make love all through the night? How would she live it down?

Mortified, she splashed water onto her face.

The day she could see through the bay window was grey and drizzly. Extraordinary how the weather did not follow personal events. Outside it was as glum as it had ever been when everything inside her felt warm. On the morning she had found Gwyn dead, sunlight had been pouring into the room. She still remembered thinking how incongruous it was to have such a scene of devastation lit up by golden sun rays.

For a long moment she sat on the stone bench, lost in contemplation. What would her first husband think of the feelings she was developing for the Englishman she'd been forced to marry? Gwyn had known their union had not been based on love. Would he be happy that she had found it in her second marriage? She wanted to think so.

Eventually, she stood up. She had to walk out at some point, and face the day, she could not stay in the room indefinitely. Steeling herself, Esyllt descended the spiral staircase. In the great hall there was no one to meet her.

Relief flooded through her. As it was much later than usual, everyone would have broken their fast already, which suited her perfectly. She sat down and helped herself to a loaf of bread that had been left for her, along with some cheese, honey and dried fruits.

She was just finishing her cup of ale when spurred boots were heard on the stone floor behind her. Such a masculine, evocative sound. Her heart leapt in her throat but the man facing her when she turned around was not the one she had hoped for. In fact, he was one of the last ones she wanted to see.

"Gruffydd."

"My lady." His bow was perfunctory.

"What brings you here?"

The smile he gave her had all the warmth of a snarl. "What do you think? Our plans. There has never been a better moment to strike."

"Strike?" She blinked at him.

"Your husband. He's been here for months now, he will

have dropped his guard. I hear he was attacked by Morgan the other day at the village. Methinks it is time to put our plan to execution. Clearly nobody will miss him."

I will miss him! she almost shouted.

The lump in Esyllt's throat threatened to choke her. Foolishly she had started to hope that the Welshman had forgotten about his original plans and instead chosen to build on Connor's unexpected willingness to act as mater of Castell Esgyrn and its domains. She had been married for nigh on three months and Gruffydd had stayed in the shadows all this time.

She understood now that she had only been lulled into a sense of false security. He had been hiding, biding his time like an adder waiting for its prey to get near so as to strike at the opportune moment.

"But, I thought we'd agreed it would be best to—"

"No, you were the only one believing such nonsense! Cooperation between our two people is simply impossible. Really, how naïve can a woman be! That is why they should never be privy to important conversations. There can be no accord between us and the wretched English, do you hear, no compromise! They are leeches bleeding the honest Welsh folk dry, nothing more, and they need to be squashed. I hear that your *husband*," he spat the word, "could not even bestir himself to come to the reeve's election yesterday."

Anger rose in Esyllt's chest when she recalled Connor's pain and the reason for his absence. She would not reveal it to a man who would never understand, but she would defend him tooth and nail. "He had every intention of coming," she said hotly, "but at the last moment he was prevented from—"

"Oh, the mighty Lord Sheridan had every intention of coming, did he?" Gruffydd cut in with derision. "Well, that's all right then. I had every intention of speaking in his defense to the other lords when we devised our plan the other day, but would you believe it, at the last moment I..."

Esyllt didn't hear the rest of the sentence as a noise coming from the solar above suddenly caught her attention. A mouse? Or worse, someone spying on them?

She felt exposed, as if the walls could hear them, as if the very air around her was witnessing her treachery. Simply talking about betraying Connor, even if she had no intention of doing so, made her feel guilty. Motioning to Gruffydd to follow, she led the way into the bailey. Out in the fresh air, it seemed to her she could breathe marginally better. Still, she was forced to endure more of his ranting.

"After our defeat in '83, the land was taken over by the blasted English. People have been driven away from their homes and replaced by the enemy's families, castles have sprouted everywhere to shelter the soldiers sent here to subdue and crush us. This is even worse than in '77. You were only a child then, but I was a man already and I can tell you as much."

"Well, perhaps the English have reason to fear a revolt and prepare for it," Esyllt could not help but reply. "Look at what happened last December with Madog ap Llewellyn. Perhaps they—"

"Perhaps nothing." Gruffydd made a cutting gesture. "Madog only did what we were all itching to do, and Gwyn would be ashamed of you."

"Of *me*? I have done nothing wrong."

"Speaking like you do is wrong. Even trying to explain or understand the workings of the enemy's mind is wrong."

Esyllt knew many would agree with him, but try as she may, she could not. Peaceful cohabitation between the two people didn't seem such a bad option to her. No doubt Gruffydd would accuse her of thinking like a woman, but she thought she preferred prosperity to bloody war. Independence was all very well, but it did not put food in people's bellies and allow children to grow up safely.

"And don't think I haven't seen how you look at that new husband of yours. Fye, are you such a harlot that a pretty face should be enough to make you forget where your allegiance should be?"

"You were the one who chose my husband!" she spat, incensed that he should dare remonstrate with her for having found happiness in her marriage, despite the overwhelming odds. "If you were so worried about my falling for his charms, you should have chosen a man who looked like you."

Gruffydd glared at her. Indeed, with a husband as ill-favored and intractable as the Welshman, neither her senses nor her mind would have been seduced. She might have been only too glad to be rid of him. But Connor... She didn't want to be rid of Connor. She wanted to be with him every moment of every day, and night. She wanted to start their married life in earnest, with their two daughters. And after last night, she felt they finally could.

"Perhaps I should have chosen more wisely. Well, no matter, 'tis done now, and we will never surrender," Gruffydd replied, eyes narrowing. "Every Englishman who presumes to come here and take possession of our land, our possessions, our women—"

"Women and possessions are not the same thing!" Esyllt gritted her teeth. "And Lord Sheridan did not come here uninvited. He came because *you* arranged this marriage," she reminded him once again.

"I did because if it hadn't been him, it would have been another, more powerful lord, one we could have disposed of less easily," he snarled. "I did it so that it could serve us, not so that you could fawn over him and open your legs like a bitch in heat."

The words were like a slap. How dare he speak to her in that manner? "Don't you go accusing me of wantonness for doing my duty to the man you chose for me. You used me as a pawn in your ambition!"

"And what of it? A woman is useless except as a wife. Why, would you have liked me to use you in a different way?" Gruffydd leered at her, eyes roving over her body, lingering on her breasts. Esyllt fought the urge to cover herself up. She had no reason to be ashamed of her body, it was not her fault he was a lecherous pig. He would not make her feel soiled when only last night Connor had made her feel the most beautiful woman alive.

"How about not using me at all?" she suggested with hauteur. He would not have the satisfaction of seeing she had understood the not-so-subtle hint. "And allow me to deal with my husband as I see fit? It might be in everyone's interest to let him administrate the domain. He's proved to be a competent, lenient ruler, and he's even started to learn Welsh. Surely, that shows he intends this to be a peaceful cohabitation? If you really must, focus your attention on Englishmen who do abuse their power. Heaven knows there are enough of those around."

"I will focus on whoever I can reach, and you will do what you agreed to do," he snapped. "You will do the one thing you can do to aid us in our enterprise. Tonight you will open the castle to us so we can slip in and take him in his sleep."

"No. I will not betray my husband thus." Esyllt did not even hesitate. "If you want to capture Lord Sheridan, do it in a fair fight. I won't do anything to stop you." She would enjoy watching them try, at least.

Gruffydd made a gesture of exasperation. "You know full well that capturing him is not as easy as it sounds. Your husband is not quite the preening, posing courtier we took him for when he arrived." Esyllt almost let out a snort. How could they have thought that for a moment? It seemed that, just like Morgan the other day, they thought that braveness and strength could only come in the guise of rugged, gnarled men. The fools. "He will not be so easily subdued. Not to mention that his brother is never far from him and just as fierce."

Yes. A dozen men would be needed to overcome men like Connor and Matthew. Alone they were formidable, together she imagined they would be virtually invincible.

She waited, hoping Gruffydd would leave at last. He didn't, instead carried on exposing his plans.

"However, if we catch him while he's sleeping, we might stand a chance."

She bit her lip. That was exactly what she had thought the night before their wedding. She had ordered her men to seize the man she thought to be the squire while he was at his most vulnerable. And it had worked. Gruffydd was not to know it, and she was certainly not about to tell him as much, but Connor slept like the dead. The middle of the night, when he was oblivious to everything around him, would be the perfect opportunity to strike.

While they continued to glare at one another, the clouds overhead finally collapsed under their own weight and a cold rain started to fall, pricking Esyllt's skin.

"So," Gruffydd asked, taking a step forward. "Will you do it? Will you open the side gate?"

"No."

Her mind would remain unchanged. From the start she had been unsure she could obey Gruffydd's foul orders, but now she was certain she would never send a man to his death, even if he had been a despised stranger, and Connor was anything but. How could she betray him after what they had shared the night before? How could she hand him over to bloodthirsty savages when she had finally accepted that they could be happy together, and that he would be a good lord to her people? She wanted to give her marriage a chance and her tenants a good master. Neither of those things would happen if she betrayed Connor. If he died at the hands of the Welshmen, then she would have deprived herself of the husband she wanted and her people of a fair ruler. If he survived, he would never forgive her betrayal.

Either way, she would have lost everything.

"Very well." Gruffydd planted his gaze into hers. "Let us hope you do not live to regret it, Lady Sheridan."

She smiled sweetly, not in the least ruffled. Why would she regret making sure Connor would remain by her side instead of being handed over to men who would hurt him? No. She would never regret such a thing.

"Thank you for your visit," she said, walking him back to the stables. Now that she had made her decision clear, she could not wait to be rid of him. "You need not worry yourself about Castell Esgyrn. It is in good hands. As am I."

Perhaps the provocative words were unwise but she could not resist them. Her discussion with the stubborn old fool who saw women as pawns to be used in all senses of the word had brought home just how lucky she was to be married to a man like Connor.

As they reached his horse, Gruffydd whispered something to the man on his right then turned to face her.

"My lady, it is raining too heavily for you. Please go back inside, I would hate for you to be inconvenienced."

Would he really? Rather she would have sworn he'd relished the prospect. "Thank you. I wish you Godspeed."

If he could lie about worrying about her comfort, then so could she.

Walking back to the great hall and the warmth of the hearth, Esyllt wondered at Gruffydd's lack of anger at her refusal. Why had he taken it so well to be thwarted by a mere woman, a woman he'd thought to control? Everything she knew of the man indicated that he should be furious. And yet, he'd just left without uttering any threats, save to say that she would regret her decision when they both knew she would not.

She shrugged. It mattered not what he thought. As long as Connor slept inside the castle walls and she did not open the gates, the Welsh rebels would not be able to do anything to hurt him, especially if she warned him about the danger they posed to him. Yes... Perhaps it was time she told her husband what he was up against, and what Gruffydd had in mind. After last night, when they had shared the secrets weighing on their minds and made love so passionately, she did not feel as if she could withhold anything from him.

As she opened the door to the great hall, she came to an abrupt halt.

Matthew was staring at her from the side of the hearth.

All the blood drained from her veins. She'd been right. Someone *had* been in the solar, spying on her. He had seen, heard everything. Even if, mercifully, he would not have understood a word of the conversation, he would not have missed the hatred in Gruffydd's voice, or the mention of Lord Sheridan. Simply the fact that they had been involved in a discussion would have raised his suspicion.

"Still not plotting, I assume," he said quietly, walking forward. His brown eyes were gleaming. "The weather must have been particularly noteworthy of late for you two to raise your voices thus. Why, it sounded positively enthralling. I wish I could have understood what you were saying."

Esyllt felt herself flush. She knew it would only make her appear guilty but she could not help it. "I hope you will agree that what I discuss with my friends is of no concern of yours," she managed to say.

"Is that what Gruffydd is then, a friend?"

"Of course, what else do you think he is? My lover? Even you cannot be that deluded. I doubt he has managed to woo a single woman with those rough manners of his." She shrugged, choosing to behave as if he were accusing her of adultery instead of treason. At least this charge she could dismiss with total conviction. But he was not so easily fooled.

"Indeed, him bedding you is not what I am most worried about."

There was no prize for guessing what he was most worried about. The two of them plotting against Englishmen. She gave a swift smile to hide her embarrassment and looked around.

"Where is my husband?" She had better get to him before his brother poisoned him against her.

"Why do you need to know what Connor does during the day? You know where he is at night, that should be sufficient."

Esyllt flushed further when she remembered that the night before she had definitely known where he was. Over her. Deep inside her. Matthew's eyes narrowed as he observed her more closely. Could he see that something had changed between them? Probably not. He probably assumed, like everyone else, that Connor was bedding her regularly, had done so for months, ever since they'd gotten married.

"Spare me your useless comments. Do you know where he is or not?" She needed to see him without delay. Being reminded of the role Gruffydd expected her to play had sent her into near panic and his presence would help restore some calm into her.

"Who wants to know? Your 'friend'?"

Oh God. Matthew was even more suspicious than she had feared. A thought crossed her mind. Did he speak, or at least understand Welsh? Was he only pretending to be ignorant of what had been said? She wouldn't put it past him to have learned the language in his bid to protect his brother. He was relentless in his loyalty to Connor and he'd been here for months, time enough to gain some knowledge at least.

Fortunately, she had declined to help Gruffydd. She could not imagine how she would have faced Matthew had she just agreed to betray her husband. She was already uncomfortable when she had done nothing wrong.

Just then hooves clattered over the drawbridge, heralding Gruffydd's men's departure. Esyllt allowed herself to breathe more freely. She had nothing to blame herself for. The Welsh lord had indeed been plotting to harm Connor but she had refused in no uncertain terms to aid him. If Matthew really understood Welsh, then he would know it. If he did not, he would simply have to take her word for it. Soon enough, he would have to accept that she would never do anything to harm Connor.

When she spoke to her husband and warned him about the plot against him, she would demand he tell his brother to stop considering her as a traitor.

"If you will excuse me, I still haven't broken my fast." This was a lie but he was not to know it. Or perhaps he did, perhaps he was spying on her at all times. It was not impossible.

"Of course. Enjoy your feast, Lady Sheridan."

After one last murderous glance in her direction, Matthew left the room. Heart beating hard, Esyllt fell on the fur-covered bench behind her. Her situation was odd to say the least, for the person she had to win over in her marriage and who could make her life hell was not her husband but her brother-in-law, a man as intractable as any she had ever seen. How was she to earn his trust? Earning his affection was most likely an impossible task, but at least she could make him see she did not have to be his enemy.

Though she had indeed already eaten, she helped herself to

another piece of bread. After last night's exertions, she was ravenous. A moment later, Jane ran into the room.

"Are you on your own? Where is everyone? Father, Uncle Matthew?"

"They had some important matters to attend to," Esyllt told her, offering her a slice of bread smothered in honey.

The little girl accepted it absent-mindedly. "I, too, am on my own. But I want Siân," she said before taking a bite. "Do you know where she is?"

"I don't." Esyllt frowned. "Didn't you wake up together this morning?"

"Yes, of course, we did. But then I went to speak to the cook and when I came back she was nowhere to be seen."

"I'm sure she cannot be that far. Finish your bread and we will go and look for her."

"I'm not very hungry." Jane placed the slice of bread back on the table.

"Very well. Let's go now then."

Esyllt stood up. She couldn't wait to find her daughter. It was the first time in days Siân had left Jane's side. The two little girls were constantly together and, without knowing quite why, the fact that Jane didn't know where she was worried her.

Picking up her skirts, she rushed out of the great hall and almost collided with one of the watchmen who was opening the door at the same moment. He took a step back with an apologetic nod.

"My lady. This is for you."

Matthew, who was cleaning his sword just a few feet away, let out a snort. "Another 'friend', Lady Sheridan?" he sneered, glancing at the missive in her hand. "My word, you are a very busy woman. If I were your husband I would—"

"You are not my husband, so stop behaving as if you were. You remember your brother's warning, I wager? He will not have you inconveniencing me in any way, and suggesting I have too many lovers to count certainly qualifies as such. I will not stand for it." She had the satisfaction of seeing his jaw tighten. He knew she was right and Connor would not countenance him harassing her thus. "Now, if you will excuse me, I have a letter to read. And yes, before you make any remarks, we Welsh savages do know how to read."

She made a point of leaving the bailey before opening the missive, as if she truly had something to hide. Let Matthew think what he wanted of her morals, she knew she had nothing to blame herself for. Her satisfaction did not last long, however.

When she finally opened the letter and saw the short sentence scribbled inside, Esyllt's heart ceased beating.

Clutching at her chest, she fell to her knees in a puddle of skirts.

Chapter Thirteen

onnor had never felt better in his life. Or at least, not since he'd been a carefree boy roaming the land with his partner in crime, Matthew. And after his night of passion with Esyllt, he had expected her to be radiant, too. But when he entered the great hall late in the afternoon, she looked nothing like the woman he had left in bed at dawn, exhausted by their energetic lovemaking but glowing. She was pale and drawn, and it seemed to him that her hands were trembling.

This was not what he wanted to see. Immediately, he wrapped his arms around her.

"Is anything the matter?" he asked, speaking into her ear.

That was a stupid question. It was clear that something had upset her. What? Who? His guts seized as a thought crossed his mind. Not him, surely? Had his ardor last night frightened her? True, he had been quite relentless in his attentions, but she had welcomed every caress, and sometimes even initiated them. After all they had done, he didn't think she would refuse to be held in his arms again, but she quickly disentangled herself from his embrace, as if she couldn't bear to be held.

"No. I'm fine." Her voice was strained, and there was an edge of panic in it.

"Don't lie to me, I can tell something is wrong," he said, stroking her cheek. "Let me help."

In the corner of his eye he saw Matthew scowl at this unusual display of tenderness on his part. No surprises there. His brother would not have the patience or the inclination to listen to a woman's complaints. But he would. He wanted to ease Esyllt's burden. Something was bothering her and if Matthew could be excused for brushing it away, he could not. As her husband, it was his responsibility to be there for her. Even more pointedly, he *wanted* to be there for her.

"Well?" He peered into her eyes.

"'Tis nothing, I assure you," she mumbled. "Mayhap I ate something that did not agree with me this morning."

This was a blatant lie, but before he could press her further, Jane burst into the hall, momentarily diverting his attention.

"Father! There you are! I looked everywhere for you, but I couldn't find you."

"You couldn't have, sweetheart. I went to the village by the coast to apologize for my absence yesterday."

Jane didn't seem interested by this piece of information, which did not surprise him. Besides, it had not really been aimed at her but at his wife, who, he hoped, would not fail to appreciate the gesture. But she didn't seem to have heard him.

"I cannot find Siân anywhere, either!"

At the mention of her daughter, Connor looked back at Esyllt. If possible, she had gone even paler. Was the Devil was wrong with her?

"I'm sorry, Jane, I forgot to tell you, but Siân has gone to my mother's for a few days," she said, her voice hoarse.

"Oh." Jane's face fell.

Connor tilted his head in disbelief. Esyllt had not thought of telling his daughter, whom she knew relied on Siân and why, that her new best friend would be away for a few days? That didn't seem possible. Matthew caught his eye. Judging from the expression on his face, he was thinking the same thing. But then again his brother was always ready to think the worst of his wife, so he could not let this sway him.

"How about a game of hide and seek with your favourite uncle before we eat?" Matthew scooped Jane into his arms and proceeded to tickle her when the silence in the room threatened to become awkward. The little girl squealed with delight and jumped back down to the floor, agile as a squirrel. "You will see that I am better at it than your father."

"It's not that difficult! He's terrible. But I know all the hiding places here now, so you'd better beware," Jane warned before dashing out of the room.

Connor threw his brother a grateful look for distracting his daughter. Matthew always knew what was needed when it concerned him or Jane. If only he could extend the same skill to his wife, it would be a tremendous help, especially right now.

"Where does your mother live?" he asked Esyllt as he poured himself a cup of spiced wine. He hated to insist, but he could not rid himself of the impression that something was not right. "You never said."

"Just on the other side of the village," she said in a quiet voice. "Siân asked to see her this morning, so I took her. The two of them are very close. I suspect she wanted to tell her all about her new friend."

"Yes. I suspect so," he said, handing her a cup of wine. Could that be the truth? It was plausible enough.

But when Esyllt emptied the wine in one gulp, Connor's suspicious were renewed. She had never been able to dissemble and it was clear something was weighing on her mind. Should he press her? Would she answer? It was far from certain.

For now, perhaps it was better not to insist. She had proved last night that she would confide in him if she felt the need to.

"I will get back to the stables if you don't need me. I think Storm's saddle needs to be replaced. I'll have a word with the groom about it."

Esyllt nodded absent-mindedly. She was surprised Connor had not pressed her to know the reason behind her odd behavior, but relieved he had not, because she wasn't sure she would have been able to withstand the assault without crumpling. Would she have told him about the events of the day, warned him against Gruffydd, as she had planned earlier that day? It was not impossible. But she could not, not now.

Now it was not about her, or even him, so she stayed silent and watched him leave the hall.

It was not long before he came to find her again. When she saw him in front of her, all tall and brooding, she almost reached up to him. In three short months he had become such an integral part of her life that she could not believe what she was about to do.

To add to her distress, he had never looked better than he did tonight. Clean-shaven, dressed in a tight velvet tunic the color of ivy leaves, he cut an impressive figure. There was also a gleam in his eyes she had never seen before. He seemed... happy. And he was looking at her with a newfound tenderness.

She almost fell to her knees and begged for his help.

"Night is falling fast. Shall we retire to your room now, little wife?" he purred, leaning toward her. "My longing for you has not quite been satisfied. We could ask for food to be brought up to us."

"No!" she almost shouted, as panic flared inside her. He needed to sleep in his own chamber tonight. No matter what, she could not welcome him into her bed.

Connor frowned, and Esyllt mentally kicked herself. Damn,

she had been too forceful, and renewed his suspicions. "Are you sore?" he asked in a breath, sounding appalled at the possibility. "Is that what it is? Was I too rough with you last night?"

"You weren't, and I'm not sore." Esyllt flushed, remembering how thorough his lovemaking had been. Thorough, intense, demanding, but never painful. "I'm sorry. I'm tired that's all. I think I need a good night's sleep t-tonight," she stammered, already knowing she would not sleep a wink. Her fingers closed on the letter hidden in her sleeve, hoping it would give her the strength to hold on to her resolve.

"Of course. I will do what you wish." He lifted her hand to his lips and kissed it tenderly, lingering over the gesture.

"Yes, please, sleep in your own bed tonight. But know that..." Her heart breaking, Esyllt reached up and placed a brief kiss on his lips. "*Rwy'n dy garu di.*"

Before Connor could ask her what she had said, she fled.

~

I love you.

Connor stared at Esyllt's retreating form in confusion. His wife had just told him for the first time that she loved him. He could not have mistaken the words. Jane had taught them to him only two days before.

"Siân told me how to say 'I love you' in Welsh!" she had announced excitedly. "*Rwy'n dy garu di.*"

"Very good, poppet. But why are you telling me this? I thought Welsh was supposed to be a secret language between you and Siân, so that Uncle Matthew and I could not understand you?"

"Yes, but this you need to know, for you will want to tell Esyllt. I'm sure she would prefer to hear you say you love her in her own language."

His throat tightened and he gave his daughter's cheek a stroke. "That's very sweet of you. Thank you."

"Oh, Father, I'm so glad you married Esyllt," Jane enthused. "Now we will both be happy with people we love."

The whole encounter had unsettled him deeply. Had Jane noticed something in his behavior that made her think he was in love with Esyllt? She sounded so certain that her father loved his new wife... Was the little girl right?

Yes, she was. He did love Esyllt. After last night he could not doubt it anymore.

What they had done had been more than consummating their marriage or even simply making love. They had allowed their bodies to express the feelings they had never spoken out loud, or even fully accepted before.

But he did love her.

Perhaps he should follow his observant daughter's advice and tell her as much. He smiled again. Next time he saw Esyllt, he would tell her that, as unlikely as it was, he loved her too. After all, if she had been brave enough to tell him she loved him, albeit in Welsh, he could certainly find the guts to tell her she was not alone, and he returned her feelings.

He had fallen in love with her and, in typical male fashion, had only realized it when he'd been buried deep inside her. Connor gave a snort. When he told Esyllt he loved her, he would not specify that making love had been what had triggered the realization, as she might take it as a slight on her other qualities.

But it wasn't. True, he thought her the most desirable woman he had ever seen, and he craved the pleasure her body could offer him, but it did not make him blind to her other accomplishments. She was also generous, caring, forgiving, an efficient administrator and a fair mistress to all. The people at Esgyrn Castle respected her, which was noteworthy in itself, but they also seemed to love her, which was more unusual. She had welcomed Jane with warmth, without stifling her or acting as if she wanted to replace her mother. With Matthew, who God knew had not been the easiest of men to deal with, she had shown patience without ever cowering.

And with him...

She had given him a chance. English though he was, she had welcomed him into her life, her castle, her arms—and now her heart.

It was the greatest gift he had ever received, and he would strive to be worthy of it.

Connor strode to his chamber with a smile on his face. The hard times were over. No doubts, no secrets, no distrust remained in their unlikely marriage.

From now on, everything would be all right.

Chapter Fourteen

"Not asking where my brother is this morning, Lady Sheridan?" Matthew's voice, never warm at the best of times, was today reduced to a snarl. "Could that be because you already know he's nowhere to be found within the castle?"

Her heart was beating so hard in her chest that Esyllt feared he would be able to hear it. She felt as if guilt was etched all over her face. It certainly was carved deep into her soul, so deep she wasn't sure she would ever be able to take it out, even if by some miracle Connor survived his abduction and then managed to forgive her.

"I... I do not—" Her mind was in so much turmoil that she had no idea what she could say, but in the end it did not matter, since Matthew cut her short.

"Spare your breath. I know that *someone*..." His eyes glittered dangerously. There was no doubt as to who he thought that elusive someone was. "Someone gave intruders a way in into the castle last night and those intruders abducted my brother. They left a message nailed to the gate as a warning to me."

Though she knew all that already, Esyllt forced herself to act surprised. She could tell he wasn't fooled, which made her insides curdle. Up until today he had only been wary of her intentions, and unpleasant as a result, but not truly dangerous. Now that his suspicions about her loyalty had been proven correct, there would be no quarter.

He planted himself in front of her. Despite herself, Esyllt recoiled. How had she not noticed before that he was just as tall as Connor, and even more muscular?

"Gruffydd was here yesterday and today my brother is missing. Not only that, but you look about to faint when talking to me when hitherto you were brave enough to stand up to me. It doesn't take a genius to work out what might have happened." He paused. "Fool that I was, after the other day I thought you two had…"

Matthew eyed her up and down slowly and she knew he was thinking of the night of passion she'd spent in her husband's arms.

He had thought then, as she had, that this would be a new chapter in their lives.

She swallowed hard at the notion of all she had lost. It was her fault that Matthew was now her declared enemy and Connor in mortal danger. But how could she have done otherwise?

"It's not what you think," she said, her voice so low that he likely didn't hear her.

"I told Connor not to trust you. But did he listen to me?" He shook his head. "Fuck, I should have—"

"Mam!" At that precise moment Siân came bounding into the room and all the air left Esyllt's lungs. Finally!

She fell to her knees in one heap. "My love! Oh, *cariad!*" She caught her daughter in her arms and started sobbing uncontrollably.

"What's wrong, Mam?"

"Nothing. Nothing." Esyllt covered the little girl's face with kisses. "I missed you, that's all."

"My, knowing that your daughter was with her beloved grandmother sends you in a frenzy, does it not, my lady? What exactly is the old woman? An ogre?" Matthew snarled, not in the least moved by the reunion. "What sort of a fool do you take me for? I will find out what is afoot here, you see if I don't. But for now, I have to go get my brother."

After one last glare at her, he stormed out of the hall. Esyllt guessed he was going to mount an expedition to get Connor back and her heart leapt in hope. If one man could find her husband, it was Matthew. She hoped to God he would get him back before it was too late.

Oblivious to her turmoil, Siân was looking at her with a frown. "I don't know what Uncle Matthew is talking about. I wasn't with Nain, but at Gruffydd's house." Oh, yes, unfortunately, Esyllt knew this all too well. "He said you'd join me later, and left me with his niece. She's very nice, but she's not you. I wish you had been with me."

Her chest squeezed. She had thought exactly the same thing all night.

"Me, too. Forgive me, I did mean to come, as he said, but at the last moment I was detained here." It was better if her daughter did not realize she had been abducted, or how close she had come to disaster. For some reason she could not fathom, Gruffydd had chosen not to frighten her, and he had taken her to his niece for safeguarding while he dealt with Connor. Knowing that her child would not be traumatized by the events was small consolation, but at least it was something. "But we are together now."

"Yes. This is for you, by the way. The woman gave it to me before I left, to give to you."

The little girl gave her a piece of folded parchment. There were just a few words on it, scribbled in haste.

You held out your part of the bargain so you can have your daughter back.

As she read, Esyllt could almost see Gruffydd's satisfied smirk. The letter was scrunched into a ball and thrown into the fire in an angry gesture. Yes, she had her daughter back. But Connor, her husband, the man she loved, was still held prisoner. What would happen to him?

Tears in her eyes, she watched as the piece of parchment was slowly reduced to ashes. Though she had burned the other letter, she still remembered its exact wording. She would never forget it for as long as she lived.

We have your daughter. If the postern gate on the east wall does not open tonight, you will never see her again.

It had been a terrible choice, one she wished on no one.

Save her husband or her child.

Sacrifice a strong man, a knight who would have a chance at defending himself or an innocent child who could do nothing and whose loss would traumatize her for life. In the end it had been no choice. Heart breaking, she had ordered Alun, the steward, to give her the keys to the castle. In the dead of the night she had gone to open the small door to Gruffydd and his men. Silent as shadows, they had stolen to the top of the tower, to Connor's chamber. A moment later they had come back, carrying a limp form between them.

They would have immobilized him before he knew what was happening, perhaps even killed him. No. They would not have killed him outright, as they would no doubt intend to make him suffer first. She had to hold on to that slim hope, if hope it was.

She let out a howl and ran after Gruffydd.

"Siân! Where is she, you beast? You said you would—"

"Hush, Lady Sheridan, you don't want to alert the whole castle, do you, and have them witness your betrayal? Fret not, you will get your daughter back tomorrow. Now get back inside. It's raining. You don't want to be wet." He let out a scathing laugh and made to join the men who had thrown Connor across the saddle of a sturdy Welsh pony.

She hit hard at his chest, heedless of retaliation. "And just what are you going to do to my husband?"

"That is none your concern, but be sure he will treated as he deserves." The voice was icy cold. "Go back to bed where you belong and leave us men to do what needs to be done."

A moment later the company had vanished into the darkness.

And now Siân was back, but Connor was still in Gruffydd's hands. It was all her fault. What could she do? Nothing.

Her gaze raked over her daughter, who was looking at her. It was obvious that she had not been harmed, or even suspected what could have happened to her. Siân knew Gruffydd well, that was why she would have followed without too much difficulty if he'd told her he was acting on her mother's orders. Esyllt barely refrained the urge to curse the man to hell for what he had forced her to do.

"Are you hungry, sweetheart?" she asked, stroking her cheek.

"No, I ate some fruit and bread before leaving. But I want to see Jane," the little girl answered, oblivious to her distress. "I've missed her."

Jane. Oh, God. Esyllt's insides collapsed anew. What would she tell her stepdaughter when she demanded to see her father? It would not be long before she asked about him. There would be no other choice but to lie, at least until they knew what had happened to Connor.

"Go to her then," she told Siân. "She will be happy to see you."

As she watched her daughter go, a sudden surge of hope pierced through Esyllt. Gruffydd had made a mistake. With her daughter restored to her, her hands were not tied anymore, and if *she* was powerless, she knew someone who was not, someone who would not rest until his brother was restored to him.

Picking up her skirts, she ran to the gates.

"Wait, Matthew, please, I need your help." Esyllt was struggling to keep up with his long strides as he made no effort to slow down. She'd found him by the stables, as she'd suspected, shouting orders to the men, getting horses and weapons ready. But he was not paying her any attention.

"I have nothing to tell you. Connor is the one who needs my help." He stormed toward his stallion, saddle already in hand. "I have to get him back."

"Yes, but you don't know where to find him, so you will have to listen to me, or you will lose precious time," she pleaded. "I can tell you where he is."

This stopped him in his tracks. "Keep talking," he said, not looking at her.

"I think I know where Gruffydd would have taken him. If we hurry than we can—"

"Where?" he cut in, finally facing her.

Despite the blazing eyes piercing through her, Esyllt let out a sigh of relief. With a man like Matthew on her side, even momentarily, she would get Connor back. It was all that mattered. He could unleash his anger on her later, she didn't care. Whatever he thought of her, he would not let his brother down.

So she told him everything, how Gruffydd had not taken Connor back to his home, unlike what she had suspected at first. When Siân had told her she'd been left alone with the man's niece, she had immediately guessed he would have taken him to Castell Ewloe instead, the residence of one of his vile friends. The castle, with its unusual location in the middle of the woods, would pass unnoticed to anyone who didn't know where to look. It was the perfect place for a discreet execution.

Matthew nodded once she had explained where to find the hidden fortress and shouted his last orders. Hope surged anew inside her. Perhaps he would arrive in time to save Connor. Moments later, Matthew was thundering away down the east road on his stallion, followed by five men at arms. Wary to the last, he had refused to take her with them.

Esyllt settled herself for a long, agonizing wait.

It was only as the last rays of the sun were disappearing behind the horizon that horses were seen into the distance. Seven, to be precise. It was one more than the number of men who had left earlier that morning. Esyllt's heart skipped a beat. Whoever was on the seventh horse, and she knew in her heart it would be Connor, was at least able to ride. If that was the case, then he could not be too seriously injured, much less dead.

She ran to the gate.

Please Lord, let him be whole.

A moment later she gazed into Connor's green eyes. Her whole body sagged with relief and she had to lean on the barbican's wall for support. He was here, he was safe. Then she realized he was looking at her as he would to an enemy.

So he knew what she had done.

Her heart seized in her chest while he dismounted, his movements less fluid than usual. He had been hurt then, just as she had feared.

"There, Brother. You cannot ignore it any longer," Matthew

said, jumping down from the saddle in turn. "Your wife is the one who sold you to the Welsh. She told me so herself. Now will you accept her responsibility in the whole affair?"

Well.

Connor had guessed there would be a traitor in the castle. His abduction had been too easy, the hue and cry had not been raised. He simply had not wanted to believe that the traitor would be Esyllt, not after the night they had spent together, not after they had bared their souls to one another. It had seemed too cruel a betrayal.

He bunched his fists, remembering her gasp of delight when he had entered her and the piercing realization that he loved her. For a moment, he had thought that everything would change between them, that they could start their marriage in earnest, but it had all been for nothing.

Fool!

Before addressing a single word to Esyllt, he made for the great hall. He needed food and ale as a matter of urgency. After a whole day spent without a drop to drink or a bite to eat, he was both parched and starving. Fortunately, he found everything he needed on a trestle table by the hearth. It seemed that his wife had been about to partake in a veritable feast, alone in her castle, while he faced his tormentors. The thought did little to lighten his mood. Ignoring her, he chewed on a piece of bread while he poured himself and Matthew a cup of ale.

Esyllt watched him warily all the while. She seemed to think it was better if she waited to let him speak first, in which she demonstrated great wisdom. He felt about to rip her head off and this would achieve nothing. He needed to calm down first.

"Is it true?" he asked once he had satisfied the worst of his thirst and hunger.

Mayhap against all odds there was an explanation for what

had happened. His brother had never warmed to his wife and he was biased against the Welsh in general. Connor didn't think Matthew would lie to him outright, but perhaps he'd gotten the wrong impression. He clung to this hope because thinking that Esyllt was responsible for his capture was just too painful. Still, he could not quite dismiss the possibility out of hand.

There was only one way of knowing. He needed to hear her version of events.

"You need to understand..." Esyllt started, wringing her hands, the very picture of a distressed woman. He hardened himself against the urge to go to her. This could all be an act. He needed facts.

"Is it true?" he repeated. "Did you open the door to the rebels so they could get to me?"

The color invading her cheeks was the only answer he needed. Never had anyone worn their guilt more blatantly on their face, and his question had been too precise for misunderstanding. She had been the one opening the door, no one else. *That* was a fact. When she started to answer, he interrupted her.

"It's—"

"I should have guessed anyway. Having a man taken from his bed in the middle of the night seems to be your method of choice. I should know. How did I not see it coming?"

She took a step toward him. "No, you must listen to me!"

"I think I've heard enough for now. Matthew, will you go and get Jane please? I'll meet you back at the stables in a moment. Have our horses saddled again and ready to depart. We're going back to Sheridan Manor." As he spoke, he kept his eyes firmly on Esyllt.

His brother left without a word, leaving them on their own for the more private part of the discussion.

"You cannot be leaving right now," Esyllt gasped. "You've

only just arrived. You need to eat, the horses need a rest, and we need to talk."

"I've already eaten, the horses will only go at a walk, and we've done all the talking I needed to do."

"Connor, please, you can't go like this, you're hurt!"

Yes, he could well guess he looked a fright. There would be cuts on his cheeks and at least a couple of bruises on his jaw. And this was nothing compared to how the rest of his body would look. Connor would be surprised if there was a single place untouched. What would have happened if Matthew had not found him in time? He might well have died, reduced to a bloody pulp by a mob of infuriated Welshmen.

The memory of what he had endured that day hardened his resolve. It was all because of her, the woman he had been married to, who was now acting the concerned wife, but who had opened the postern gate to his enemies, surrendered him to their cruelty for them to amuse themselves with. Gruffydd had given his orders, then inexplicably left at dawn. At the time, Connor had been relieved, as he'd guessed that the men would not resume the torture without him. But unfortunately, his absence had meant that Matthew and his men at arms had not been able to kill him, unlike they had his torturers.

Not to worry. He would find him soon, and get his revenge.

"It's a bit late to worry about my health, don't you think? I only got these injuries because of what you did."

Esyllt opened her mouth as if to protest but no sound came. Good. So she did feel some shame over her actions. It did not exonerate her, but it proved she possessed some conscience at least. He turned around, determined to dismiss her from his mind.

"Wait! You cannot go like this!"

"I can and I will. I doubt you will miss me very much. After all, had Matthew not come for me in time, I would have been gone more permanently. You didn't seem to have a problem with it then."

To his surprise, she walked around him to come face him again. There was fire blazing in her eyes.

"You wouldn't be saying that if you knew the truth about your rescue! But I see that your brother conveniently forgot to mention that I was the one who told him where to find you." Connor stilled. Indeed he had not known that. But he would not let it bother him. Matthew was very good at extracting information from people. If she had given in to his entreaties or surrendered to his threats, then it was no cause for congratulations. Besides, her knowing where he had been imprisoned only made her guilt clearer. She'd known, and she'd done nothing to get him back. "That alone should tell you I had no intention of letting Gruffydd harm you."

"It does not. Do I appear unharmed to you?" In an angry gesture, he lifted his tunic and undershirt, revealing his battered body. The beating he had received had been severe, even though he had not been cut. That had been reserved for the following day. He knew because his captors had delighted in informing him of their plans. Little by little they would increase the severity of the beatings, and see how much he could take.

When she saw his bruised flesh, Esyllt blanched so much he feared for a moment she would faint. He almost reached out to steady her.

Almost.

Instead he bunched his fists and covered his body once more.

"I knew they would not kill you outright," she said after a while. "I knew they would torture you. That's why after you left, I—"

"It matters not what you did *after* you opened the gates to my enemies and allowed them to take me in my sleep!" he snarled. She'd known! Good God, all day she'd known he was being tortured and she had not lifted a finger. That blow hurt more than all the ones he'd received at the hands of the Welshmen. "The damage had been done by then. And don't go accusing my brother of wrongdoing when he was the one who came to my rescue. I know who I can rely on in this castle—and you're not one of them."

That seemed to silence her. He'd thought she might faint a moment ago, now he wondered if she was not about to retch.

He stormed to the stables, followed at a distance by an unsteady Esyllt. Though he was the injured one, she seemed to be the one having difficulty to walk.

At that moment Matthew came back with Jane.

"Father!"

His heart almost gave out when his daughter ran up to him. For a dreadful moment last night he had thought he would not see her again. She was all he had left now that his wife had been exposed for the traitor she was. To think the prospect of being reunited with Esyllt had been what had sustained him while he'd endured the beating! The irony of it twisted at his guts.

"But you're hurt!" Jane cried out.

"'Tis nothing, sweetheart. I fell into a ditch whilst chasing after Uncle Matthew but don't worry, I eventually caught up with him, as I always do." Ignoring the pain in his body, he knelt down by her side. "Now, go get ready. We are leaving for Sheridan Manor. I have urgent business there."

The little girl made a face. "Now? It's almost dark."

It was, but he could not stay another moment in the castle. They would stop outside the village to camp but he had to go now. He could not risk staying too close to Esyllt because he feared her beguiling ways. He needed time to think about the implications of what had happened and decide where they could go from there, or even if they could. He could only do that away from her.

"Yes, we're going now. There is not a moment to lose."

"But I don't want to go back to Sheridan Manor on my own. I wish to remain here with Siân," Jane glanced back toward the great hall where he guessed her stepsister was waiting so they could resume their game.

Connor hesitated. Could he tear her away from the little girl who had given her her life back? Alone at Sheridan Manor, surrounded by memories of her dead mother and sisters, Jane would be miserable. He never wanted to see her miserable ever again, even if it meant he would suffer a separation.

Besides, his daughter remaining here meant he had an excuse to come back to Esgyrn Castle sooner rather than later. He refused to think he was being weak by leaving the possibility of a reunion with Esyllt open, but he could not deny that a part of him hoped they could one day overcome this setback, severe though it had been.

"Very well," he relented. "Then give me a kiss, for I shall miss you."

"Me too."

After a suitably fierce hug, Jane ran back to the great hall, her mind already on the game ahead. Connor wished he could be like her. Unfortunately, he was not about to forget his wife's treachery.

"I trust I can leave my daughter here without fear of seeing her abducted by your friends?" he asked Esyllt.

What little color had gone back to her cheeks drained away once more. "How can you even suppose—"

"I don't," he said more amenably. That had been a low blow. "Even I know you wouldn't go as far as hurting an innocent child."

"Connor, please." The use of his name almost undid him.

But he could not falter now. Using his heart to think instead of his head had almost cost him his life. He could not afford to make the same mistake twice. "You cannot leave like this. We need to talk."

"Not now." She was right, explanations would have to be given. But not now, when he was aching so much, body and soul. What difference would a few weeks make? He needed time to heal and come to terms with what had happened. Then there would be a reckoning.

He turned and vaulted on his horse without another glance at his wife.

His treacherous wife.

Chapter Fifteen

Despite her fatigue Esyllt kicked her mare on.

She had agonized about this trip for weeks. Should she go and find Connor? Would he not send her back from whence she'd come with a curse? No, he would never be so callous. And he had told her he was going to Sheridan Manor, when he could have kept silent about his destination. She wanted to see this as a sign that all was not lost, that she was allowed to go visit.

Besides, it wasn't all about her. Jane was missing her father dreadfully. It had surprised everyone when the little girl had elected to remain in Wales instead of going with him, but it might now prove her salvation. She had used the little girl as an excuse to set off for England and see her husband before the rift between them became a gulf. A few weeks without him she might have been able to handle, but it had now been months.

She needed to see him.

The journey had been longer than she had anticipated, though, taxing both physically and mentally. Not only was she constantly tired and sick on occasion, but as days went past she started to worry about the reception she would get from

Connor. At first, the idea of seeing him had filled her with anticipation, making the first few miles easily bearable. But soon her mood had turned to diffidence. Would he not be angry to see her when he had not called for her? Shouldn't she at least have written to announce her arrival?

Perhaps, but it would not have made much difference. She had to see him. What she had to say was not easy to put down on paper and she wasn't even sure he would read a letter coming from her. He would assume she was trying to justify her terrible betrayal with more lies. Encouraged by Matthew, he might well throw the letter into the fire instead of opening it.

No. There was only one way to break the news to him, in person. But even if she hadn't had any reason to go and find him, she would have wanted to go.

Because she missed Connor, missed everything about him.

Her body missed his heat at night, her mind missed their complicity by day, her heart missed all of him day and night. She missed the sparkle in his eyes when he teased her, the sound of his laughter, the jolt of recognition her body gave every time he entered a room, the warmth of his hands on her waist, the way he looked at her. She missed everything.

Against all odds, she had fallen deeply, irremediably in love with the husband who had been forced upon her.

Without him she was irritable, and her days had no purpose. She spent her time waiting for something to happen, for the excitement only Connor could provide. Every day she woke up full of hope before crumbling slowly when it became clear that today would not be the day she would be reunited with him. It had been the same as when he had left the first time, only a hundred times worse, for she hadn't been in love with him then.

As days had become weeks, then months, she felt had the weight of his absence more and more keenly and the guilt of her betrayal had threatened to crush her.

Although she'd had her reasons for handing him over to Gruffydd, there was no denying that she had woefully betrayed him. Worse, she had done so the day after they had spent their first night of passion together.

How perfect Connor had been with her that night! First, sharing his grief, then reassuring her when she had exposed her innermost secret, and finally so passionate, so loving when he had made love to her. Far from being appalled at the strength of her desire, he had assured her it was normal, he had stroked her as if she'd been the most precious creature in the world.

He had made her body explode and her uncertainties vanish. She wasn't a wanton, there was nothing wrong with her, there was no shame in desiring her husband.

How could she not love a man like this, who made her feel safe and cherished?

But... What now? Would she have to spend the rest of her life away from him? Would they become estranged? Was he even now working to have their marriage annulled? Did he still want her? Was he courting someone else? There were so many questions torturing her by day, and such a burning desire keeping her awake at night that she could not have waited another moment before setting off on the long road to Sheridan Manor.

There was only one way to put an end to all the uncertainties, the doubts.

Go and confront him, have it all out in the open, try and win him back, because she couldn't live without him.

She even missed *Matthew* for pity's sake!

"When are your handsome husband and his dashing brother coming back?" Branwen had asked her one day. Esyllt had asked herself that very question so many times that she had burst into sobs.

"I don't know."

"Oh, no, Esyllt, I'm sorry, what have I said?" Her friend was horrified by the sudden outburst.

"It's not something you said. Only, I have no idea when he will come back or even *if* he will want to!" Crying, she had explained everything to Branwen, who'd listened without passing any comment or judgment.

"You could always go and find him, I suppose," she'd said eventually.

"Yes..." Esyllt had stared at her. How had the idea not crossed her mind before? It went to show how upset she had been, so upset she couldn't think straight. "I suppose I could."

And here she was at last, in Sheridan Manor's great hall, waiting for her husband to appear. One of the Englishmen who had elected to come live at Castell Esgyrn had led the retinue and indicated the way across Wales and into unknown English territory.

Right now Connor was in the solar with Jane, who'd been beside herself with joy at being reunited with her father. Esyllt had not wanted to intrude on the father and daughter reunion and decided to stay in the great hall.

Finally, after an excruciatingly long wait, he joined her.

"My lady."

She could barely breathe. The look in his eyes was uncompromising, the voice icy. Evidently, he was not pleased to see her. It was a bad start but she forced herself to calm. At least Matthew was not with him, so they would be able to have the all-important conversation in private.

"Good day, my lord," she answered slowly.

"What are you doing here? I do not recall requesting your presence."

"You did not. But we agreed we needed to talk, and I didn't think it wise to wait much longer." It had been almost three months.

"If I had been of the same opinion, I would have come to you already."

Everything inside her withered. Why had she thought that coming here would make any difference? The time apart had done nothing to ease his anger and resentment. Defeated, she lowered her eyes and bit her lip to stop herself from crying. Alone or not, they would not have that conversation right now, not when she felt on the verge of tears.

"After a trying journey, I would be grateful for a rest," she said, resisting the urge to cradle her belly.

"Of course. I shall have a room readied for you. Will you require anything else?"

"No, I thank you."

The exaggerated politeness was chilling. She was treated with all the deference due to a female guest, but nothing more. There was nothing personal in his welcome, no warmth in his voice, no tenderness in his eyes. She could have been anyone. The only consolation was that Matthew had not witnessed her humiliation. She would not have been able to keep tears at bay if she'd seen him smirk at the cold welcome she'd gotten from her husband.

Esyllt followed the maid who had been called and instructed to lead her to the chamber at the top of the tower. The message was clear.

They would not be sleeping in each other's arms tonight.

He would have to go and see her without delay, Connor realized as he watched Esyllt disappear though the door. He would not be able to wait long before wanting to hear what she had to say. Of course, it might be about her betrayal, but he sensed there was something else. If she had only meant to sway him, it would have been in her best interest to wait until he'd calmed down enough to go back to Esgyrn Castle. The mere fact that he'd gone to her would have indicated that he was ready to hear her out. Instead, she had risked reawakening his wrath by coming here unannounced.

That was another thing. Why had she decided to come without warning, or without requesting a proper escort? She'd brought half a dozen men at arms with her, which was hardly adequate protection for a woman and child traveling through rebel country. He would have to have a word with John to ask why he had heeded his wife's instructions and not insisted on taking more men with them. He should have remonstrated with the man upon arrival, but he had been unable to think.

The shock of seeing Esyllt in the great hall had made it impossible for him to know how to act. Worse had been his reaction. His heart had leapt, his whole body had surged in recognition.

He still loved her, fool that he was.

It was the only explanation for it. If he did not, he would not have felt the urge to run to her and crush her in his arms as soon as he'd seen her. It had been safer to assume a cold demeanor and keep a safe distance between them. Matthew's presence just behind the door had helped as well. Without him, Connor might well have started to blurt out unwise words, and behaved like he could not afford.

As soon as he was alone, that door opened, allowing his brother into the room.

"Are you going to listen to her explanations then?" Matthew crossed his arms over his chest in obvious disapproval.

"I don't know." He had not requested her presence, but she was here now, so what harm could it do to have the discussion they needed to have?

"You almost died a painful death because of her. You'd be a fool to allow her feminine wiles to sway you."

Connor did not try to repress his irritation at this unfair comment. He had never allowed anyone to sway him, he was not about to start now. And Esyllt's beauty was not the only reason he was drawn to her. His brother should have guessed that.

"I will do no such thing. But if she were a man, I would want to hear what she has to say for herself and judge accordingly. I think the least I can do is extend the same courtesy. We are married. I cannot discard her on a whim."

Over the last three months he'd had time to heal and think, and he could not shake the feeling that something was not quite right. It was time to get to the bottom of what had really happened. Suddenly, he was very glad Esyllt had come.

Matthew was not so easily impressed. "If she were a man, you wouldn't be married to her, would you, and she wouldn't be in a position to ensnare you with what is hidden under her skir—"

"I will thank you for keeping your lewd comments to yourself," Connor snarled, goaded beyond endurance. "*You* are a man, so I won't hesitate to send you to the ground if you show her any disrespect or speak of her in those terms again. Regardless of what happened, she is still my wife. Do not make the mistake of forgetting it ever again."

With those words, he ran out of the room. He would give Esyllt time to rest, but then he would go find her.

~

The feeling between her legs was not normal.

Upon waking up from her well-deserved nap, Esyllt had started to feel odd. Attributing it to her nervousness at the idea of facing Connor after his unpromising welcome, she had done her best to push her discomfort from her mind. She had to focus on the mission ahead. This time, no matter what reception she got, she would not get defeated, she would speak to him.

And he would listen.

By the time she had reached the bottom of the spiral stair-case on legs that felt unsteady, however, she could not ignore her instinct any longer. Something wasn't right. Holding her breath, she slipped a hand underneath her skirts. When she brought her fingers up for inspection she found them stained with blood. It was not much but it was unmistakable. Esyllt stared at her hand in horror and then started to tremble. This was not her monthly courses, could not be. It could only be one other thing.

"No! No, no, no!" she whimpered.

What had she done? Surely a week of relentless riding was not the best thing she could have endured in her condition... And here was the result.

A noise made her lift her head and she found herself staring straight into Connor's green eyes. He was standing by the door, a frown on his face. Lost to her despair, she had not heard his approach. For what felt like an eternity, they both looked at her hand, which was red with her blood.

"What the devil is—" he started.

"I don't want to lose my baby," Esyllt said, feeling as if she were about to faint. All thoughts of breaking the news gently to him vanished as she leaned on the table for support. There was only room for wild panic inside her. "I don't... I can't... Please. I don't want to lose my baby."

The floor opened under Connor's feet. Baby? Esyllt was with child, and she was bleeding?

Oh, God.

He'd been champing at the bit all afternoon, desperate to go to her. Eventually, deciding she was rested enough for a discus-sion, he had elected to go and speak to her. At first, he had been relieved to see her already up and in the great hall. Relief had quickly morphed into horror when he'd seen the red stain on her hand.

Blood. Unmistakable. And now he knew where it came from.

In three strides, he had reached her. Cursing his earlier intransigeance, he swept her into his arms and carried her to the nearest bed, his own, in the chamber just behind. Against him he could feel her tremble, and heard her murmur to herself incessantly, as if by doing so she could to stave off tears. 'My baby' was all he could hear.

His baby, too.

Conceived that night he had thought they might be able to come up with an understanding, the only night they had made love. His baby, the baby he had fathered onto his wife, the woman he loved. And now he had endangered it by forcing its mother to come and find him hundreds of miles away from her home because he had been too proud, too stupid to relent and listen to her in three long months. No wonder she'd given up hope of a reconciliation. No wonder she had undertaken the dangerous journey. He should never have left her alone for so long, whatever his recriminations, he should have written at the very least, he should not have let her believe he cared nothing for her.

Well, now was not the time to think about all that. Now was the time to do what had to be done. He could drown in self-loathing later, once Esyllt had had the help she needed. He would not fail her a second time.

"Matthew!" he bellowed, feeling like a murderer. His brother appeared at the end of the corridor a mere moment later. "Go and get Mistress Annie in the village. Now!"

The woman had attended to his late wife and baby daughter the previous year. She would know what to do. He, by contrast, had never felt more powerless. Esyllt was lying on the bed, curled up in a ball, eyes closed. He came to lie beside her and took her into his arms, rocking her, murmuring soothing words into her ear.

"I don't want to lose my baby," was all she repeated, tears streaming down her cheeks. No other words passed her lips, and he was sure that no other thought crossed her mind. It was the same with him.

"I don't want you to lose this baby, either," he said, speaking against her temple. "I'm so sorry."

His hands landed on top of hers, cradling her stomach, which still felt flat. He guessed she would have set off from Esgyrn Castle as soon as she had missed her courses, intent on telling him about it. In any case, he knew exactly when the babe had been conceived. No more than three months ago, in his bed. Not for a moment did he think to doubt her and attribute the paternity to an elusive lover.

At long length there was a knock and the door opened. Connor raised his head. Matthew was staring at him with a creased brow.

"Mistress Annie has arrived," he announced cautiously.

His brother would be wondering why a midwife had been summoned. Then his eyes darted to Esyllt's bloodied hand still cradling her stomach. He blanched when he realized what was going on.

"Let her in," Connor said, standing up.

A plump woman wearing a crisp linen dress entered. She was smiling, which seemed almost sacrilegious to Connor. How could anyone smile right now?

"My lord, how can I help?"

Instead of answering, he turned to look at Esyllt, who had barely stirred. "Please, my wife," was all he said.

The smile disappeared, replaced by a very welcome sense of focus. "I need a moment with her ladyship."

Connor would have stayed but Matthew pulled him to the door. "Your wife will not thank you for it if you stay now," he said gently. "This is woman's work."

"I have to stay. You don't understand, it's—"

"It's not your fault," Matthew cut in immediately. "Come. Let the woman do what she does best. You can come back to see your wife afterward."

He led him to the great hall and proceeded to pour him a glass of ale, then another when the first one was emptied in one gulp. Mercifully, he stayed silent all the while. There was nothing to say, nothing to soften the horror of what was happening. Then Jane burst into the room.

"Guess what. I've just shown Siân our bed and she immediately fell asleep on it. The travel was rather tiring for her, I suppose."

Yes. It had been. For her and her mother. And now Esyllt might be paying for it with their baby's life.

"Come here, sweetheart. I've missed you so much!" He almost crushed her in his arms, needing the comfort of her small body now more than ever.

"I've missed you, too. I'm sorry I wanted to stay at Castell Esgyrn instead of coming here with you. But you see, I did not know you would be gone for so long and Siân needed me. I could not leave her, not after what had happened to her."

"What was that?" He frowned. What had happened to her? He'd not been told anything.

"She was taken by that horrid man Gruffydd to spend the night at his place and was left almost on her own. She'd thought Mother would be there at first, but there was only his niece, who was nowhere near as nice." The little girl leaned in to whisper into his ear. "Do not tell her I told you as much, but she said she'd been rather afraid."

Connor stole a glance at Matthew. The expression of horror

on his face mirrored what he felt. Because now he understood everything. Esyllt had been blackmailed, and that was why she had handed him over to the Welsh rebels. Before abducting him, Gruffydd had abducted Siân, thereby forcing her to obey his instructions for fear she would never see her daughter again. Her betrayal had not been motivated by anything other than the need to save her child from harm, something any mother would do.

"Jesus," Connor mouthed.

A moment later Jane was distracted by the arrival of her favourite greyhound, whom she hadn't seen in months. While animal and child started to chase after each other in fits of giggles, Connor took Matthew to a corner of the room.

"You know something I don't," he immediately accused. After the initial shock, his brother's face had gone ashen. He never went that color unless something was very wrong.

"Your wife received a letter the day before you were taken, just after Gruffydd met with her. He had come to see her that morning and they argued," Matthew said slowly. "At the time I thought they had been plotting together but now I see that he was angry because she had told him to go to hell and he did not take it too well. Christ, how could I have guessed, though? I only understood two words of their heated conversation. Lord and Sheridan. I should really start to learn that barbaric language."

Connor ignored the disparaging comment. "She told me on our wedding day that Gruffydd was the one behind our union, that he had all but forced her into it."

Matthew nodded. "And now we know why. He wanted a way to get to you. I think that after months of pressure, she may have agreed to give it to him." Though Connor threw him a warning look, he carried on. "But she changed her mind a few weeks into your marriage and decided not to play into Gruffydd's hands after all, and the reason for it is obvious. She has fallen in love with you."

Hearing such words in his dour brother's mouth were startling, but Connor did not even think of teasing him. "I know she has. She told me so in Welsh that day, thinking I would not understand what she'd said. Fuck, Matthew, this is a disaster!"

He started to pace around the room, feeling like a prize fool.

Now he knew why Esyllt had not wanted him to go to her bed that night, why she had been so pale that day, why she had been unable to stop herself from telling him what she felt before he was taken. Obeying Gruffydd's orders to open that postern gate had been the only way to get her daughter back, but it had killed her to do so. She would have died a thousand deaths knowing she was betraying him and very possibly sending him to his death, but she'd had no choice.

And he had abandoned her without even listening to her explanations!

"She was the one who told me where to find you," Matthew said, his voice low. "As soon as Siân had been restored to her care, I imagine, she came to ask for my help, revealing the hide out where Gruffydd had taken you. It would have taken me days to find the place without her help."

Connor froze, then very deliberately strode over to his brother. He only stopped when their foreheads were almost touching.

"And you never thought to tell me this before?" he asked in a low hiss. In all the weeks they had spent at Sheridan Manor, Matthew had let him think Esyllt had betrayed him, he had not thought of informing her of what she had done to help?

For the first time in his life, his brother had taken a decision he could not support, and the anguish he felt did not help him keep a cool head. With a curse, he sent his empty cup of ale crashing against the wall.

Matthew did not flinch, but he lowered his eyes.

"Forgive me. I did what I thought right, what was needed to protect you, because even if your wife loves you, she can still be a danger to you. People will use her to get to you."

"Let them try!" Connor roared. "I care not! I would rather face a dozen Gruffydds than let anyone harm her child, touch a single hair on her head, or make her lose the baby she is carrying!" He was a man and a knight, he could defend himself. He had known what he was getting himself into when he had agreed to marry a Welsh woman, but Esyllt had not asked to be used thus, should not have been placed in that impossible situation.

She had been forced to marry a stranger and then to betray him when, against all odds, she'd fallen in love with him, all the while knowing he might never forgive her even if he survived the ordeal. It would have been agony.

And now she might be losing their child because he had refused to listen to her.

"Dear God, Matthew, can't you see? I couldn't bear it if anything happened to her."

"So it's like that, is it? You love her too?" For the first time Matthew sounded unsure of having taken the right decision. "Then I'm sorry. Whatever I thought, I should have talked to you."

Connor's anger deflated. He could not blame Matthew, who had always been loyal, for wanting to protect him and doing what he thought was best. Besides, he was right in his reasoning. Loyal or not, Esyllt could be used to get to him. Matthew would be thinking in strategic terms, like a warrior, not a husband, he would only see her as a liability. He was not married and in love, so he had no idea how it felt. It made sense that he would not place anyone above his love for the brother he had grown with.

But *he* owed his loyalty to Esyllt. Not just because she was his wife, but because she was the woman he loved.

"Yes, I do love her. I have for a while now. And now through my fault…" He shook his head in despair. "How will I ever forgive myself if she's hurt? How will I bear to lose another child?"

"It is I who will never forgive myself," Matthew said slowly. "You have done nothing wrong, I'm the one at fault here, the burden will be mine to bear. Listen, I—"

Mistress Annie walked into the room, cutting his declaration short. Connor's heart went to his throat. What was she about to announce?

"Jane, come here, sweetheart." Matthew immediately went over to the little girl and led her toward the courtyard. "We have a new foal you will want to see, born just after you left. Take Arnold with you," he added, nodding at the dog. "The two of them are great friends, you know."

Connor threw him a grateful glance. As usual, his brother was doing exactly what was needed.

As soon as they were alone, he turned to face Mistress Annie. "What news?"

"My lord, your lady wife requests your presence in the bedchamber."

Requesting. So she was alive, she was conscious, she was not refusing to ever see him again. Life flowed back in his veins.

"Is the…" He rubbed a hand over his face and could not finish the sentence.

"Everything is fine. She only experienced some light bleeding. It can happen at these early stages, and she told me she spent days on the road. That might account for it. It doesn't mean anything will happen, though. I can understand your worries, given what happened with your late wife but the new

Lady Sheridan is a woman of uncommonly strong constitution. She will be just fine, as will the babe."

It was only then that Connor realized the woman was smiling again. She wouldn't be smiling if she were worried in any way. His knees almost buckled from under him. Everything was fine. Esyllt was asking after him, their baby was safe, he was not being told he had lost another child. Everything was fine.

"Oh, God," he murmured.

"Go to your wife, my lord, she is most anxious to see you."

"So am I. Thank you, Mistress Annie. You have given me my life back."

"It was my pleasure." She paused. "But I think I'm not the one who gave you your life back, my lord. Well, I'm glad at any rate. It was time someone did."

He rushed out of the room.

Chapter Sixteen

When Connor walked in through the door, Esyllt was sitting up in the bed, feeling herself again after the dreadful fright she'd had. Seeing him enter the room, she flushed. Very little time had passed since Mistress Annie had left, which meant he had rushed to her side as soon as he'd been told she wanted to see him. Dare she hope it was a good sign? Would he listen to her at last?

There was so much she needed to tell him. But first, she would have to apologize for frightening him.

"I'm sorry. I panicked."

He closed the door and took a step forward, looking uncharacteristically hesitant. "Don't be sorry. I panicked too."

Yes. Having lost two children already, he would have. Which only added to her guilt.

Once the kind woman had reassured her, Esyllt had felt like a prized fool for scaring Connor unnecessarily. He would have thought his worst nightmare was coming true again. After the horrific losses he had endured, seeing her lose this child in front of him would have been too awful for words.

"I was tired, aching from my ride, I saw the blood and I—"

"Please," Connor interrupted. "You don't need to explain yourself. I'm so sorry you had to go through this. You shouldn't have been on the road in the first place. You shouldn't have been worrying yourself over the reception you would get from me, your husband. It was all wrong, and it was all my fault."

He shook his head in dismay.

"This had nothing to do with the travel. Or the anguish of wondering what you would tell me. Mistress Annie assured me it was perfectly normal, and no cause for concern." She stroked her stomach tenderly. Though she had only just found out about this baby, she already loved it fiercely. "Thank you for sending her to me. I could not think what to do, I just—"

"Oh, Esyllt, there is no need to thank me." In two strides he was by the side of the bed. "I will always take care of my wife and child, how can you doubt it? I was so relieved when she told me you were both all right. I could not bear the idea that I would be responsible for yet another death."

"Another death?" Her heart skipped a beat. "Who else have you killed?"

He stared at her, the expression on his face grave. "My late wife. You could argue I killed her. Had I not made her with child, she would never have—"

"Stop. Husbands and wives make children together, it is the way of things and sometimes it ends up tragically. It is awful but one thing is certain, it is not your fault." Esyllt took his hand in hers, wishing she could erase the haunted look in his eyes.

"No, I know." He sighed and gave her hand a squeeze. "But it doesn't necessarily make it easier to deal with the notion. And I think you of all people understand exactly what I mean."

"Yes. I do." She still bore the burden of Gwyn's death, though many would argue she had not really killed him.

For a moment they remained silent, fingers entwined. Then Connor glanced at her stomach. A dreadful thought tore through her mind. Was he about to ask her who the father of this child was? Had Matthew mentioned his suspicions about her supposed numerous lovers? For a moment she feared it might be the case.

But the look in his eyes reassured her before panic could suffocate her once more. It was one of awe and love, not suspicion.

"So you are carrying my child. That's why you could not wait to see me, why you came to Sheridan Manor, not just because you wanted to talk about what had happened with Gruffydd. It was because you wanted to tell me about this babe you're about to give me."

Esyllt's shoulders relaxed. He didn't doubt the paternity of the child for a moment. She should have known he would trust her. Still, he didn't seem confident enough to come sit on the bed next to her, as if he weren't sure of the reception he would get if they got too close. She placed a hand on the cover, indicating she wanted him on the bed with her.

"Yes. I thought I had better tell you without delay, and I didn't think this was the kind of news a man wants to read in a letter."

"No, you were right." He did not comment, but the way he twisted his lips told her he didn't think the way he had found out was ideal either. She could only agree. No sooner had he found out that she was with child than he'd had to face the possibility of losing the babe. It should not have happened that way.

"I'm sorry. In the end, it might have been better to send a message," she mumbled as he took another step forward.

"No. I thank you for coming to tell me in person. It was very brave of you, and I'm not sure I deserve the discomfort you suffered as a consequence." He leaned in slightly. Perhaps once the conversation was over he would finally sit down next to her.

She hoped so, as she dearly needed to touch him. "When did you realize you were with child?"

Esyllt smiled at the memory of that day. Her whole body had felt lit up from within when she'd understood she was to have another child. "I knew almost immediately."

It had not been her first pregnancy, so she had been prepared for the signs. Even more pointedly, she had been watching for them. Secretly, she had wished that her passionate night with Connor had borne fruit. She could not bear to think that there was nothing left of the bond they had briefly shared. If she gave him a child, he would have to come back to her, and perhaps if she gave him an heir, he would even agree to listen to her.

Listen to her. Yes, they still needed to have the all-important conversation.

She glanced at the place next to her and, to her relief, he sat down. "I came to tell you about the child, but there is another reason for my presence here, as you might have guessed. I need to explain what I—"

He cut her explanation short with a raised hand. "Please. Just tell me this. Did Gruffydd take Siân from you? Is that why you opened the postern gate? To get her back? That's all I need to know."

Esyllt gave a cry when all the awful tension left her body in one rush. He knew! Then if he knew, he might find it in himself to forgive her. "Oh, Connor! I thought my heart had stopped beating that night."

Before she could think, she threw herself into his arms. Connor placed his chin on top of her head, holding her tight, and she melted into the embrace. How she had missed this, the comfort of being in his arms!

"Is that why you handed me over to him?" he murmured in her ear, rocking her slowly against him.

She nodded against his chest, ashamed of not having been stronger, of not having confided in him. They would surely have found a solution together. Matthew would have helped to, she knew it.

"I had no choice, or so I thought. He came to see me at Castell Esgyrn, asking me to hand you over to his mob of men. I refused and I thought, fool that I was, that he had accepted my refusal. But then he sent me a letter telling me he had abducted Siân and I would only ever see her again if I agreed to open the castle to him and his men that night. I could not think, I could not breathe. I panicked, just like I did now. I should have come to you and told you, I should have—"

"Hush, love," he soothed. "I understand. You did what you had to do to save Siân. Of course you could not leave your child in the hands of that bastard. Better to hand over a knight, a man capable of defending himself, than leave a vulnerable, frightened little girl alone with Gruffydd even for a moment."

Relief swept through her. He understood her thinking and even seemed to agree that it had been the only choice available to her. If he did, then everything would be all right. "Exactly. Still, no matter my reasons, I placed you in mortal danger. Will you ever forgive me?"

"Only if you forgive yourself."

Oh, the wretched man! He knew guilt was gnawing at her. "I... It might take me a while," she said honestly.

"Take all the time you need, I'll be there. Would it help if I told you I love you too?" he purred, looking straight into her eyes.

Esyllt inhaled sharply. Had he said he loved her *too*? That meant he knew she loved him. But how? "What do you mean?"

"Don't pretend you did not say you loved me that night," he said, stroking her cheek. "But even if you did not, I can see it in your eyes now, wife."

She smiled at the way he said the word she had ranted against many a time, knowing it would be the last time he ever called her that. From now on he would call her Esyllt.

"You can?"

"Yes. But tell me again."

"I love you. I have loved you for weeks. I should have realized it before."

"As long as you did." His hand found its way to her stomach. "And now you are going to give a me a child. It is perfect, the marriage I always wanted and never dared to hope for."

"Yes." She blushed. They had only spent one night together but it had been enough for her to conceive. It had to be a sign that their marriage was blessed. "An heir, perhaps."

Connor waved Esyllt's words away. Though many of his male friends thought him odd for it, he cared nothing about fathering the all-too important heir. All he wanted was a healthy child who was the image of its lovely mother. He knew all too well that a successful birthing was not guaranteed.

"An heir will come, in time, I'm sure of it, because I mean to fill you with my seed over and over again."

The way she blushed at his crude declaration made it impossible for him not to kiss her. And kissing her with all the fire he was capable of made it impossible not to want more. Blood started to pump in his veins and he nudged at her gently until she was lying on her back, under him, right where he needed her.

"Is it safe, do you think?" he asked, his lips hot against hers. He wanted her more than his next breath, but was he not being too hasty? Esyllt had just suffered a scare, and he had seen the blood on her hand earlier. Perhaps she needed time before she welcomed him inside her body. "If you preferred to—"

"I'm sure it's safe. Stop talking. Make love to me."

Everything inside Connor roared. His wife wanted him to stop arguing and take her? He would do just that.

"Forgive me, love, but this is going to be fast," he said, gathering the hem of her skirts in his hand. He already knew he would not last long.

"Good, because I need you now," she rasped, opening her legs wide while he freed himself and settled his shaft between her thighs. He was glad to see that all fear about appearing wanton had disappeared. She wanted him and she wasn't afraid to show him as much, without worrying about he would think. Finally, she had accepted the wilder side of her.

Nevertheless he didn't dare flip her over onto her stomach and pound into her from behind, as he'd dreamed of doing for many a night. After what she'd gone through that day, he would have to be gentle with her. He could not resist telling her what he wanted to do, though. Words inflamed the body as well as the imagination.

"Next time I will show you all we can do together, my love." He slid inside her, savoring both the hot tightness wrapping around him and the moan she gave. "I want to slide inside you while you press your delectable breasts into the mattress underneath." Another thrust, more forceful. Another moan, even more arousing. "I want you to ride me like I ride my stallion and take your pleasure with me." Thrust. Esyllt lifted both her legs to cradle his waist. "I want to bend you over and make you take me in all my urgency." Thrust, thrust. "I want you to keel at my feet and—"

"Connor, please! You are going to kill me with such talk," she whimpered.

"Oh, no, I will never kill you, with words or otherwise. I'm going to make you come. Now."

Right on cue, she erupted around him, spasming with delicious force. The feeling was so extraordinary that he had no choice but to follow her in ecstasy. Arms straight, chest heaving, head rolled back, he emptied himself into her softness, forgetting the past and all the hurt he'd ever felt.

Then he collapsed and allowed darkness to claim him.

Connor had no idea how long he'd slept when he woke up to a smiling Esyllt.

"Well, husband. All those things you want to do to me might have to wait if you cannot even muster the strength to take me in the normal way without passing out."

"Witch," he growled. "I'll show you that it takes much more to floor me. Usually," he added when she arched a brow in challenge. When she laughed, he drew her to him. "Which reminds me. I never asked you, but why did you allow me inside your body that night before our wedding?"

She didn't have to actually let him take her to give anyone the impression that they were "coupling", to use her delightful expression. But she had surrendered to his entreaties all too readily. He had always wondered why.

"Why do you think?" He guessed, rather than saw, that she had blushed. "Because I wanted you inside me. When you suggested it, I could not resist. I had never seen anyone like you. I was fair transfixed."

"I know exactly how you felt," he groaned. "It was the same for me. I could not believe my luck that the wife I had chosen at random could be so alluring. I know I should never have suggested making love to you, never mind actually possessed you but I could not resist, as you say."

"I too have a question about that night." Esyllt sounded shy. "Why did you not carry on until you had reached your release?"

He stared at her for long moment, not sure what to say. Why had he stopped? He had asked himself the same questions often enough. Eventually, he gave the only answer he could think of.

"Because I'm a fool."

~

"Esyllt."

Her name in Mathew's mouth was so unexpected that Esyllt's eyebrows shot all the way to her forehead. Had her disapproving brother-in-law just used her name in such soft tones? Yes, he had.

Behaving as if this was not an earth-shattering event, she turned around slowly.

"Yes, Matthew?"

"I never said... Well, I never apologized..."

She had never seen the man hesitate before, much less appear at fault in front of her. Was he embarrassed?

"Why should you apologize?" she asked, barely refraining from smiling. The devil in her refused to make this too easy for him, even if in her heart she had already forgiven him. There were worst crimes than indefectible loyalty. Besides, she knew from his behavior toward everyone else that he was a good man at heart.

The brown eyes gleamed. "I should never have doubted you. I know now why you let Gruffydd and his men into the castle, and I understand why you would have thought it better to gamble on my brother's ability to survive the torment inflicted on him rather than expose your daughter to harm. What you must have suffered when you realized she was the Welshman's captive doesn't bear thinking about." He ran a hand through his blond hair. "Well. I guess I'm trying to say I'm sorry."

"You must be, to call me by my name," she could not help but tease. This was rather enjoyable. "Although you are still a long way from pronouncing it properly, you know." To her relief, he smiled at the provocation. "Don't be sorry. I am reassured to see that Connor has such a loyal brother by his side. And it was thanks to you that we could get him back in the end. I owe you his life. Be sure I shall never forget it."

"It was thanks to me *and* you. Without you we would never have known where to search for him, and we might have reached him too late. It took courage to come face me in all my wrath." He took her hand in his to kiss her fingers. Esyllt felt absurdly moved and she knew from then on they would be the best of friends. "I am reassured to see that Connor has such a steadfast, loving wife by his side. With a woman like you to watch over him, he has no need of me anymore."

The wistfulness in his tone told her he was only half jesting. He did fear he would be left on the side, but she knew that would never happen.

"Nonsense. You are Connor's only brother. Mark my words, he will not let you out of his sight."

"You do know that I'm not, though, not really?" Now he sounded racked with doubt. Esyllt could not help but place a light hand over his arm. The vulnerable side to her brother-in-law she was quickly discovering was endearing him to her.

"You are his brother by choice. That is just as significant, if not more, than being his brother by blood. Families come in many different forms. I already love Jane like my own and I'm sure Connor considers Siân as his second daughter. There is room for more than one person in someone's life and heart, and Connor loves you. Do not doubt it."

Her words had the desired effect on Matthew. All tension left his body.

"Thank you, my l—Esyllt. If I ever wondered why Connor loved you, I don't anymore. And may I offer my most heartfelt congratulations?" he said, glancing at her stomach. The move was bold, even if he was her brother-in-law. Most people would never dare allude to anything to do with her body, never mind look directly at it. "I cannot wait to meet my new niece."

"Or nephew," she said in a breath.

Matthew gave a slanted smile. "We shall see. I told you, Connor doesn't seem to be able to father boys."

"It matters not if he does not. I will be perfectly happy with another girl, and so will he." Indeed, she couldn't wait to see her husband holding their baby in his arms.

"Of course. Just make sure you remember what I told you. It will be another girl, and what's more, she will have green eyes."

Chapter Seventeen

"Leave us."

Heart thumping hard in her chest, Esyllt approached the chair Connor was tied to. His eyes were flashing in the candlelight, clear and pale as jade. Her core tightened at the sight. How could any man be so handsome—and hers?

Here they were, back in her bedchamber in Castell Esgyrn, with him tied to a chair, just the way they had been in February when she had ordered him to be brought up to her. So much had happened since then... and the best was yet to come. In less than three months, they would meet their first child.

She couldn't wait.

"What is the meaning of this, my lady?" Connor asked in a low voice.

"When they are with child, women often get cravings, you know," she answered, walking up toward him as slowly as she could. The urge to nestle against him was hard to resist. "So far I hadn't experienced any but..."

"Oh? And what have you found out? A sudden longing for

figs steeped in wine? The need to eat peppercorns a handful at a time?"

"No, nothing like that. Fortunately, my cravings can be satisfied more easily, as you're about to see."

She smiled. Connor groaned when she approached and started to undo the ties of his undershirt. She was only wearing a thin shift that hid nothing of her new voluptuous shape. Being with child had made her body bloom, a fact that delighted her husband. He'd whispered in her ear many a time that she had never looked more glorious. And she certainly felt it.

"It seems that you are entirely at my mercy," she said, straightening back up.

"Which is exactly where I want to be."

The perfect answer. Esyllt melted. Her husband had a way with words, especially in bed, where he indulged his penchant for crude talk. It had not taken her long to try and follow his lead, going as far as discovering she had a talent for it.

She shuffled closer to him. At first, she had been unsure whether she could pull this off but now she cared not. Her body was on fire and, one way or another, she would make this work. In any case, she doubted there was a wrong way to do what she wanted to do. With her hair tumbled over her shoulders, her rounded stomach, her nipples peeking from under the shift, her lips parted in longing, she hoped she presented a picture of such decadence that her husband would not be able to resist her seduction.

If the bulge at the front of his hose was any indication, it was working.

"Shall I free you?" she asked, running her hands over his bound arms. "Are you in pain, my lord?"

"No. And don't you dare stop what you're doing," he answered in a growl. "I'll be just fine."

"I'm going to do what I've wanted to do for months, ever since before our wedding."

"Are you? And what is that?" His voice had acquired a distinctive ragged edge, one that frayed her nerve endings.

"I'm going to take my pleasure with you, and ignore your protests, if protests there are. I'm going to show you how much I want you."

"Dear God. What have I done to deserve such a fate?"

Esyllt tilted her head in mock consideration. "Looking sinfully handsome for one. Sending me mad with longing for another. Giving me another child to love. The list is endless."

"Wait. Before you do this, please, remove your shift. I need to see you. It will make whatever you have in store for me even more unbearable."

Unbearable. She almost laughed out loud at his choice of word.

Pushing aside a vestige of modesty she had never been able to rid herself of, Esyllt lifted the sheer garment over her head. The look in Connor's eyes was ample reward for her efforts. They looked positively ablaze with desire.

Slowly, she came to kneel in front of him and reached for his braies. He sucked in a breath when she freed him and licked her lips suggestively, her intent clear. Never once in all their nights together had she dared do such a thing. Every time she thought she might build up the courage to finally do it, Connor distracted her with his own daring caresses and by the time he was finished with her, she was too spent to lift even a finger.

Tonight she would indulge herself—and him, with any luck. She had not forgotten his claim that men liked their lover to take them into their mouths and she now had a better idea of what he meant by that. The only thing left to do was see if she could manage it. As much as she wanted to please him, she was not certain she would.

Well, there was only one way of knowing, and practice did make one perfect.

"Don't do this, Esyllt," he growled. It wasn't hard to guess he would find it excruciatingly hard to remain in control. He already sounded about to burst.

"Why not?"

"Because I don't think I will be able to stand it."

She stilled her hands and made a grimace of mock dismay. "Oh, dear, am I supposed to feel sorry for you?"

"No. And forget what I said. Please don't stop."

She could not repress a smile. He really was losing his mind. And he had alluded to the act often enough while making love to her that she knew he wanted it, even if he had not yet dared to ask for it.

"Very well, Lord Sheridan. If I remember correctly, the first time you bedded me you sent me to the edge of madness and then refused to allow me the release I needed. It is time I paid you back for this cruelty. Let us see how *you* handle frustration."

Connor groaned. "Esyllt, please."

"No, there will be no quarter." She opened the laces to free his straining manhood. It was as hard as she had ever seen it, which was saying something, because true to his word, he had made sure she got used to seeing him naked in various state of arousal. "Well. Someone is ready for his punishment, whatever you say."

Connor let out a curse when she wrapped her lips against the tip of his shaft. Again and again she teased him, first with licks and then by welcoming him into her mouth, tentatively at first, then as deep as she could manage. Before long she'd brought him near to climax. She could hear and feel it against her tongue. His breathing was coming out in ragged breaths, his moans were getting louder and his thighs had gone almost as hard as his shaft. He was about to erupt. It was time to put an end to the torture they were both feeling. Because pleasuring him in that manner had brought her to the brink as well, and now she needed him inside her, deep inside, where he could spill.

With one last moan, she released him.

"Shall I walk away now?" she asked, straightening back up. Where was she finding the strength to goad him, she wondered? She could not have walked away now if her life depended on it.

"You wouldn't dare!" he rasped.

With a smile she hoped looked seductive, she came to straddle him. "I would dare, but it would not be in my best interest right now. I'm desperate for you."

"Good. Take me. Dear God, now, Esyllt, take me now, before I expire."

She wanted to be gentle, she wanted to torture him, she wanted to lower herself onto him one inch at a time and make him beg for more, just like he had done for her that first night, but she lacked his strength or his iron control to do it.

In one bold move, she buried his hardness into her heat. They groaned at the same time at the relief of it.

It was bliss.

"Yes. Just like that. Ride me, my love, give me what I deserve."

She did, riding him with a fierceness verging on desperation. He was so hard, she was so wet, he felt so good and she felt so tight, they were so perfect together that she wished this moment could last forever. And yet at the same time she wished she could explode now. It was an impossible situation.

Delicious.

"Kiss me."

She wasn't sure whether she or he had spoken but she complied all the same. The kiss, sensual and passionate, pushed her over the edge.

When she cried out her release into his mouth, Esyllt thought she was going to collapse. Two arms closed around her waist when she finally sagged, holding her in place with her face in the crook of Connor's neck. He pumped into her more forcefully a few more times then stilled, panting hard while his seed shot deep inside, warming her to her core.

She remained there a long while, dazed, enjoying his rhythmic caresses on her back—then bolted upright when she realized what had just happened.

"You wretched thing!" she cried out, lifting his hands from her to illustrate her point. "You were free all along and you never said!"

He gave a low rumble of a laugh. "I don't think your men put their hearts into it. They did a much better job of tying me up last time, when I was a despised enemy instead of their lord and master and your husband. It was easy to free myself."

"And I thought I had you at my mercy." She pouted in disappointment. That had been the whole point. "Why didn't you say anything?"

"What sort of a fool do you take me for?" he growled. "Why on earth would I have wanted to put an end to what you were doing to me?"

She rubbed her cheek against his chest, soothed by the words. Her husband loved and desired her. Her heart was full, her life perfect. "You didn't let me fall and injure myself though."

His hands tightened around her. "Never. I will always be there to catch you."

They stayed locked together for a long time. Then Connor stood up and brought her to the bed. While she watched, he discarded the few clothes he was still wearing. Oh, yes, she was more than used to the sight of naked men now, she was craving it. Well, craving the sight of a naked Connor at least. No one else held any interest for her.

After he'd lain her next to him, he stayed a long moment by her side, looking at her exposed body.

"What are you doing?" The intense scrutiny was starting to make her uncomfortable.

"Watching you like you once watched me during the night while I slept. Do you remember?" Of course she did. It had been the first time she had thought they might have a chance at a real marriage. And how right she'd been. "You are so beautiful, my love. I will never get my fill of you."

He traced a finger along her collarbone then came to tease her pointy nipple. Esyllt moaned. There was nowhere she'd rather be than naked in bed next to her equally naked husband.

"I watched you in candlelight, but it is broad daylight. I think I would prefer it if you indulged in your cravings for the sight of me at night." Next to his perfect form, she felt at a disadvantage.

"Not a chance." He placed a kiss just above the swell of her breast. "I'm not risking dropping hot fat on your delicious skin and marking it."

She winced. "I'm sorry about that. I never meant to hurt you."

"I know. You told me enough times." Connor smiled. "But I'm not sorry. Every time you think about that day you kiss the scar on my pectoral and inevitably, things get out of control. I rather like that, if you must know."

Oh. If that was the case, then perhaps she could make her peace with what had happened. She smiled and stretched, feeling more beautiful than she had ever felt with their child blooming inside her. Perhaps she did not feel at such a disadvantage after all.

"Watch me then, husband. And then it will be my turn."

Epilogue

"Let me help you."

With a smile, Esyllt accepted Matthew's hand to negotiate her way down the steps. Her eight-month-old belly made the undertaking more hazardous than she would have liked and she was somewhat unsteady on her feet. She was so heavy she often wondered if she was not carrying twins. But the midwife insisted she could only feel one babe.

"Thank you. Who would have thought a few months ago that my dour English brother-in-law would have turned into such a thoughtful escort?" she teased.

"No wonder my brother fell in love with you, lady. You are just as unbearably smug as he is." The gruffness in his voice was not enough to mask the affection in his eyes. "But be careful, don't push me too far. I am not as soft as Connor. I will not hesitate in putting you back into your place."

Esyllt smiled to herself. Could Connor be called soft? Mm. Perhaps, where she was concerned.

"Oh, I have no doubt you will snap one day, and I am looking forward to it. I will enjoy watching Connor reduce your pretty face to shreds if you dare lay a hand on me or even speak to me the wrong way."

"Pretty face!" Matthew almost choked on the words. She had known the very feminine compliment would hit him more than an insult would.

"Yes, pretty face. Don't tell me you haven't seen the effect you have on women?" Her included. If she weren't head over heels in love with her husband, she might well have fallen for the rogue's charm. "Now, before you commit the irreparable, would you please run ahead and inform my friend, Branwen, that I shall be with her presently? In my condition I'm afraid I cannot move as fast as I wish, and I have kept her waiting for long enough."

With a nod, Matthew vanished in the direction of the great hall.

"I know exactly what you're doing, you she-devil."

Esyllt gave a startled laugh as Connor appeared from the shadows behind her. He leaned a shoulder against the wall and pursed his lips.

"What would that be?"

"Do not play the innocent with me, my sweet. I know you are not as inconvenienced by your belly as you would have Matthew believe. There was only one reason for you to send him ahead to Branwen. You have, like me, come to the conclusion that a Welsh bride is the very thing to make my stubborn brother see that your countrymen—or should I say *women*—are not all devious schemers."

"How very ambitious of me if that were true!"

"Yes. But you have chosen your weapon well. Branwen is lovely. Eyes like dark honey and skin like cream."

"In other words, good enough to eat." Esyllt's eyes narrowed. Connor was so handsome and so many women lusted after him that she could not help but feel jealous and vulnerable, never more so than now, when she was huge with child.

"Yes, good enough to eat." He let one hand slide lovingly over the curve of her stomach. "Thankfully, I'm not hungry in the least. I've everything I need at home, and I've never felt more sated." He kissed her full on the mouth, lingering long enough to send her knees wobbling. "Mm. Perhaps on second thoughts, I could be convinced to have a bite of my delicious wife."

"Connor! Not here!" she giggled, fully reassured. Big as she was, her husband only had eyes for her, as he proved most nights.

"No, not here, of course," he said with a seriousness that did not stop his eyes from sparkling. "But it would not take me long to carry you over to our bed where I could devour you whole."

"You are jesting," Esyllt said, rendered breathless by the fire in his eyes. "You would carry me, heavy as I am?"

"I would carry you if you were twice as heavy. You have never looked more glorious, my love. So stop provoking me," he growled.

"I'm not sure I should if the punishment for it is you devouring me. I rather like it when you do, if you must know. Or hadn't you noticed?"

"Esyllt, I swear you will send me mad."

"I am well on the way, or so it seems," she answered with a meaningful glance at his bulging groin.

"Father, there you are!" Two little girls' excited screams reached them from the other side of the courtyard. Connor ran his hand through his hair and positioned himself behind Esyllt before Jane and Siân could reach them.

"Is something the matter, husband?" she murmured, mightily amused.

"You know perfectly well there is. And I am trying not to frighten our daughters," he answered through gritted teeth.

"Oh. It must be hard."

"Hard, indeed." He gave a snort. "Just be thankful that your emotions don't show as easily. I wager you're not better off than I am right now."

She gave a sigh. Indeed, she was hot all over, and slick with need. But the proof of her arousal was hidden safely under her skirts, thank the Lord.

"Guess what, we have just seen Uncle Matthew kiss a woman!"

"On the *mouth*!"

The two little girls dissolved into scandalized laughter.

"My, that was quick work!" Connor laughed in turn.

"Will they be married before our baby sister is born, do you think?" Siân asked excitedly. She had taken Matthew's word that the baby would be a girl as nothing less than truth.

"I don't think so, for the babe will be born before too long, you know."

"Oh. But perhaps in the new year?" Jane asked hopefully.

Esyllt and Connor looked at each other and smiled. "Who knows? Perhaps."

A Savior for Branwen
Read about Branwen and Matthew

About the Author

As far back as I remember, I have been attracted to the Middle Ages, to knights in shining armour and their ladies in spectacular dresses. Now I get to write about them, I feel like the luckiest woman in the world. Being French and married to a Brit makes each book I write extra special, as our countries share a long and sometimes painful past. But in the end, in life as well as in fiction, love conquers all!

I have published several medieval romances under my own name, including series, and also have a pen name, Judith Falcon, for spicier projects, still in historical romance.

Join my newsletter and check out my other books on virginiemarconato.com.

Also by Virginie Marconato

The Welsh Rebels

A Husband for Esyllt

A Savior for Branwen

The Noble Norsemen

Taming the Wolf

Soothing the Beast

Wooing the Devil

Baiting the Bear

Tempting the Saxon

Seducing the Warrior

Loving the Blacksmith